Crashing Tide

Holly Ash

Also by Holly Ash

The Journey Missions Series
Crystal and Flint
Family Binds
Thicker Than Blood
Shattered Refuge
Divided They Fall – Coming 2023

The Cleansing Rain Duology
Cleansing Rain
Crashing Tide

For Mike, I couldn't do any of this without you.

«« Chapter 1 »»

Cole Wilborn eyed the perfectly decorated room with suspicion. It was clear that it belonged to his mother — her signature style was everywhere — but he had never set foot inside until her armed guards shoved him through the door. He slowly walked around the large living room, his eyes jumping from a family picture above the fireplace to a framed candid shot of him and his fiancée, Zoe, on the end table.

Cole picked it up and ran a finger over Zoe's face. God, he hoped she was all right. She had lost so much blood after his mother shot her. He knew sending her away with Ian was the best hope to keep her safe, but he had no idea where Ian had taken her or if they had access to medical treatment. It wasn't like they could go to any of the local hospitals. Cole was sure his mother's terrorist group, the Arrow Equilibrium, had plants at all of them who would see to it that Zoe didn't survive.

He took the picture with him as he went to sit on the

couch. What was he going to do? Cole stole a glance at the armed men standing in the doorway, watching him. Would they stop him if he tried to leave? He was fairly confident they weren't allowed to kill him. At least not yet. His mother still thought there was a chance to win him over to her side, but he had no idea how much pain they were allowed to inflict before it crossed the line.

He looked at the picture of Zoe and let out a breath. He needed to find her, though part of him wondered if he should even try. The last thing he wanted to do was lead the Arrows to her. He had no doubt his mother would have Zoe killed if they found her.

"Cole? What's going on?"

Cole tore his eyes away from the picture to see his older sister, Victoria, walking in with her three kids. Even with a baby's car seat in one hand and a diaper bag slung over her shoulder, she still looked like the stylish, confident businesswoman she was, even if her face was etched in confusion at the moment. Her two older sons, Finn and Maverick, had their faces buried in their tablets. She shooed them to the other side of the room while carefully setting down the car seat so as not to wake up the baby.

"You can drop the act," Cole said.

"What act? I was on my way to the airport when Dad called and told me to come here instead. That there was some kind of emergency." Victoria scanned the room, her eyes stopping on the family picture before turning back to Cole "Whose house is this?"

"I assume it belongs to the Arrow Equilibrium," Cole said in an offhanded way.

"The what?" Victoria sat down next to him on the couch. She was looking at him like he had lost his mind.

Cole sat up and turned to his sister. "I'm done with

the games, V. I know everything." Victoria ran the London branch of the family's company. Was Cole really supposed to believe that she didn't know about the terrorist group operating in their midst? Though, he was head of North American operations, and the vaccine had been manufactured at one of his facilities without him knowing, so he guessed it was possible that she didn't know.

Victoria crossed her arms and glared at him. "Then you're way ahead of me, because I have no idea what's going on."

"Cole!" Jackson's voice echoed through the whole house. Jackson had been in the parking garage when Ian released him back to his family. Cole wondered how far behind him their parents were. He wasn't ready to face Gordon and Alana Wilborn. He wasn't sure he would ever be ready.

"Cole!" Jackson burst into the room, leaping over the armchair to get to Cole. Jackson pulled him off the couch and into a hug. "Thank God you're okay."

"I'm fine." Cole brushed his brother off and sat back down.

"Why wouldn't he be fine?" Victoria looked from Jackson to Cole. "Someone needs to tell me what the hell is going on."

Jackson sat down on the coffee table in front of the couch. He looked over to make sure Victoria's kids weren't listening, then leaned in. "They broke into Wilborn Holdings this morning."

"Who did?" Victoria asked in a whisper.

"Ian Sutton, the guy who kidnapped Zoe. When I got to work, he was standing in the parking garage with a gun to Cole's back."

"Are you serious?" Victoria turned to look at Cole,

but he just rolled his eyes. They really had no idea what was going on. "What did he want?"

Cole didn't answer, instead turning his focus back to the picture in his hands. He would give anything to know that Zoe was alive right now. He should be out there trying to find her, but instead he was stuck here.

"Dad wouldn't tell me," Jackson said. "He just told me to come here and wait for him."

"Is that why we have a security detail?" Victoria nodded toward the two guards at the door.

"Not exactly," Cole said under his breath. How could he tell them that the guards were there to keep him from leaving, not to protect them? That the people they really needed protection from were their parents, not Ian?

"Cole." Jackson reached out and touched his knee. "I saw other people in the car that Sutton drove away in. Did they take Zoe again?"

"No." Cole let out a sigh. He had to tell them something. They deserved to know what was really going on before their parents arrived and told Jackson and Victoria their warped side of the story. "I mean, Zoe's with them, but they didn't kidnap her. They were trying to save her."

"Save her from who?" Jackson asked.

Cole hesitated. He had no idea how to tell them this. "Mom shot Zoe."

"What are you talking about?" Victoria demanded.

"In the control room at Wilborn Holdings. Zoe broke in to try to stop the field test, and Mom shot her in the leg."

"Why would she want to stop the field test? It was her experiment," Victoria said.

"That was just a cover so Mom could release something else into the environment without anyone knowing. A toxin that will bring about the end of humanity. And she did." His voice had a faraway quality that made it sound like it was coming from someone else.

"Cole, you aren't making any sense." Jackson looked at Victoria, concern clear in his eyes. They thought he had lost his mind. He really couldn't blame them; it was probably how he looked when Zoe first told him the truth.

"That's why Ian broke into Green Tech in the first place. He was trying to stop her. Zoe found out while they were holding her and started helping them after she was rescued." Cole locked his gaze on Victoria. "Mom runs a terrorist group called the Arrow Equilibrium."

"We're not a terrorist group."

Cole turned his head to see his parents standing in the entryway. They both looked like they had just wrapped up a business deal instead of ending the world.

"I thought I asked you to keep him separated from the others until we got here," Alana said to one of the guards at the door.

Cole wanted to get up and run from the room, but he was frozen in place. He hadn't admitted it to himself until this moment, but he was terrified of Alana. How could this be the same woman who had raised him? The woman who claimed to love him unconditionally? Had any of it been real, or was it all an act?

"Sorry, ma'am."

Alana shook her head and went over to her grandsons, who were still playing on their tablets on the other side of the room. "Boys, I asked the housekeeper to lay out an ice cream sundae bar in the kitchen. Why don't you go and get started? We'll be there in a little bit. I need to talk to your mom and uncles first."

"Sure thing, Grandma," Finn said, and took off running with Maverick in his wake.

Alana came over and joined Gordon by the couch. Cole refused to look at them. "Now, Cole is right; I do run an organization called the Arrow Equilibrium, but we aren't a terrorist group."

Cole laughed, anger displacing the fear he'd felt when Alana first arrived.

"We're a group of people who care about the environment," Alana continued, ignoring Cole's outburst, "and are willing to do what needs to be done in order to ensure it flourishes."

"Killing billions of people in the process," Cole said.

"That's enough, Cole," Gordon warned with a look that normally would have filled him with guilt—but now it held no power over him.

"So, Cole's wrong?" Victoria asked. "You didn't release some kind of toxin that will kill everyone?"

"It's not that simple." Alana sat down on the coffee table next to Jackson and took Victoria's hands in hers. "Earth is overpopulated. Something drastic had to be done to restore the balance."

"Wait, so what Cole said is true?" Jackson looked from Alana to Gordon in disbelief.

"Yes, I released the toxin this morning after Zoe's attempt to stop me." A small smile crossed Alana's lips. "I will say, she got closer than I thought she would."

Victoria pulled her hands from Alana's grasp. "What about my kids? My husband? How could you do this?"

Cole got up and walked to the other side of the room. "Oh, don't worry." His voice dripped with venom. "There's a vaccine, and we've all had it already."

"So, they pieced that together too," Gordon said. Cole could have sworn there was a hint of pride in his voice. He had always been impressed by Zoe's intelligence.

"You mean that you put the vaccine to your toxin in RiverLife so that your customer base would be saved? Yeah, she figured that out."

Alana turned back to Victoria. "See, you have nothing to worry about."

"Other than the fact that our parents are genocidal maniacs!" Cole snarled.

"That is enough out of you, young man," Gordon yelled.

"I don't have to listen to you anymore. I'm thirty-five years old. I should have stopped listening to you a long time ago, but I thought you had my best interest at heart, so I was happy to take to your advice. That ended when Mom put a bullet in my fiancée's leg and killed billions of people with the press of a button."

Alana rose to her feet, a coldness in her eyes Cole hadn't seen before. "Everything I did, I did because I love you. Do you really think Zoe would be alive right now if I didn't?"

"I don't have to stay here and listen to this." Cole held up his hands and started toward the door, but the guards blocked his path.

"I'm sorry, Cole, you're not going anywhere. Everyone is staying here until this first phase is over." Alana nodded to the guards, who seized Cole's arms. He tried to pull free, but it was useless.

"What are you going to do, lock me in my room?" Cole spat at Alana.

"As a matter of fact, that's exactly what I'm going to do." Alana made her way over to him. "I know you're upset right now, but soon you'll see that what I did was for the good of everyone, and you'll forgive me."

"I will never forgive you." Tears ran down Cole's face. In the course of a few hours, he had lost the love of his life and his family. The only thing that mattered now was living long enough to make sure they paid for everything they had put him through.

Alana pursed her lips and nodded to the guards, who dragged Cole from the room. He didn't bother to fight them.

«‹‹›»

A stale, musty smell filled Zoe's nose. She had no idea where she was. The last thing she remembered was being in the back of Ian's car as they fled from Wilborn Holdings.

Zoe stretched out her hand and felt rough, cheap fabric as far as she could reach. She wasn't in the car anymore, though she was fairly certain she wasn't in a hospital either. Maybe she had died, and this was the nothing that waited for her in the afterlife?

She was surprised by the effort it took to open her eyes. A small part of her hoped that when she did, she would find herself back in Cole's bed. That breaking into Wilborn Holdings Headquarters, getting shot, the toxin, and the Arrow Equilibrium had all been a bad dream. When her eyes finally opened, the off-white popcorn ceiling above her confirmed that wherever she was, it wasn't Cole's bed. She didn't recognize anything about the room, but she could tell from the drab curtains and the muted floral comforters on the two full-size beds that she was in some kind of motel.

On the other side of the room, Ian sat backward in a chair with his shirt off. Iris sat across from him, holding his hand, while someone Zoe didn't recognize dabbed something on the blisters covering his tan skin. She knew Ian had gotten burned when the Arrows set her apartment on fire with them in it, but it looked far worse than she'd realized. She felt a pang of guilt as she remembered him covering her with his body as the ceiling came down around them.

Zoe turned her head expecting to see Blake, but he wasn't the one sitting in the chair next to her bed. It took her a moment to place the older man sitting next to her. She had only met him a few times.

"Dr. Sami," she said in a soft whisper. She shouldn't have been surprised to see Ian and Iris's uncle there. He was probably the best asset they had right now. Hamid Sami had been hiding from the Arrows for ten years.

"Easy, child, you're safe now," Hamid said in a voice just as soft.

Zoe nodded, though she knew she would never really be safe again. Not as long as the Arrows were in power.

"How are you feeling?" Hamid looked at her with a kindness in his eyes Zoe knew she didn't deserve. It was her fault they were here. Why did she think she could stop the Arrows on her own? The last thing she wanted was to drag the others into this. She had no idea how Ian had known where she was, but she was glad he had shown up. Otherwise she would be the Arrows' prisoner. It was thanks to them that she still had a chance at life, even if she had no idea what that life would be now that Alana had released her toxin.

Zoe tried to take stock of her body. She was tired, and there was a dull, throbbing pain in her leg, but it wasn't anything like the pain she had felt when Alana shot her. "All right, I think." She tried to sit up, but weakness made it impossible. Hamid helped her up, putting a few lumpy pillows behind her back. "The pain's not nearly as bad as it was," she confirmed.

"That would be the pain killers." The man who had been treating Ian's back walked over to her with a smile on his face. He looked to be in his early thirties, clean shaven with neatly trimmed light brown hair. There were bags under his eyes, but they radiated kindness.

"Who are you?" Zoe eyed him suspiciously.

The man opened his mouth, but Ian cut him off from across the room as he pulled his shirt back on. "He's a friend. It's best to leave names out of it, just in case. We don't want the Arrows to connect you back to us."

Zoe crossed her arms. "But you all know who he is, so what you're really saying is you don't want me to know his name because I can't be trusted."

"That's not what he means," Hamid said.

"No, Uncle, that's exactly what I mean." Ian came to the end of her bed. "How many people told you not to go up against the Arrows by yourself? That you couldn't win? And did you listen to any of them?"

"I was trying to save people," Zoe said with a conviction she didn't really feel. If she had listened to Cole or Ian or even Detective Pearson and left things alone, everything might be different right now.

"How did that work out for you?" Iris asked, coming to stand next to her twin.

"There's no use worrying about that now," Hamid said. "What's done is done."

Zoe turned her head away. She didn't have the energy to fight.

"I'm a doctor," the unknown man said as he took a step closer to the bed. "Ian asked me for help."

Zoe turned her head back to look at him. "Well, Doc, am I going to survive?" She put what she hoped was a friendly smile on her face.

"You need rest, and it's going to be a while before you've built up the muscles in that leg again, but yes, you'll survive." He pulled two pill bottles out of his pocket. "A pain killer and antibiotic, just in case." Doc handed the pills to Ian. "They're for both of you."

"Thanks for all your help." Ian clapped Doc on the shoulder.

"I'll be back in a couple of days to check on you, and I'll bring more pills if I can manage it."

"Don't do anything too risky," Iris said, tucking her long black hair behind her ear. If Zoe didn't know any better, she'd say Iris was trying to flirt with the good doctor.

"I'll be careful, I promise." Doc picked up his bag from the foot of the bed and walked over to the door with Iris following close behind.

"Did you start drinking RiverLife like I told you to?" Iris's voice was laced with concern as she looked at the doctor with a softness Zoe had never seen from her.

Doc nodded. "This is really happening, then?"

"I hope we're wrong, but it doesn't hurt to be on the safe side." Iris shrugged.

The doc smiled down on her. "That is something I never thought I'd hear you say." He leaned down and kissed Iris on the cheek. "Be careful."

"You too." Iris closed the door behind him.

Ian crossed his arms and glared at Iris from his post next to Zoe's bed. "I thought you two broke up."

"That's really none of your business." Iris sauntered back over to the table to clean up.

Ian rolled his eyes. "I should go keep an eye out for Blake."

"Where is he?" Zoe asked.

"He had to ditch the car, and then he was going to pick up some supplies."

"Supplies for what?"

"For the end of the world," Ian said with a shrug. "You should get some sleep. We'll stay here as long as we can, but there's no telling when the Arrows will send someone after us. You'll need to have your strength back by then."

"They already won. Do you really think they'll come after us?" Zoe desperately wanted Ian to tell her that the Arrows would leave them alone now that they had released the toxin, but she knew in her gut it wasn't true.

"Of course they will. It's not like they're going to want us around when they start to rebuild the world. Now get some rest." Ian pointed to the door next to the head of her bed. "We'll be in the adjoining room. Yell if you need anything."

Hamid turned off the lamp and followed Ian and Iris out of the room. Zoe wasn't sure how she would rest in the semidark room with all the thoughts currently running through her mind, but she felt herself drifting off the moment she closed her eyes. Doc must have given her some strong drugs to quiet the dread that had overtaken her.

«Chapter 2»»

Cole had been his mother's prisoner for three days.

He knew every inch of the second-story bedroom, from the empty closet to the windows that only opened four inches. The attached bathroom meant he never got a reprieve from his cell. Guards brought him meals three times a day. He had been excited when the first tray arrived, thinking he could use something on it as a weapon, but the only utensil was a plastic spork. Everything had been cut into bite-size pieces before being brought to him. He barely touched the trays after that.

He leaned on the counter in the bathroom and stared in the mirror. He didn't recognize the person looking back at him with sunken eyes and a full beard. He used to never let a morning go by without shaving, except for the morning he'd woken up to an empty bed and realized Zoe had snuck out to try to stop the Arrows on her own. He considered asking the guards for a razor, but he very much doubted they would give it to him.

He left the bathroom and headed back to the bedroom, where the television was blaring. He had started to watch it obsessively, trying to get news on what was happing. News on the effects of the toxin his mother had released; news on if Ian had been found; news on if Zoe was alive. But he found no answers on any of the stations. He was sure the Arrows were somehow behind the lack of information. Still, he kept the TV on to fill the empty space.

Cole lay on the bed, spread his arms out, and stared at the ceiling. Was this what it had been like for Zoe when Ian had kidnapped her? Had the isolation made it easier for her to accept that they were telling her the truth about the Arrows? To help win her over to their side? Cole was confident that his mother was willing to hold him here until he was broken enough to accept that what she had done was for the greater good.

As if killing billions of people was justifiable. As if shooting Zoe was justifiable. He knew no matter how long they kept him locked in here, he would never be able to forgive Alana for that.

A soft knock on the door stirred him from a daydream of him and Zoe. It was too early for dinner, not that any of the guards had ever knocked before entering. The only warning he ever got was the sound of the many dead bolts opening. He rolled off the bed and made his way over to the door.

"Uncle Cole, are you in there?" A small voice whispered on the other side of the door.

"Finn, is that you? Are you all right?"

"Yeah, I'm okay. Grandma said you're sick, and that's why you can't come out of the room. Are you going to die?"

That was an awfully big question to come from an eight-year-old. "No, buddy, I'm not going to die. I don't know why Grandma is keeping me in here." Cole thought about asking Finn to let him out, but he wasn't sure it was worth the risk. He had no idea how many guards were at the house. Cole doubted he'd even be able to make it off the property before he was caught. Besides, he couldn't put Finn in danger like that.

"Maverick and I made some cards to help you feel better. Mom told me to slide them under the door."

Cole's heart beat so fast, he was sure it would burst from his chest. Victoria must have some kind of plan. He watched eagerly as a small stack of cards made from computer paper slid under the door. He picked them up with shaking hands and looked over the crayon-colored drawings the boys had done for some kind of hidden message, but there was none. Maybe he was wrong, and his nephews really were bored enough to make him cards.

"Thanks, little man. These are great," Cole said, trying to hide his disappointment. That's when he saw a small piece of paper on the floor. It must have fallen out of one of the cards. Scribbled on it in Victoria's handwriting was one word: *midnight*.

"I better go. Mom says we can't let Grandma's friends see me outside your door."

"Thanks, Finn. I'm sure I'll be out of here soon, and we can hang out. Play some video games or something." Cole leaned against the door and listened while Finn walked away. He fingered the piece of paper with Victoria's message on it. For the first time in days, he had hope.

«‹›»

Zoe sat up on the bed in the run-down motel room, flipping through the channels on the TV. She was desperate to know what was happening with the Arrows' toxin, but of course the news wasn't covering it. Ian had told her the Arrows controlled the airwaves when she suggested they take their findings to the press, but part of her didn't believe him. Unfortunately, it seemed he had been right about that as well. In fact, everything Ian had told her turned out to be the truth, which was comforting and depressing all at the same time.

Zoe threw the remote down in frustration.

"Nothing good on?" Blake came in from the adjoining room on crutches.

"What happened to you?" She watched him in amusement as he fumbled to get a sandwich out of the bag he carried and tossed it to her.

"Nothing, just taking them for a test drive. These are for you." Blake crutched the rest of the way over to the bed and handed them to her.

Zoe tentatively took the crutches. "Do you think I'm ready? It's only been three days."

"You need to get ready," Ian said as he walked in from the next room with his doctor friend. "We can't stay in one place for too long, or the Arrows will find us."

"But first, let me see how you're healing," Doc said as he made his way over to her. Zoe leaned back and watched as he carefully unwrapped the bandages. She expected to see her skin ripped to shreds, but it was just a small red hole. "It doesn't look infected, which is good. It needs time to heal." He began applying clean bandages. "Keep it clean and dry."

"I will. Can I give these a shot?" Zoe grabbed the crutches, excited to be able to move around on her own again. Having to have Ian, Blake, or Iris help her to the bathroom was starting to make her feel like she was their prisoner again.

"Sure." Doc helped Zoe to her feet. She really couldn't put any weight on the leg that had been shot, but she managed all right with the crutches. She slowly made her way to the other side of the room before collapsing into one of the chairs. The amount of energy it took her to cross the room was shocking. If the Arrows showed up now, there was no way she would be able to get away.

"I promise it will get easier. Try not to push yourself too much." Doc picked up his bag and walked over to Ian, who had been watching from the other bed. "There are bandages, pain killers, and some antibiotics in here. It should last you a while."

"Thanks." Ian took the bag. "What's happening out there? Have you started to see the effects of the toxin?"

"It's hard to say. There's been a huge uptick in what looks like heart attacks in the last couple of days; most people are dead before we can get them to the hospital."

"It has to be the toxin," Ian said, his face hard.

"Maybe, but there's nothing to prove it," Doc countered.

"We need to tell people that there is a vaccine out there," Zoe said as she looked from Ian to Blake. "Try to save as many people as we can."

"It could be too late for that," Blake said in between bites of the sandwich he was eating on her now-vacant bed.

"We have to try," Zoe insisted.

"How?" Iris said from the doorway to the connecting

room. "It's not like we can go to the media."

"Then we do it ourselves. The Arrows can't stop us from posting the truth online."

"It's a risk," Ian said.

"The Arrows already know who we are, it's not like we can make ourselves a bigger target at this point," Zoe countered, pleased by the smirk that crossed Ian's lips.

Blake got off the bed and started to pace. "We'll have to make sure it's untraceable, or at least as untraceable as possible. They might know who we are, but hopefully they don't know where we are."

"Can you do it?" Ian asked.

"Of course I can," Blake said with a wicked grin.

Ian nodded. He grabbed the complimentary notepad and pen off the table that separated the two beds and handed them to Zoe. "Start thinking about what you want to say."

"Me?" Zoe hated public speaking. Surely one of them would be better suited to deliver the message.

"The public thinks I'm a kidnapper; they'll never trust anything I have to say," Ian said.

Iris pushed off the door frame and came to stand next to her brother. "On the other hand, the public fell in love with you while you were kidnapped. Didn't I say it would be great PR?"

"Like it or not, you're kind of a celebrity. If you tell people what's going on, they'll believe you. It's the only chance we have," Ian finished.

"I'll set up a space in the other room where we can record. Make sure there isn't anything in the frame that might give our location away," Blake said.

Zoe nodded and looked down at the pen and paper in her hands while the others left her to her thoughts. She could do this. She had to. She needed to save as many people as she could. More importantly, Alana needed to know that she hadn't broken Zoe, that she was still fighting, even if her first attempt to stop the Arrows had failed. Alana needed to see that she was still alive. Cole needed to see that she was still alive and fighting. Maybe it would give him the strength he needed to break away from his family and come find her. Maybe they could still have a future together.

After two hours, the table in front of her was covered in scraps of paper, but Zoe felt like she had captured what she wanted to say. She read through the message one more time before slowly making her way to the other room.

The beds had been pushed to the edges of the room. White sheets were pinned to the walls and spread over the carpet. They had made a blank canvas for her to record her message on. She had no idea how many people would see this, or if they would believe her; what she was going to tell them was insane, but at least she was finally doing something to help. She had failed at saving the world, but if she could save one more life, that would be enough.

"Do you want to stand or sit for this?" Iris looked more determined than Zoe had seen her in a long time. They had a purpose again.

"Sit. I'm not sure I have the strength to stand for more than a few minutes."

Iris placed the chair in the middle of the sheet.

Blake threw another white sheet over the chair. "Can't be too careful." The odds of someone recognizing the chair and knowing exactly what cheap motel they were in seemed impossible, but Zoe didn't say anything.

She started to make her way to the chair, but the crutches slipped on the sheet. Ian rushed forward and grabbed her before she hit the ground. "Can I help you?"

Zoe nodded as Ian gently picked her up and placed her in the chair. "Thanks," Zoe said softly as she looked up at him.

"Are you two done?" Iris asked, pushing Ian out of the way. "Let's get you camera ready."

"Is that really necessary?" Zoe eyed the makeup bag in Iris's hand.

"Have you looked at yourself recently? You look like you're moments away from death. If you're going to be the face of our little resistance, you need to look strong, powerful."

"I'm not sure you have enough makeup to achieve that," Zoe said with a small laugh. "Then let's settle for healthy. The Arrows need to see that they can't get rid of you that easily."

"Okay." Zoe leaned back and let Iris apply what felt like an absurd amount of makeup to her face.

"Do you want to practice?" Hamid asked from the table where he sat, watching them.

Zoe shook her head. "No. I want to get this done before I lose my nerve."

"Let me know when you're ready." Blake held out a phone. It looked different from the one she had seen him using before. How many burner phones did they have? She wondered if she should ask to use it to let Cole know she was alive.

She pushed the thought from her mind. It was far too risky.

She quickly read through her notes again. She didn't want to read them on camera if she didn't have to. "All right. I'm ready."

Blake held up three fingers and slowly counted down. When he pointed at her, she assumed he had hit record.

Zoe took a deep breath and looked directly at the camera. "My name is Zoe Antos. You might have heard about me in the news recently. I'm the woman who was kidnapped from Green Tech Laboratories three weeks ago. What the news won't tell you is that my kidnappers aren't the real bad guys. They were trying to stop the Arrow Equilibrium, a terrorist group that wants to save the environment by killing off a vast majority of humanity. The Arrow Equilibrium is run by Alana and Gordon Wilborn. They've been using their research facility, Green Tech Laboratories, as a front to produce a deadly toxin."

Zoe glanced down at the notes she had crumpled in her hand. She closed her eyes and tried to block out everything except for what she was doing. This would help people—that was the only thing that mattered.

She looked back at the camera. "Three days ago, I broke into Wilborn Holdings Headquarters and tried to stop the Arrows from releasing their toxin. I failed, and Alana Wilborn put a bullet in my leg. With the help of the people who kidnapped me, I was able to get away, but the toxin was released." Zoe glanced at Ian to see if she was making any sense, only to find a rare smile on his lips. "This toxin will kill billions of people. I wasn't successful in stopping the release, but we did uncover the Arrows' vaccine. It's in RiverLife water. I know this all sounds insane, but I promise it's all true. I urge you to start drinking RiverLife water immediately. I don't know how fast the toxin works or how it kills. I'm just trying to save as many lives as I can." She nodded to Blake, who lowered the phone.

"That was great," Ian said.

Zoe slumped back in the chair. "Do you think

anyone will listen?"

"It's possible, people believe all kinds of crazy things these days," Iris said.

"Once more people start dying, they'll start looking for a cure anywhere they can," Hamid said. "This will save lives."

"I hope you're right, Dr. Sami. I can't stand the thought that my work has been twisted to hurt people," Zoe said.

"Work that I started," Hamid said with a knowing smile. Zoe kept forgetting that Hamid had been the one to help Gordon start Green Tech and was in charge of her department before he decided to part ways with the Arrows, at which point they'd tried to have him killed.

Ian turned to Blake. "How long before we can get it posted?"

"A few hours, maybe. I need to make sure it can't be traced back to here. The second the Arrows see it, they'll try to use it to find us. You sure we're ready for that?"

Zoe looked around the room as everyone nodded.

"We'll plan on moving in a day or two just to be safe," Ian said.

"We should all get some rest while Blake works," Hamid said.

Zoe reached for the crutches. Ian handed them to her and helped her to her feet. He didn't release her until she was back in the other room. She lay down on the bed, completely drained, and closed her eyes, willing the darkness to take her so she could get a reprieve from the pain and guilt that were her constant companions.

«Chapter 3»

Cole paced in front of the door. It was nearly midnight, and he wanted to be ready when his siblings came for him. He had no idea what they were planning, but at this point he was game for anything that would get him out of this room. He wanted to believe they had found a way to break out, but he tried not to let his hopes get too high.

The soft clicks of the locks turning froze him midstep. This was it.

He waited for the door to open, but it never moved. After a few seconds, he reached for the doorknob and turned.

He peered through the crack in the door, expecting to see guards in the hall, but it was empty. He opened the door farther, his heart racing as he crossed the threshold into the hallway. He braced himself for something to happen — for gunshots to ring out or guards to rush at him. The silence that met him only increased his nerves.

"Cole, in here," his brother whispered from across the hall.

He closed the door to the room that had been his prison and quickly crossed the hall. He didn't know what he expected to find, but it was just another bedroom, almost exactly the same as the one he had been locked in for the last three days. The only difference was the crib on the far wall. This must be Victoria's room. Sure enough, his older sister was sitting on the bed, holding her youngest son in her arms.

"So, what's the plan?" Cole looked eagerly between his brother and sister. "How are we getting out of here? Where are Finn and Maverick?"

"It's the middle of the night, they're sleeping." Victoria got up and put the baby down in the crib. "And we aren't leaving."

"What do you mean we aren't leaving? Mom and Dad admitted everything. We have to get away from them before they pull us down with them. They're insane, genocidal maniacs!" Cole gestured wildly around the room.

"I think insane, genocidal maniacs might be exaggerating it a bit," Jackson said as he leaned against the dresser.

Cole crossed his arms and looked at Jackson in disbelief. "Really? Because they're responsible for the deaths of billions of people." Did Jackson really not understand the magnitude of what their parents had done? "If that's not genocide, then I don't know what is."

"They're still our parents. I'm sorry if I'm having a hard time seeing them as anything else."

"You aren't one of them, are you?" Cole took a step back toward the door.

Jackson stood up straight. "What exactly are you accusing me of, Cole? Do you think I had something to do with this?"

"The thought had crossed my mind."

"Enough, both of you," Victoria whispered harshly. "We're all on the same side here. Mom and Dad kept us all in the dark, and the only way we are going to get through this is if we trust each other."

"Fine," Cole said as he came back over to the bed. "Then why isn't there a plan to get out of here?"

"Because we can't." Jackson resumed his casual position leaning against the dresser. "This house, compound, whatever they call it, is heavily guarded. There are security cameras everywhere and armed guards patrolling all the exits."

"Wait." Cole looked from Jackson to Victoria. "You're prisoners too?"

"Yeah, just with a bigger cell than you have." Even in the dark, Cole could tell that Jackson was rolling his eyes.

"Then why bother letting me out of my room at all?"

"We're working on a plan to get out of here, but it's going to take some time," Victoria said. "In the morning, Mom and Dad are going to come talk to you, to see if you've started to see things their way. You need to make them believe that you have."

"What good will that do?" The idea of going along with his parents, even if it was an act, made Cole sick. It was their fault he had lost Zoe. He didn't even know if she was alive or if his mother had killed her.

"They might let you out of your room, for starters," Jackson said.

"And once we can convince them that we're on their side, maybe they'll start to trust us with their plans. Then

we can figure out how to get away from them for good,"
Victoria added.

Cole let out a sigh. It made sense, even if it meant
spending far more time here than he wanted. "I'll play
along for as long as I can, but the moment I see a chance
to leave, I'm out of here. I need to find Zoe."

"We'll do everything we can to help you, but for
now, we all have to play our part."

"You should get back to your room. The guards
should be making their rounds soon. We have no idea
what will happen if anyone realizes we let you out,"
Jackson said.

Cole got up and made his way over to the door. "You
guys be careful," he said, then slipped out the door. His
legs grew heavier with every step he took back to his
prison until it took all his concentration to simply put
one foot in front of the other. He collapsed on top of his
bed and curled into a ball, willing the sweet oblivion of
sleep to overtake him so he could forget, for just a
moment, the hell that had become his life.

«‹›»

Zoe stirred in bed. Her leg was throbbing, keeping
her from completely succumbing to the blissful
unconsciousness she desperately desired. The pain meds
Doc had given her that afternoon had worn off a long
time ago. She considered getting up and searching for
more, but she wasn't sure where they were, and she
didn't want to wake the others. Ian was lying on his
stomach on the bed next to her. His shirt was off,
exposing the burns on his back. He probably needed the
pain meds more than she did anyway.

She adjusted her pillows for the twentieth time and

willed herself to go to sleep. She was almost there when she heard a soft click coming from the front door.

Had one of the others come to check on them? It seemed unlikely they would come through the front door instead of the door connecting the two rooms. Maybe she was just imagining things. The noises coming from outside the motel were anything but familiar.

She lay perfectly still with her eyes shut as she listened. She heard footsteps on the worn carpet and what sounded like the lock turning on the connecting door. Someone was definitely moving around the room.

Zoe opened her eyes to see a piece of cloth moving toward her face.

She screamed and shoved the hand away from her, knocking the rag to the floor. She rolled away from the man standing next to her bed, sending a jolt of pain through her leg. That's when she noticed a second intruder in the room. He was standing over Ian with a syringe in his hand.

"Ian, wake up!" she screamed, but Ian didn't move. She grabbed wildly for the lamp on the table next to the bed, but of course it was bolted down. Instead, she yanked the phone from the wall and threw it at the man standing over Ian. It wouldn't take him out, but she needed to buy some time for the others to come in. They must have heard her screaming by now. Where were they?

"Damn it! I dropped the toxin," the man standing next to Ian said as he bent down to search for it. "Will you get her under control?"

"I'm working on it." A hand wrapped around Zoe's arm and yanked her back across the mattress. The next thing she knew, a pillow was covering her face. She flailed wildly trying to break free, but she couldn't get it to budge.

"We aren't supposed to kill her. Mrs. Wilborn wants her alive."

"I'm just going to knock her out." The pillow pressed harder against her face.

In the distance, she heard someone calling her name, but she couldn't pinpoint where it was coming from. She focused all her strength on pushing the pillow away from her face, managing to move it a few inches so she could get a few breaths of fresh air.

"You have some fight in you," the man said as he pushed the pillow back down with greater force. It felt like he was lying on top of her face.

A knocking sound filled her ears. At first, she thought it was coming from inside her head before she realized it must be the others trying to get into the room. Why were they wasting time knocking? Zoe tried to scream again, but it came out as a muffled croak. She was getting dizzy. She needed air soon, or she would pass out.

"Have you found the toxin yet? We're running out of time," the man on top of Zoe called.

"It's too damn dark in here. I'm turning a light on."

"Well, hurry up, she's losing her fight. It won't be much longer."

Zoe continued to struggle but was getting nowhere. She knew he was right; she wouldn't be able to hold out much longer — then they would bring her back to Alana to be killed. She couldn't let that happen.

Zoe's fingers brushed against a thin metal tube. Her crutch. She grabbed it and swung with all the strength she had left. It connected with something solid, and a moment later the pressure on the pillow lessened. She shoved it aside and gulped in air. Her attacker was sitting on the ground next to the bed, still conscious. She swung the crutch again, this time aiming for his head. After two more blows, he collapsed to the ground. One down.

Zoe turned her attention to the man by Ian's bed. He appeared to be still looking for the toxin. Zoe used the crutch to pull herself out of bed, stumbling the moment her injured leg hit the ground.

Where were the others? Had the Arrows gotten to them first?

"Hey!" she yelled, getting the other man's attention. The man stopped searching and stared at her. She had no idea what she was going to do now.

He crossed the room in three steps and clamped his hands around her neck, lifting her from the ground, sending her crutch clattering to the floor. She tried to pull his fingers away as they tightened around her throat, but she couldn't move them. "Mrs. Wilborn said she wanted you alive, but I'm not sure she'd care too much if I brought her your lifeless body," he growled in her face.

The front door swung open. "Let her go!" Blake howled, a gun in his hand. The man turned his head to look at Blake but didn't release her. "I mean it. I'll shoot."

"Do it," Zoe managed to say as her field of vision narrowed. If he didn't, she was dead anyway. She heard two gunshots and fell to the ground with her attacker.

Blake and Hamid rushed forward and helped Zoe to a chair while she gasped for air. She looked down at the man who had almost killed her. "Is he—?"

"Dead," Hamid confirmed. "Are you all right?"

"I think so." She gently touched her throat as she tried to catch her breath. She glanced at the bed. Ian still hadn't moved. Iris was at his side, checking his pulse.

"He's alive," she said with a sigh of relief.

Hamid joined Iris at Ian's bedside. "He's probably been drugged. He'll be out for a while."

"They had a syringe," Zoe said. "I heard them mention something about a toxin."

Iris bent down and pulled a syringe out from under the bed. It was still full.

"But they have to realize we're immune," Blake said as he secured the man Zoe had knocked out with her crutch.

"I'm sure it's such a concentrated dose that it wouldn't matter," Hamid said.

"How did they find us?" Iris asked as she sat down next to her unconscious brother.

Zoe looked at Blake. "Was it the video?"

"I doubt it." Blake ran his hand through his hair. "It only went live ten minutes ago. There's no way they could have found it and tracked it back to this motel that quickly."

"It doesn't matter how they found us," Hamid said. "We can't say here. It won't be long before they come looking for these two. We don't want to be here when they do."

"I'll go get us a ride," Blake said. "Can you pack up?"

"I'll handle it," Iris said. "Zoe, will you sit with Ian? I don't want him to be alone when he comes to."

"Of course."

"What should we do with this?" Iris held up the syringe.

"Maybe we should keep it," Zoe said. Blake handed her the crutches, and she slowly made her way over to the bed. "You never know, it might come in handy."

"All right. I'll go figure out a safe way to pack it." Iris got up and left with Blake and Hamid while Zoe sat down on the bed next to Ian. She wished she knew what they had used to knock him out, and more importantly, how long it would last. She stared at his face to avoid looking at the dead body on the floor.

She had no idea how much time passed. If it wasn't for Ian still lying on the bed, she would have feared they had left her behind. Not that she would blame them. She had put them all in danger. They would be safer if she wasn't around.

Ian started to stir. "What's going on?" he asked groggily.

"The Arrows found us. We think you were drugged."

"What?" Ian shot up. His gaze landed on the dead body. "Are you all right?"

"I'm fine. I was able to hold them off until Blake got in with a gun. You were no help, by the way." Zoe gave him a small smile.

Ian smirked. "It doesn't look like you needed my help. Where are the others?"

"Iris and Hamid are packing. Blake's getting a car."

"Good." Ian slowly lowered himself back down. "Thanks, Zoe. I have a feeling I'd be dead if it wasn't for you."

"Believe me, it's the least I can do. Now rest. We'll be leaving soon."

«‹«Chapter 4»››»

Cole spent all morning preparing himself for his parents' visit. He had no idea how he was going to make them believe that he was starting to see their side, let alone forgive them. The very idea made him sick. He couldn't keep the image of Zoe sprawled on the floor covered in blood from his mind. He could never forgive Alana for that—but if he ever wanted to see Zoe again, he had to convince his mom he had done just that.

When his door finally started to open, everything he had prepared vanished from his mind as his anger came flooding back. He wasn't going to be able to pull this off; he would end up spending the rest of his life locked in this room.

"Cole, darling," Alana said as she made her way over to him. Cole took a step back without thinking, and Alana held up her hands. "That's fair."

She sat down on the bed. Gordon shut the door before he joined her on the bed.

Cole didn't move. His gaze shifted to the door. Would it be possible to make a run for it?

"There are guards outside the door," Alana said, guessing his thoughts.

Cole's gaze shifted back to her. "How long are you planning on keeping me prisoner here?"

"You're not a prisoner," Gordon said.

"Oh, really?" Cole walked over to the door and opened it. Just as his mother had said, a guard was waiting on the other side with a rifle in his hands.

"Sit down, and let's talk like adults," Alana said.

Cole fought not to roll his eyes. They had been treating him like a child since he got here, and now they wanted him to act like an adult?

He tried to remember what Jackson and Victoria had told him. If he ever wanted to get out of here, he needed to play along.

"Fine." He shut the door and sat down in the armchair across from the bed. "How's your plan to end the world going?"

He was really bad at playing along.

Alana sighed. "We've been over this. We're saving the world, not ending it. If things had gone on the way they were, humans would have destroyed the planet. What we did will ensure that there is a thriving planet for generations. The sooner you accept that, the easier it will be for you to adjust to the new world we are creating."

"We want you to be part of shaping that new world," Gordon said kindly. "You can help us make the planet better for everyone." Cole looked his father in the eye and nearly broke down. He wanted to see a monster staring back at him, but all he saw was the man who always went out of his way to make sure his children were taken care of. How could his eyes still be filled with love when he was in the process of killing billions of people?

Cole leaned forward and put his head in his hands. He had to turn this conversation around. "I'm trying," he said in what he hoped was a convincing tone. He looked back at his parents. "It's just hard for me to believe that this was the only way. What about all the work being done at Green Tech? Aren't they supposed to be finding solutions to save the planet that don't involve killing billions of people?"

"The work being done at Green Tech is amazing, but it isn't enough to reverse the damage that has already been done to the environment," Gordon said.

Alana reached out for Cole's hand, and he had to stop himself from pulling away. "We need a reset. Then we can build a society that values nature and works to protect it. The technology Green Tech has developed will go a long way in helping us achieve that goal."

Cole leaned back in his chair to escape Alana's grasp without offending her. "Is that why you started Green Tech? To develop the technology you'd need for this society?"

"Partly," Gordon admitted. "We had hoped that we could find a way to save the environment from destruction without resorting to a complete reset, but it became clear that wasn't possible. That was when we shifted Green Tech's focus to developing the technology we would need to rebuild and rehabilitate the environment once the destruction stopped."

Cole put a hand over his mouth to stop himself from laughing. His parents really believed this was the only logical answer. Had they always been this insane, and he had somehow missed it?

He racked his brain for a response that would show his parents he understood, but nothing came to mind. Thankfully, a knock at the door saved him from having to say anything.

"Mrs. Wilborn," one of the guards said as he stuck his head into the room. "You have a call."

"Not now," Alana snapped.

"They said it was important."

"Fine." Alana rolled her eyes and got up. She took the phone from the guard and stepped out into the hall.

Cole turned to Gordon. "Dad, you have to talk to Mom. I'm going crazy in here by myself." Cole figured if he couldn't make them believe he was on their side, he might be able to play on his father's love for him. Gordon had always been the softer of his parents.

"All I care about right now is keeping this family safe. I know you want to go out there and look for Zoe, but doing that right now might end up getting you both killed, and I can't have that. Things are going to get dangerous out there. Once they calm down, I'll help you find Zoe."

"What do you mean they got away?" Alana's voiced traveled into the room. Cole turned away from Gordon and looked at the door, which Alana had failed to close all the way. "Explain to me how an injured scientist was able to overpower you!"

Zoe. The call was about Zoe. Alana had people out there trying to find her. Cole's stomach tightened as he thought about what they would do to Zoe if they found her.

"Just find them," Alana said, the tension clear in her voice. A moment later, she reentered the room with a smile on her face that didn't quite hide the stress in her eyes.

"You have people out there looking for Zoe." It was a statement, not a question. He really shouldn't have been surprised that his mother wanted to find Zoe. She had tried to stop the Arrows' plan and probably gotten closer than anyone thought she would.

Alana's smile faltered slightly as she retook her seat. "Yes, we do."

"Why? What are you going to do to her?"

"I want to bring her home, of course," Alana said.

"We all love Zoe," Gordon added. "We want her home safe. We want the two of you to be able to build your life together. That hasn't changed."

"The people she's with are dangerous. They've manipulated her to believe that we are the villains here," Alana said. Cole had to force himself not to laugh in her face. Of course they were the villains. "They'll use her to try to stop us from rebuilding the world the right way. They don't care about her. That's why we need to get her away from them and back with the people who love her."

Every word coming out of Alana's mouth was lie. Zoe was a threat that Alana wanted to eliminate. But at least he could use this angle to get his parents to believe he was coming around to their side. "That's all I want. Zoe is the only thing that matters to me. If she was here, safe with me, I know we could find a way to move forward." Cole put as much emotion into his words as he could. As much as he wanted Zoe back, she would never be safe if she was here with him.

"Good." Alana got to her feet. "How about we all go have some lunch?"

Cole nodded and followed his parents out of the room. He'd won the first battle and was a step closer to getting away from them for good.

«‹›»

Zoe had no idea where they were. They had been driving all day, only stopping when they were getting low on gas, at which point Blake or Iris would steal another car. They always targeted older models, claiming they were harder to trace. Zoe tried not to think about all the people they had left stranded at a roadside gas station. She hated that they were adding stress to the short amount of time they had left to live.

It was dark when they finally stopped. So dark Zoe could barely make out the edges of the trailer they had parked next to. The full moon overhead was the only source of light. "Where are we?" She slowly climbed out of the back of the rusted-out minivan. Her injured leg was throbbing, and she stumbled when she tried to put weight on it.

Ian carefully draped her arm over his shoulder and wrapped his other arm around her waist to support her. "We're in Kentucky. This is a safe house we set up in case the Arrows ever discovered what we were trying to do."

"Why didn't we come here sooner?" Zoe slowly made her way to the trailer with Ian's support.

"You were kind of bleeding to death." Ian carefully picked her up and carried her up the three steps into the trailer. He didn't let her go until he had carefully set her down on the couch.

Zoe looked around the trailer while the others brought in the few things they had in the car. It was old, and given the quarter inch of dust covering everything, hadn't been used in a long time. The style was similar to the house they had held her at while she was kidnapped.

It had only been a month since Ian had taken her from Green Tech, but it felt like a lifetime ago. Still, she was happy to see that there was no way to secure her wrist to the couch.

Iris came in looking very proud of herself. "I hooked up the electrical. No use wasting the propane. Zoe, see if the TV still works. We might be able to catch the evening news."

Zoe found a dust-covered remote on the table next to her. She picked it up and hit the power button. She was a little surprised when the giant cube television sprang to life. She hadn't seen a TV like it in years. The picture was blurry, but it wasn't terrible. She flipped through the channels looking for a news broadcast.

"I got something," she called once she found a station playing the national news. Everyone gathered around to watch. It had become a ritual as they waited for the fallout of the Arrows' toxin. Blake passed around a plate stacked with sandwiches before taking a seat next to her.

"A mysterious illness sweeps the nation," the newscaster said after the opening. Zoe set her sandwich down on a napkin and leaned forward so she wouldn't miss anything. This was what they had been waiting for. "As death numbers in the US quickly rise to half a million, the public wonders what can be done to slow the spread. We take you now to our chief medical correspondent."

Ian adjusted his position in the chair next to her. "This is moving faster than I thought it would."

The image on the screen changed, now showing a man standing outside of a hospital. "Doctors are still unsure what is causing the recent uptick in deaths. Most cases present as a heart attack, but there appears to be no correlation between people with known heart conditions and the deaths. Doctors have yet to find a treatment method and are urging people to stay home and isolate themselves until more information about how this new disease spreads is determined."

Iris scoffed. "Do they really think people are going to do that?"

"The government is putting together a plan to address what can only be called a global pandemic," the newscaster continued. "Hospitals are already reaching capacity, and staffing shortages mean that many who show up for treatment die before they see a doctor. Back to you, Chuck."

The news went to a commercial. Zoe looked at the others in stunned silence. This was really happening. Everything they told her had been true. Cole's parents had brought about the end of the world. Even after everything, part of her hoped they had been wrong, but there was no denying it now. Zoe carefully got to her feet, adjusting the crutches so they supported the weight her injured leg couldn't.

"Where are you going?" Iris asked.

"I can't watch this anymore. I need to get some air."

Ian jumped to his feet. "It's not safe."

Zoe rolled her eyes. She wasn't their prisoner anymore — at least, she didn't think she was. She appreciated everything they had done to get her away from Alana and help keep her safe, but right now, she needed space. "I thought you said this was a safe house."

"I did, but . . ." Ian looked to the others for backup.

"Let her go," Hamid said with a nod.

Confusion hung heavy on Ian's face, and Zoe spoke up quickly. "It's dark out, and no one knows where we are. I'll be all right. It's not like I can go real far." She glanced down at the crutches.

"Be careful," Ian stressed, "and if you need anything, yell." He opened the trailer door and helped her down the three steps to the ground.

Zoe crutched to the tree line and sat down on a decaying log. She closed her eyes, tilted her head back, and breathed in the crisp night air. All around the world, people were dying, and they had no idea why. She imagined the fear they must be feeling, watching their loved ones die while they could do nothing to stop it.

At least they wouldn't have to grieve too long before they joined them.

Tears formed in Zoe's eyes, and she didn't hold them back. She had tried to save them, to save them all, but she had failed.

She wondered what her life would be like right now if Ian had never tried to steal from Green Tech. She would probably be sitting at home with Cole, watching the news, ignorant that they were protected from what was happening. Would Alana and Gordon have confessed what they had done, or would they have left them in the dark? It would almost be worth not knowing the truth if it meant she was back in Cole's arms again. God, she missed him.

The tears fell faster. Zoe leaned into the sadness, allowing sobs to rake through her body. It felt good to let go. To embrace all the pain and despair that she had been keeping at bay. She had lost everything that mattered in her life; her friends, her family, her job, and Cole. And the Arrows had still won. She had paid such a high price for nothing.

"I thought you might be cold."

Zoe looked up to see Ian standing in front of her with a blanket. "Thanks," she said through her tears.

Ian draped the blanket around her shoulders and turned to head back inside.

"Do you regret any of it?" Zoe said softly.

Ian turned back toward her. "Yeah, maybe." He sat down next to her. "I regret not paying attention to where I was going that day at Green Tech. If I hadn't run into you and dropped that box of files, things might be very different right now. At least for you, anyway. I feel like I ruined your life that day."

"And here I was thinking I was the one who ran into you," Zoe said, trying to break some of the tension that had built up between them.

"Oh, I'm sure I made it seem that way. I was so paranoid that the Arrows knew I was there that I wasn't watching where I was going."

Zoe took the blanket off her shoulders and spread it across her lap before offering Ian the other side. He scooted closer and let her place the blanket over his legs. "Do you think you would have been able to stop the Arrows if I hadn't gotten involved?" It was something she had been struggling with for days.

Ian shook his head. "I doubt it. And there's no way we would have figured out that RiverLife contained the vaccine. Without you, we'd all likely be dead by now."

Zoe swallowed hard and nodded while looking out into the night. "It still feels like it's all my fault."

Ian reached up and gently turned her face to his. "Listen to me. None of this is your fault. You're amazing, Zoe." He brushed the last of her tears off her cheek.

"Thanks." Zoe didn't really believe him, but it was nice to hear him say it. She leaned her head on his shoulder and let herself relax for the first time since this had started. "There sure are a lot of stars here."

"Yeah." Ian wrapped his arm around her and pulled

her closer as they both stared up into the night sky.

««Chapter 5»»

Cole took his time getting ready. His first day of freedom had been tense, and he wasn't exactly looking forward to a repeat. His parents had spent the day acting as if they were all on some family vacation, barely leaving him alone. At one point, he had snuck away — feigning having to use the restroom — and tried to get out of the house, only to find every exit blocked by guards. Despite letting him out of his room, he was still his parents' prisoner.

He paused with his hand on the doorknob. Part of him expected it to be locked, and he nearly fell on his face when it opened freely.

Cole slowly made his way toward the kitchen, hoping to find something for breakfast, but voices coming from the dining room distracted him — voices that didn't belong to his family. He stopped outside the room, and the tension emanating from it vibrated through him. Something had happened.

"We need to get ahead of this," William Conner's voice carried over the rest. "It's an added layer of panic we weren't anticipating."

Conner was a board member for Wilborn Holdings and clearly part of the Arrow Equilibrium. Had the whole company been in on it?

"We always expected there to be some panic once things began to progress. This doesn't change anything," Alana said.

"But they're going after the vaccine," Conner stressed.

"Our RiverLife stockpiles are secure. We have more than enough to meet our needs without reclaiming what's on the store shelves." Cole would recognize that voice anywhere, and it nearly destroyed him. It was Tyrone Roberts, the plant manager from the RiverLife bottled water plant.

He had taught Cole everything he knew about manufacturing. Cole had looked up to the man for years. It never crossed his mind that he might be an Arrow.

"This is a massive overreaction," Gordon said, boredom clear in his voice. "Zoe's message will save a handful of people at best. It's irrelevant. We have more important things to focus on."

Cole inched closer to the room at the sound of Zoe's name. He needed to know what she had done. If she was still fighting, then she must be all right, but he would give anything to know for sure.

"She's still a risk. She knows too much," Conner insisted.

"Should we have her eliminated?" That sounded like Brett, Zoe's boss from Green Tech. Cole wasn't surprised that he was an Arrow, but he was blown away by how casually he suggested having Zoe killed. Cole had never liked the man, but he thought Brett and Zoe had been close. Zoe certainly looked to him as a mentor.

"No one is going to have her eliminated. She's Cole's fiancée." Frustration brimmed in Gordon's voice. "We have people trying to find her and bring her back safely. That way we can contain her until things finish playing out."

"Cole."

He almost jumped out of his skin at Jackson's whisper behind him. His brother waved him away from the dining room; reluctantly, Cole followed.

"Victoria found something you're going to want to see," Jackson said once they were farther away.

"What did she find?" Cole looked over his shoulder at the dining room. Whatever Victoria had to show him couldn't be more important than what was being discussed in there.

"Zoe's message." Jackson smiled at him, picking up the pace.

Cole's breath caught in the back of this throat. He was going to see Zoe again. He would be able to see for himself that she was all right, even if it was just a recording.

Jackson led him to a part of the house he hadn't been in yet. Victoria was waiting for them in the most elaborate playroom he had ever seen, with a full ball pit in one corner and a pool table in the other. His nephews were nowhere in sight.

"What are we doing in here?" Cole joined her in front of a large TV screen mounted on the wall.

"Mom and Dad took our cell phones, and the cable went out last night," Victoria started. "I figured there was something they didn't want us to see. Fortunately for us, they forgot that the kids' gaming systems are connected to the internet." She reached down and picked up a controller and waved it at them.

"So, you found whatever it was they were trying to keep from us?"

"Yep." Victoria turned toward the screen and brought up a video. Paused on the screen was an image of Zoe; the whole background was white, but Cole could tell she was sitting on something. She must not be able to support herself on her injured leg.

"She's alive." The words escaped Cole's lips like a prayer.

"She's not only alive, she's still trying to save as many lives as she can," Victoria said.

Jackson plopped down on the couch. "Zoe always was stubborn," he said with a smirk.

Cole nodded to Victoria. "Play it."

Victoria clicked a button on the remote and sat down next to Jackson. Cole didn't move as he watched. He wasn't really hearing what Zoe was saying, it didn't really matter to him anyway. Instead, he focused on her eyes, which looked tired — she must not be sleeping well — and her mouth, which she kept even except for when she shifted her weight. A small flinch showed she was trying to hide the pain.

He had always known she was strong, but watching her now, still standing up to his mom after she put a bullet in her leg, was inspiring. No wonder William Conner was concerned. Anyone watching this would follow Zoe.

For a moment, Zoe disappeared from the screen, and pictures of his parents took her place as she called them out as the ones responsible for the deaths sweeping the planet.

"Mom and Dad aren't going to like that," Jackson

said.

"Who cares? They are responsible, and everyone should know it." A moment later, the video ended, and Cole finally took a seat in the armchair next to the couch. His mind was going in a thousand different directions, but they all came back to the same thing: Zoe was alive and fighting. "I need to find her."

"And we'll help you," Victoria said, "but we have to wait for the right time to make our move."

"She might not have that kind of time. I overheard the Arrows talking about this video and debating whether or not she should be eliminated." Cole waved his hand at the screen. "They're hunting her, and if they find her, they'll kill her."

"I don't think Mom or Dad would let that happen." Jackson picked up the video game remote and switched to some war game. "Despite everything, I think they still love her. They might not be thrilled that she's fighting against them, but they won't kill her."

Cole got up and started to pace. "You don't know that. You weren't in the control room that day. You didn't see what Mom was like. She'd do anything to see this through to the end."

"If that was the case, then why didn't she kill Zoe then?" Jackson wasn't looking at him, his full attention on the video game. "Where are the boys?"

Victoria sighed. "They're with their dad. You know, I think Trevor knew about this all along. He might even be one of them. Can you believe he never told me?"

"It makes sense. Didn't Mom set you two up? She probably wanted to make sure she had people she could trust in the family. Makes me glad I never went out with anyone Mom tried to fix me up with. I could have ended up married to a terrorist like you," Jackson said.

Victoria smacked Jackson on the back of the head. "You're an ass." She picked up a game controller and started to play.

And just like that, his siblings had moved on, the risk to Zoe's life forgotten. They might be on his side, but it was clear they didn't fully understand the scope of what was happening. People were dying en masse outside the walls of their fancy prison, but inside they might as well be on vacation.

How could they not understand everything Zoe had risked to get that message out? Despite what Gordon had said, Cole didn't believe they would spare Zoe when the time came. It was up to him to find her and keep her safe. He just had no idea how to do it.

«‹›»

Zoe tried to help as much as she could as they cleaned the trailer, but she was limited to the tasks she could do while seated. She really needed to work on getting the strength back in her leg. It was fine to sit on a stool to wash dishes, but if the Arrows showed up, she would be helpless. It was a fluke she had gotten away unharmed the last time. If Blake hadn't gotten into the room when he did, she would be dead right now.

"Uncle and Blake went to get groceries," Iris said as she walked in with a basket full of wet laundry. "Want to help me with these before they get back?"

"Sure." Zoe grabbed her crutches and followed Iris out of the trailer. She was getting pretty good at navigating the steps with the crutches, though she never turned down the help when Ian offered.

"It's a pain to do things this way, but Ian insists we try to save fuel." Iris set down the basket and handed

Zoe a container of clothespins. Iris had been nothing but nice to Zoe, but she still couldn't stop her nerves from resurfacing whenever they were alone. She really needed to find a way to not feel like a captive whenever Iris was around. "Though I guess we better get used to it. Who knows how long the electrical grid will be maintained once the toxin runs its course?"

Zoe had never thought about how they would live when this was all over. Part of her didn't think she'd make it long enough to find out. Alana and Gordon wouldn't want her messing up their perfect new world. It seemed silly to worry about the logistics of laundry when there was a terrorist group hunting you. "We'll have to learn to live like the pioneers did." Zoe reached down, careful to maintain her balance, and grabbed a wet shirt.

"God, this is going to suck. I hate all that scratch cooking, growing your own food, organic bullshit." Iris turned to look at her with such conviction in her eyes that Zoe was sure they were about to charge into battle. "Promise me we won't let these boys force us back to doing all the domestic garbage women have been saddled with since the beginning of time. It's time for the men to step up."

"I'm all for that," Zoe said with a smile. "If we're going to have to rebuild the world anyway, let's make sure we build one where the patriarchy doesn't exist."

"Hell yeah!" Iris said as she hung a pair of Ian's underwear on the line. "It's women's turn to make the rules. In fact . . ." Iris turned around and spotted her brother clearing some dead branches away from the generator. "Ian, come here."

Ian jogged over to them. "What's wrong?" He looked them both over, clearly assessing them for injuries.

"I need you to finish here." Iris motioned toward the basket of wet clothes that still needed to be hung up.

"Why? What are you two going to do?"

"I'll go tune up the generator. I am the one with an engineering background after all, and Zoe can go monitor the news while she rests her leg."

"I have the generator under control," Ian said. Zoe smirked at the confusion in his voice. She wondered how often Iris did things like this to him.

"I don't care, I'm taking over." Iris walked away without another word.

"What the hell was that all about?" Ian asked as he watched his sister leave.

Zoe shrugged. "Down with the patriarchy," she said with a laugh, and handed him the clothespins before heading back inside the trailer.

She sat down on the couch and propped her foot up on the arm of the chair next to it, wincing as a wave of pain surged through her leg. She was pushing herself too hard. For a moment, she considered searching for the painkillers but decided against it; she could handle the pain for a while. Besides, they might need them for something more important, and who knew if they would be able to find more?

Iris was right, they needed to start preparing for life after the toxin.

She picked up the remote and started to flip through the few channels they had. It was still too early for the midday news, and Zoe couldn't find anything else worth watching. She left some talk show on and dropped the remote on the couch next to her. It was better to have some background noise rather than being left alone with her own thoughts for too long. She didn't want any flashbacks to her kidnapping.

Iris came in after a few minutes and grabbed a bottle of RiverLife water from the fridge. They had transferred a few cases from car to car as they made their way here. They had no idea how much of the hidden vaccine they would need to have in their systems to keep them safe, so they had decided to drink a bottle a day until they were sure the threat was over.

"The generator is ready should we need it." Iris sat down on the couch next to Zoe. "Anything new yet?" she nodded toward the TV.

"No, but the news should be starting soon."

The door opened again, and Ian walked in with his arms loaded with grocery bags. "Does your protest against the patriarchy extend to bringing in the groceries?" He nearly dropped one of the bags as he managed the three steps inside.

"I suppose not." Iris huffed and went out to help.

Zoe got up and slowly made her way to the kitchen a few feet away. She left her crutches by the couch, gingerly testing how much weight she could support on her injured leg. "Let me help." She took one of the bags from Ian, limped over to the counter, and started to unpack the bag.

"You don't have to."

"It's okay, I can manage." She gave Ian a smile.

"Things are getting insane out there," Blake said as he entered the trailer with another load of bags. "We saw three people collapse in the middle of the store while we were there."

"Are you serious?" Iris said as she followed him back inside.

"Yes," Hamid said. "Gordon and Alana might think they're giving people a quick, painless death, but the fear out there is so much worse."

"The fistfight over toilet paper was entertaining, though," Blake said.

"What's important is that we got enough supplies to get us through the next few weeks. I don't want any of you out there in that madness." Hamid looked pointedly at each of them as if they were children.

"Yes, Uncle." Iris kissed his cheek and took the bags he was carrying.

They all paused as they heard the melody that signified the start of the news. "Hundreds of thousands of people died overnight. Doctors are still unable to identify the cause. Panic sweeps the nation as the government orders nationwide stay-at-home orders." The newscaster announced the afternoon headlines.

Zoe turned back to the groceries. She didn't need to see more proof of her failure.

"But we begin with a message that's sweeping across the globe."

"Shit," Blake said, dropping a can of soup he had been unpacking. Zoe turned to see what had happened. Her eyes landed on the television, where an image of her on a white background was displayed in the top left corner.

Ian came over to her and put his hand on her shoulder. "We wanted people to see the message. This proves they have. It's a good thing."

Zoe nodded as she watched the news play small clips of her message, leaving out everything she said about the Arrows and the Wilborns. "Scientists want to stress that there is zero proof that RiverLife water contains a vaccine and urge people not to believe theories they find online. At this time, there is no known way to stop this virus."

Zoe turned away from the TV and busied herself

with the groceries again. She wasn't sure what she expected, but hearing the news completely discredit her hurt far worse than she expected. Would anyone believe her now?

Hamid brought a bag of groceries over to the counter next to her. "The only reason the news is trying to discredit you is because the Arrows want them to. They don't want the public to know there is a way to stop the toxin."

Zoe nodded as she choked back the tears that were starting to form in her eyes. She knew he was right, or at least she hoped he was. If not, what had been the point of any of this?

«‹›»

Cole had snuck into the game room to watch Zoe's message a hundred times over the last two days. Her words played on repeat in his mind constantly. He would do anything to hear her voice in person again, but for now, this would have to do.

He sat down on the familiar couch in front of the TV in the game room and picked up the video game remote. He was about to pull up Zoe's video when he heard someone behind him. Cole held his breath as he waited for the person to identify themselves.

"Jackson said I would find you in here," Alana said.

Cole didn't turn around to look at his mother; instead, he opened a game and started to play. He had no idea what he was doing, but he needed to do something so Alana wouldn't suspect they were using the console to get uncensored information from the outside world.

Alana sat down on the chair next to the couch. "I got

this system to keep the boys occupied. I never imagined you and your brother would spend so much time using it."

"Well, it's not like there's much else I can do to pass the time," Cole said while keeping his eyes fixed on the screen. "I can't go to work anymore. You won't give me a phone. Zoe's gone. Victoria's busy with her kids, and Jackson could never hold up his end of a conversation that didn't involve sports or girls. I need something to keep myself busy."

"I might be able to help with that. Something has come up that I want your help with."

Cole paused the game and turned to look at his mother. Alana had to be pretty desperate if she was coming to him. "You want my help?" He tried to keep the disgust from his voice. He was supposed to be playing the part of loving, understanding son.

"It involves Zoe," Alana said slowly. Cole could feel her eyes searching him for a reaction.

"Did you find her?"

"Not yet. Believe me, I wish we had."

I bet you do. Cole swallowed hard to keep himself from blurting out the thoughts running through his head. He could do this. "Then what is it?"

"Zoe put out a message that is starting to gain some traction. The public is scared, and her message is only fueling that fear. It's getting people killed."

"Does it really matter at this point?" Cole said before he could stop himself.

Alana sighed. "Yes. The steps we have taken to restore balance are extreme, but we've been very careful to ensure that people experience a quick, painless death."

So it was okay to kill people as long as they didn't

suffer. At least he knew his mother drew the line somewhere, though he doubted that same courtesy would apply to Zoe if the Arrows found her.

Cole let out a deep breath. "How can I help?" He felt like he was going to vomit as he said the words. The last thing he wanted to do was help the Arrows.

"I've arranged for a press conference tomorrow to address Zoe's comments. I need you to give a statement." Alana shifted in her seat. There was something she wasn't telling him.

"What kind of statement?"

"You aren't going to like it," Alana warned. "We need to discredit her. The public needs to think she is lying to them. It's the only way I can keep her safe."

"And that's what you really want? To keep her safe?" Cole wasn't buying it. There had to be more going on than his mother was telling him. If all that mattered was keeping Zoe safe, then why should they be concerned about the effect her message was having?

"There are certain members of my organization who think she's a threat to what we are trying to accomplish, and they want to take extreme measures to eliminate that threat. I'm trying to stop that from happening. The only way I can do that is if I stay in power. Zoe speaking out against the Arrows has some members convinced that I'm not the right person to lead us into the new world we envision."

And there it was — the truth. Zoe was a threat to Alana's power. Cole knew deep down that his mother didn't really care about Zoe's safety, but the realization still hurt. "I can't write a statement like that."

"I'll have something prepared for you. All you have to do is go in front of the camera and read it. It's the only way to keep her safe."

Cole leaned back into the couch. He really didn't want to do this, but his mom was right. He would do anything to keep Zoe safe. Cole feared what Alana would do to Zoe if he didn't go along with her plan. "Fine," he said with a resigned sigh.

"Good." Alana got up and started to make her way toward the door.

"Mom," Cole said, turning around to watch her.

"Yes, darling?"

"Can I see Zoe's message?" Of course, he had already seen it, but he wanted to know what Alana would say. Zoe had said some pretty damaging things about his parents. Would his mom want him to see that?

Alana hesitated. "I don't have a copy of it on me. I'll see if I can get someone to show it to you."

She was lying. She would never show him the message.

"Thanks, Mom." He turned back to the TV and picked up the game controller. When he was sure Alana had left, he pulled up Zoe's message and started to watch it for the hundred and first time.

««Chapter 6»»

There was a perfectly pressed suit hanging on the back of Cole's door when he got out of the shower. He had barely slept the night before as he second-guessed agreeing to give a statement to discredit Zoe. He dreaded what she would think if she saw it and hoped that she knew how much he still loved her — and that he would never betray her like this unless he had no other option.

He had heard Brett, a person Zoe had trusted and depended on for years, casually mention having her killed. There was no doubt that he meant it. Cole was sure he wasn't the only Arrow who felt that way. He needed to play along to keep her safe.

With a sigh, Cole grabbed the suit and started to change. It felt like forever since he'd last worn one. He took his time buttoning up his shirt in a feeble attempt to put off what he had to do. When he couldn't put it off any longer, he left the room.

Jackson and Victoria's family were already in the dining room when he got there. The jeans and T-shirts they had been wearing since arriving at the safe house were gone, replaced with business wear. Even his nephews were in formal attire, and they didn't seem thrilled by the situation. More than once, Victoria had to swat their hands way from loosening their ties or trying to unbutton their shirts.

"Did Mom drag you guys into this press conference too?" Cole pulled out the chair next to Jackson and sat down.

"She wants us all there to show a united front against the lies Zoe is spreading," Victoria's husband said. Cole had never been a fan of Trevor Castillo, but at that moment, he couldn't have despised him more. Cole took a sip of milk to try to rid his mouth of the taste of bile.

"Trevor, can you go check on the baby? I think I hear him crying," Victoria said.

Trevor threw down his napkin and got up without saying a word; they had been fighting ever since he'd confessed to Victoria that he had been an Arrow all along and never told her.

"He didn't mean that," Victoria said.

"Yeah, he did." Cole grabbed a box of cereal from the middle of the table and poured himself a bowl.

"Trevor has always been kind of an ass, but we put up with him for you," Jackson said in between bites of his eggs.

"I know," Victoria said. "Maverick, stop playing with your breakfast."

"Are either of you speaking at the press conference?" Cole asked.

"No, I thought we all just had to stand there and look pretty," Jackson said.

"Maybe you do, but Mom wants me to read a statement to help discredit Zoe." Cole didn't look up from his cereal as he talked.

"You're kidding, right?"

"You didn't agree to do it, did you?" Victoria asked.

"I don't have much of a choice. I overheard the Arrows having a meeting the other day. They were discussing Zoe's message and if she should be eliminated. Brett was leading the charge to have her taken out."

Jackson nearly choked on his cup of coffee. "Brett from Green Tech? Brett her boss?"

"Yeah," Cole sighed.

"I never liked him. He always had to be the center of attention. I bet he's been waiting for a chance to go after Zoe. It must kill him that she was always so much smarter than him."

"He can't be that threatened by her," Victoria protested.

"Apparently, he can," Cole said. "Mom promised if I did this, she wouldn't let the Arrows kill Zoe."

"That's messed up," Jackson said.

"Do you know what she wants you to say?" Victoria asked.

"No. She said she'd have something prepared, and all I'd have to do was read it. Would be nice to see it ahead of time, though."

"She probably doesn't want to give you a chance to back out," Jackson said.

"I take it she didn't ask you to write the statement then," Cole said. Jackson was the one who usually told him exactly what to say whenever he had to talk to the press.

"She did not. They haven't let me do anything since

we got here. I'm going out of my mind." Jackson grabbed an apple and threw it over his head before catching it.

"You're worse than the boys, you know that?" Victoria scolded.

Jackson caught the apple again before sticking his tongue out at Victoria, making the boys giggle.

Gordon walked into the dining room. "Last call for the bathroom. The cars will be here any minute."

"We aren't having the press conference here?" Cole asked.

"No. This is a safe house. We don't want the world to know where we are."

"Then where are we going?" Victoria asked as she ushered her kids out of the room.

"Wilborn Holdings. I'll see you all out front in five." Gordon followed Finn and Maverick out of the room.

Cole looked excitedly from Jackson to Victoria. "We might be able to get away," he said in an excited whisper, in case Gordon was still nearby.

"It's possible, though I'm sure we'll have security detail with us," Jackson said.

"It has to be easier than trying to break out of here."

"Be alert in case an opportunity presents itself, but don't do anything stupid." Victoria looked pointedly at Cole.

"Fine," Cole said, though he had no intention of listening to her. The first chance he got, he was making a run for it.

«‹«›»»

It hadn't taken them long to develop a routine: chores in the morning, break for lunch and to check the news, work on regaining strength in her leg in the afternoon, followed by dinner and another news break. It made it almost possible to forget what was happening outside the safety of the trailer.

Zoe limped to the couch. She was able to make it around the trailer without the crutches now, though even short stretches wore her out. She eased herself down and grabbed the remote. The others would be in soon.

Blake came over, handed her a bowl of cheap, boxed mac and cheese, and plopped down next to her. They had been taking turns with the cooking and cleaning, though Iris was still protesting anything she considered too domestic. Zoe didn't mind, except for the fact that Blake seemed to have the palate of a teenage boy and Ian's idea of cooking was warming up whatever he could find to microwave. She guessed at this point, they couldn't be picky, though she would kill for a salad or Cole's homemade spaghetti sauce.

Zoe glanced up at the screen. "This is different." She had turned on what should have been the local news, only to find it replaced with a silver arrow wrapped in a green vine of leaves with perfectly balanced scales hanging off each end. "Blake, go get the others."

Blake jumped off the couch and ran out of the trailer. A few moments later, everyone came in. "What the hell is this?" Iris stared at the screen as she wiped grease from her hands with a rag.

"This is what it's all been about." Hamid sat down in the armchair next to the couch. "This is the start of the Arrows' rise to power."

The image on the screen changed, and they were now looking at a stage set up in the lobby of Wilborn Holdings Headquarters. The last time Zoe had seen it set up like this was during the press conferences while she was kidnapped. She figured there was a good chance they'd once again be asking for information on her location, though she very much doubted it was to bring her home safely.

As people began to file onto the stage, she expected it to fill with the upper ranks of the Arrows; instead she saw only the Wilborn family. Cole stood between Jackson and Victoria, his face expressionless. Zoe had no idea what that meant. Was he there because he really was an Arrow? Had he been playing her all along? Or was he there against his will?

Alana approached the podium at the front of the stage with a stoic look on her face. "Hello, my name is Alana Wilborn, and I'm the head of the Arrow Equilibrium. There have been some negative things going around about us, and I'm here to set the record straight. Despite what you might have heard, we are not a terrorist group, and we had nothing to do with the disease that is devastating the planet."

Blake snorted. "She's one hell of a liar, isn't she?"

"The Arrow Equilibrium is an environmental advocacy group. We have used our resources and discovered the true source of the toxin sweeping the globe. It breaks my heart to report that this toxin was created and released by someone whom I considered family, my son Cole's fiancée, Zoe Antos. You may recall hearing about her kidnapping from our laboratory, but we now believe that was a setup to build sympathy for her before she went through with her plan. This is the security footage we recovered showing her releasing the toxin."

Zoe wanted to laugh; Alana was really trying to pin this whole thing on her.

The screen changed, now showing a black-and-white video of Zoe standing in the control room at Wilborn Holdings. However, instead of showing her dumping a jug of water on the controls or shooting out the panel, the angle changed to show a manicured hand hitting a button and the words "Launch Successful" flashing on the screen. Zoe looked down at her unpolished, stress-bitten nails in disbelief.

The image changed again, and Alana was back at the podium. "We believe Zoe is working with Blake Cooper, Iris Sutton, and Ian Sutton. All of them are believed to be armed and extremely dangerous." Images of each of them flashed on the screen, including one of Ian holding a gun to Cole's head. "My son Cole would like to make a statement."

Zoe sucked in a breath as Cole walked to the podium. Why was he helping the Arrows blame her for their toxin? This had to be some kind of nightmare. She willed herself to wake up, only to have Blake reach over and grab her hand, confirming what she was seeing was real.

Cole picked up a piece of paper from the podium. Zoe watched, transfixed, as his eyes scanned the document before he glanced back at his mom, who nodded.

Whatever Cole was about to say, they weren't his words.

"Zoe sought me out while we were in college, doing whatever she could to make me fall in love with her." Cole's voice was robotic as he read the statement. "I realize now that I was a pawn in her plan to spread death and destruction across the planet."

Every word Cole said sliced through Zoe's heart. She knew he didn't mean any of it, Alana had to be forcing him somehow, but that didn't make it hurt any less. Blake squeezed her hand as the tears started to roll down her cheeks.

"She needed access to my family's money and resources, and like a fool, I gave her everything she wanted. Including securing her a position at Green Tech Laboratory, where she developed her toxin in secret. Zoe Antos is a heartless liar who will do whatever it takes to achieve her goal." With a small shake of his head, Cole stepped away from the podium.

Alana stepped forward again. "Zoe Antos and the people helping her need to be brought to justice. The Arrow Equilibrium will pay $50,000 to anyone who can provide information on their whereabouts or confirmation of their deaths."

"No!" Cole screamed in the background while jumping to his feet. "You promised Zoe wouldn't be hurt if I read your message! You're the real monster!" Two men rushed forward to grab Cole just before the screen went black.

"Well, that was interesting," Ian said as he turned to look at Zoe.

She was aware of everyone's eyes on her, waiting to see how she would react. She supposed she should be angry — Alana had managed to pin the end of the world on her — but anger would have to come later.

"If you'll excuse me," she said calmly. Slowly, Zoe limped her way across the trailer to the bathroom. Once inside she locked the door, slid down to the floor, and started to sob.

«Chapter 7»»

They dragged Cole off the stage, threw him in the back of a car, and drove him back to the safe house where he once again found himself locked in his room.

He collapsed on the bed. He had been a fool to believe Alana was trying to keep Zoe safe. She had proven time and again that she only cared about the Arrows, and yet he kept believing she had his best interest at heart. Cole prayed that wherever Zoe was, she wouldn't hear what he had said. Her love and faith in him were all he had left, and the fact that he could have destroyed that for nothing killed him.

Worst of all, he had blown his chances of escaping. He was sure he would be banished to this room for the foreseeable future. Everything he had done to gain back his parents' trust was gone.

Cole turned the TV on, hoping for a distraction. Unfortunately, it appeared the Arrows had taken over all the airwaves, and the only thing on was the damned press conference. His outburst at the end had been edited out. There was no chance Zoe would see it, and if she hadn't caught the live feed, she wouldn't even know that he had fought back. She would think that he had turned on her.

The thought made him sick. He grabbed a pillow and covered his face with it.

He didn't move when he heard a knock at the door. It wasn't like he could answer it even if he wanted to. He heard the door open and close.

"Are you here to give me a lecture?" Cole didn't remove the pillow from his face as he spoke.

"I should, after that stunt you pulled." Gordon sat down on the armchair across from the bed and watched Cole intently.

Cole sprang up, the pillow falling back to the bed. "The stunt I pulled? You're one to talk! Mom convinced me that the only way to keep Zoe safe was to read that garbage about her on TV, only for Mom to turn around and put out a kill order on her."

"That's not what she did," Gordon said.

"Oh, no. 'We'll pay for information on their whereabout or *confirmation of death*.' Sounds like a kill order to me."

"It was an unfortunate choice of words."

"Really? She sounded pretty sure of herself when she said it."

"I don't believe your mother wants Zoe dead. Zoe is still part of this family. We want to bring her home and help her through this so we can all move forward together."

Cole stared at Gordon in shock. "You can't possibly believe that."

"I do, and I know your mother feels the same way . . .

she's just under a lot of pressure at the moment. The Arrows believe she isn't capable of leading them after Zoe got so close to stopping their plan. She only said what she did in order to prove that she has the situation under control."

Cole rolled his eyes and turned away from Gordon. "By asking the public to kill Zoe?"

"That's not what she did. Trust me, Zoe is safer with your mother in charge than if one of the other founding members take over."

Cole whipped around. "So I'm supposed to appreciate that Mom lied to me about keeping Zoe safe because it keeps a different lunatic from taking over?"

Gordon squeezed the bridge of his nose. "I thought we were past this, Cole."

"I won't be past anything until I know Zoe is safe for good."

"I'm doing everything in my power to make that happen for you, but she's not making it easy." Gordon took a deep breath and got to his feet. "I didn't come here to discuss the press conference."

"Then why are you here?"

"I came to make sure you were all right. I know it couldn't have been easy reading that statement. I told your mother we should have let you see it ahead of time, but she felt it was better to rip the Band-Aid off, so to speak."

"Since when do you do whatever Mom says?"

"Your mother and I are a team, we always have been. We might not always agree, but we support one another anyway."

"You keep telling yourself that." Cole walked to the other side of the room. How could his dad not see that Alana was using him too? They were all pawns in her game.

"I can see that you don't want to talk, and I respect that. For now, your mother and I think it's best for you to stay in here."

Cole knew this was coming. He guessed he should be grateful they weren't locking him up somewhere else. At least the room was comfortable. "I figured."

"It won't be for long. We're leaving the day after tomorrow. I'll have one of the guards bring you a bag so you can pack up anything you want to take with you."

Cole looked at Gordon in confusion. He'd assumed they were going to stay here until the toxin had run its course. Something must have changed. "Where are we going?"

"To DC. Your mother is going to be sworn in as president," Gordon said as if it was the most natural thing in the world.

"How is that even possible?" This couldn't be happening. There had to be someone better suited to run the country. Alana had nothing to do with politics. Even if the toxin had taken out several members of Congress, there still had to be someone else in line before her.

"What's left of Congress passed a law this morning that allows them to name a new president if the sitting president and vice president die during a national emergency."

"That's insane."

"Maybe, but this has all been in the works for a very long time. If the Arrows are going to successfully rebuild with a culture that values the environment, we need to do it from a position of power that people respect."

Cole's head was spinning. This couldn't be real. He put his hand on his forehead to try to center himself. He thought Zoe telling him about the Arrows would be the most insane thing he ever heard in his life, but this was so much worse. "This is what it's all really been about, isn't it? Taking over the country."

Gordon closed his eyes for a moment before looking at Cole. "It's a necessary step in achieving our ultimate goal. And whether you agree with it or not, you will stand there and smile while it happens. Your mother has always supported you. It's your turn to return the favor."

Cole shook his head. "I won't do it. I can't support this."

"Stop acting like a child," Gordon said through gritted teeth.

"Stop treating me like one!" Cole yelled. "I'm thirty-five years old. You can't keep me locked up here! I've had enough. I'm leaving."

"I'm sorry, Cole," Gordon sighed. "You aren't going anywhere. Once you've calmed down, we can discuss your responsibilities to this family. Until then, you'll stay in here."

Gordon turned and started to make his way to the door, and Cole rushed after him. He wouldn't let them lock him in his room again. He would get out and get to Zoe before the Arrows had a chance to kill her. He would keep her safe.

He reached the door a step behind Gordon, and an armed guard blocked the door. Gordon nodded to the guard, who shoved Cole back into the room and locked the door.

«‹›»

Zoe had no idea how long she sat on the cold bathroom floor. The others didn't bother her as she drowned her pain in tears. She tried to reassure herself that Cole didn't mean any of the things he had said, that he was being forced somehow, but hearing those words come out of his mouth killed her. Every time she closed her eyes, she saw him being dragged off the stage by armed guards, and the guilt flared up inside of her. What had they done to him after he had spoken up against Alana? She had thought that he'd be safe there, but now she wasn't sure. Things would be so much simpler if they were together.

When no more tears would come, she pulled herself up, splashed some water on her face, and opened the door. The others were hanging around the kitchen doing a terrible job at pretending they weren't waiting for her.

"Are you all right?" Ian asked softly as she limped her way to the sink to get a glass of water.

"Yeah." Zoe nodded and tried to smile. They all had to know she was lying, but there was nothing they could do to make it better.

"Good." Blake grabbed a duffel bag from the closet and plopped it down on the kitchen table. "Then it's time for makeovers."

"I'm sorry, what?" Zoe looked from Ian to Iris to make sure she had heard him right. Iris was already ruffling through the bag. "Do you really think a makeover will help anything right now?"

Ian gently touched her shoulder. "It's not like that. Since the public knows who we are now, it's time to change our appearances so we aren't as easily recognizable."

"Oh." Zoe limped over to the table. "That makes sense." She looked into the bag full of hair products. She wasn't sure they would be able to fool the Arrows with some grocery store hair dye, but at least it was a good distraction.

"So, do you want to go red or blonde?" Iris held up two boxes of dye.

"Red." There was no way Zoe could see herself as blonde.

Iris held the box of red dye up as she studied Zoe's hair. "It should work, but we should probably cut it too."

"Sure." Zoe had never really been attached to her hair, but she wasn't sure how she felt about Iris cutting it. They had been getting along fine since Zoe had joined their little group, but she couldn't forget the offhanded way Iris suggested they kill her when Ian first kidnapped her. The thought of Iris taking a sharp object to her skull make her nervous.

"Got a razor in that bag?" Ian asked. Blake fished out an electric razor and handed it to him. They both disappeared into the bathroom.

Iris pulled out a chair. "Sit down, we'll do you first."

Reluctantly Zoe sat down while Iris went to fill up a spray bottle she had gotten from the bag. Zoe pulled out her hair tie as she waited, running her fingers through her straight brown hair. It had been a while since she had gotten it cut. It came down to the middle of her back.

"Ready?" Iris held up the spray bottle and scissors. Zoe nodded and closed her eyes, flinching slightly as Iris sprayed the cold water on her head. "So, I know that you and I didn't get off on the best foot."

Zoe snorted. That was the understatement of the century. She had only just begun to connect with Iris, and most of the time Zoe still felt like Iris barely tolerated her being there.

"Don't move," Iris scolded as she raised the scissors and started to cut. "What I was trying to say is that I'm glad you're here. It's nice to have another woman to talk to."

If Iris didn't have a pair of scissors to her hair, Zoe would have whipped around to make sure she hadn't been replaced with an impersonator. "Thanks." Zoe couldn't help but feel like Iris was trying to trap her somehow. "I'm glad I'm here too," she said carefully.

Iris laughed. "No, you're not, but thanks for the sentiment. How does that feel?"

Zoe reached up and ran her fingers through her now shoulder-length hair. There was no way to tell if it was even, but she wasn't sure that mattered. Did people still care about hairstyles after surviving the end of the world? "It's great."

"Then let's start on the hair dye. Have you ever done it before?" Iris said as she scanned over the directions on the box.

"No." Zoe blushed. She was sure Iris thought she spent hours at the salon, much like Victoria did. She had the money for it after all . . . or at least Cole did, and he always encouraged her to use as much of it as she wanted. But she hated going to the salon, often putting off getting her hair cut until she couldn't take it any longer.

"I'm sure between the two of us, we can figure it out."

Iris set to work wetting Zoe's hair and applying the dye. She talked while she worked, but she didn't seem to mind that Zoe stayed silent. Zoe closed her eyes and tried to pretend everything was normal. Merely a fun girls' night. What she wouldn't give for a glass of wine, though alcohol hadn't been on the supply list the last time Hamid had let any of them venture out. Zoe was starting to go stir-crazy being cooped up in the trailer.

She couldn't remember how many days they had been there, but it felt like a lifetime since she had snuck out of Cole's bed to try to stop the Arrows.

"What do you think?" Ian emerged from the bathroom with a fully shaved head. It did not suit him.

Iris burst out laughing. "You look ridiculous."

"Wait 'til you bleach your hair and see how it feels." Ian ran his hands over his bald head. "I don't think it's that bad."

"It's not," Zoe said while trying and failing to control the smirk on her face. She reached out and gently touched the side of his head. "At least it'll grow back."

"You're both so helpful," Ian said, feigning annoyance. "I don't know why I even asked."

Iris tapped Zoe on the shoulder. "Come on, we need to rinse the dye out."

Ian helped Zoe to her feet and let her lean on him as she limped after Iris to the bathroom. They all stopped in the doorway. "What did you do?" Ian asked.

Blake was standing in front of the sink with half his head shaved in a buzz cut. The other side was still long, and he was in the process of applying blue cream to the tips, tinting the ends of his dark hair teal. "What? This is the apocalypse, I figured I'd lean into the look."

"We're trying to avoid being noticed," Ian said, his arm still wrapped around Zoe's waist as he stared at Blake.

Blake turned toward them. "No, we are trying to avoid being *recognized*. There is a difference. I don't look anything like the picture the Arrows showed."

"He has a point." Zoe smiled up at Ian. Blake could always be counted on to lighten the mood.

"Well, whatever it is you are doing . . ." Iris waved her hand around Blake's head. "Can you hurry up? I need to get this dye out of Zoe's hair before it starts to burn."

"By all means." Blake picked up his tin of blue dye and moved out of the bathroom. "Want some?" he said to Ian as he passed.

"I don't have any hair left."

"I can use it to draw a picture on your head. Maybe a happy face? I mean, did you really even survive the end of the world if you don't dye your hair blue?"

«‹‹›»

Zoe ran her hand through her shortened hair as she looked at her reflection in the dark window. Blake and Iris had retreated to the bathroom to bleach her hair. Apparently, Blake had spent a year working in a beauty salon at some point. The makeover had been a good distraction, but now that she was done, she couldn't stop Cole's words from replaying in her mind.

"I think it looks good," Ian said as he came and stood next to her. He stooped down so he could see his reflection next to Zoe's. "Much better than mine, anyway."

"It's different, that's for sure." The small smile that Ian brought to her lips faded quickly.

Ian turned to face her. "Is different such a bad thing?"

"I guess not." Zoe looked at her reflection one more time before turning away. She leaned against the table, her eyes darting to the TV.

"You're not okay, are you?"

Zoe smirked. "Is it that obvious?"

"I'm sure Cole didn't mean any of what he said during that press conference." Ian jerked his head toward the television.

Zoe raised her eyebrows at him. "But he still said it. That statement hit all my biggest insecurities. He knows that and still chose the Arrows over me. It's bad enough when other people say I'm using him for his money or to get a job I don't deserve, but to hear *him* say it . . ." Her voice trailed off as a fresh wave of tears threatened to fall.

"We don't know what he's going through. You saw how they pulled him off the stage at the end, how he fought back. The Arrows had to have forced him to say those things somehow."

Zoe shook her head. "I know you're probably right, but that doesn't make it hurt any less. No one was holding a gun to his head while he was on camera. He could have said anything he wanted, but he stood there and read those lies to the whole world . . . or what's left of it, anyway."

Ian stepped in front of her and locked his eyes on hers. "You don't know that. They very well could have had him at gunpoint with the shooter just out of the frame."

"Or he could have decided that I'm not worth losing his family over." Zoe sank down into a chair as a dull pain started to throb through her injured leg. "Not wanting me dead isn't the same thing as wanting to be with me." She gently massaged her thigh, being careful not to put too much pressure on the still-healing bullet wound. "I was terrified that the cops were going to kill *you* when you were playing cocky kidnapper to buy time for Iris and Blake to get away. I didn't want you dead, and I didn't even like you at that point." Zoe gave him a small, devilish smile.

Ian pulled out a chair and sat down next to her. "Fair

point," he said with a laugh, "but I really don't think that's what's going on with Cole. He loves you. He wouldn't have said those things unless he absolutely had to."

"I really hope you're right," Zoe said as Cole's voice echoed in her head: *Zoe Antos is a heartless liar.*

««Chapter 8»»

Time seemed to move even slower than the first time Alana had locked him in his room. Each hour felt like days, and other than the intermittent meals the guards brought, he saw no one. Cole wondered if Victoria and Jackson were locked away too, or if they had been warned not to talk to him. He didn't want to believe that they had abandoned him. He didn't know what he would do if there was no one he could depend on.

There was nothing to help pass the time, so he spent an unhealthy amount of time obsessing about Alana becoming president. He was confident this had been her plan all along and that she didn't really care about trying to save the environment from the destructive nature of man. It would have been simpler if she had run for office like a normal person. Cole had always thought of his parents as logical, intelligent people. If they wanted power, they should have been able to come up with something better than killing billions of people to get it.

Cole nearly jumped out of his skin when the door opened. He glanced over at the half-eaten tray of food on the nightstand. How long had it been since someone had brought him something to eat? He looked over his shoulder, expecting to see a guard standing in the doorway, but it was Alana walking into the room.

"It's time to go."

"Go where?"

"Your father said he told you we were relocating to the White House today."

Cole laughed. "What makes you think I'm going anywhere with you?"

Alana crossed her arms. "Would you prefer to stay locked in this room and slowly starve to death?"

"Honestly, yes," Cole said in a matter-of-fact way that he hoped shocked her.

"Really, Cole, you're a grown man. This childish behavior is beneath you."

"Why do you even care if I'm there? It should be clear to you by now that you're not going to win me over to your side. Why can't you just let me live out the rest of my life in peace?"

"You are my son, and this family stays together no matter what."

"Maybe we shouldn't. Like you said, I'm an adult. I can make my own choices, and right now I'm choosing not to be a part of this family anymore."

Alana rolled her eyes. "You're coming with us, and that's the end of it."

"Then you're going to have to drag me out of here because I'm not willingly going anywhere with you."

Alana sighed. "Do you really think I won't do just that?" She gave him a look he hadn't seen since he was a child, then she shook her head before turning and opening the door. Two large guards stepped into the room, one of them holding a syringe in his hand. "This is your last chance, Cole. You can come willingly, or we can do this the hard way. The end result will be the same."

Cole let out a frustrated breath. "Fine." He didn't like the idea of Alana drugging him and dragging him to the car, which he didn't doubt she would do. At least if he was conscious, he might be able to make a break for it.

"Good." Alana came over and put her arm around his shoulder; Cole shoved it off and stormed out of the room, the guards trailing in his wake. Out front there was a line of black SUVs waiting for them. Cole turned to look at Alana. "Are we driving to DC?" There was a hint of hope fluttering in his chest. There had to be a few chances to get away during the ten-hour drive.

"Of course not. They're taking us to the airport," Alana said with an overly sweet smile, then she walked over to talk to one of the drivers, leaving Cole standing there flanked by two armed guards.

Jackson came over to him, giving the guards a weary look. "How are you holding up?" he said softly.

"Not great." Cole didn't worry about keeping his voice low. He no longer cared if his parents knew his real feelings. "I can't keep doing this."

"I know. Hopefully things will ease up once we get to DC and Mom and Dad are occupied with other things."

"What happened to you and Victoria after the press conference?"

"Just more of the same," Jackson said with a shrug.

"So you were locked in your room with minimal food and nothing to keep yourself from going crazy?" Jackson had no idea what he was going through. He wasn't a prisoner of the Arrows, at least not in the same way Cole was.

"No, but they took away my video games," Jackson said with a smirk. "Mom caught the boys using it to get online and saw the search history. She knows you've been watching Zoe's message on repeat."

"Good, I'm glad she knows." Cole glared at the woman who had given birth to him as she bustled from car to car.

"Jackson," Gordon called, and waved him over. Cole turned to see his father standing next to one of the cars with a worried expression. His phone was pressed to his ear.

Jackson shrugged to Cole, and they both made their way over to Gordon. He hung up the phone before they reached him. "Cole, you are going to ride with your mom and Victoria in the next car," Gordon said slowly. "Jackson, I need you to come with me."

"Why?" Jackson asked.

"I need you to help me with something. We'll meet the rest of the family in DC when we're done."

"What are we going to do?"

Gordon's eyes darted to Cole before returning to Jackson. "I'll give you the details once we're on our way."

"I'll come with you," Cole offered. He needed to know why Gordon wasn't coming with the rest of them. "I'd like to help if I can."

"Thank you, Cole, but I only need Jackson's help. You can help Victoria with the boys."

"Does this have something to do with Zoe?" It was the only thing that made sense. Why else would Gordon not want to talk about it in front of him?

"Just go with your mother, Cole. And please, for once, do what you're told." Gordon nodded to a guard, who came over to Cole. This only confirmed that whatever his father was doing involved Zoe. Maybe the Arrows had found her.

Cole needed to get in that car.

He tried to circumvent the guard, but he blocked Cole's path, grabbed his arms, and slammed him against the car.

"Hey, take it easy, man!" Jackson said as he tried to pull the guard off Cole.

"Jackson, get in the car. We need to go." Gordon held open the back door of the SUV.

The guard pulled Cole upright and dragged him over to the next car. He shoved Cole in the back seat and slammed the door shut behind him.

Cole sat up and watched the car with Jackson and Gordon pull away, his last shred of hope dissolving as they disappeared from sight.

«‹‹›»

The sun was just starting to set, and Zoe sat on the couch, mindlessly flipping through the channels — most of which were static. The news had not returned since Alana's press conference two days ago. Not knowing what was happening out in the world was driving Zoe crazy. She turned off the TV and threw the remote down on the couch.

Hamid was absorbed in a book at the kitchen table, looking totally at peace. Zoe got up and went to join him. She hated distracting him, but she was so bored. "How do you do it?" She plopped down in the chair next to him.

Hamid marked his place in the book before setting it down on the table. "Do what, my dear?"

"You've been in hiding for years. How do you keep from going insane? You were a scientist too . . . don't you miss the work?" Zoe leaned forward as she waited for his answer.

Hamid gave her a knowing smile. "The first few months were the hardest. I didn't know what to do with myself. But then I realized that just because I wasn't working in the lab anymore didn't mean I couldn't keep learning."

"It's not the same, though. I need something to challenge me." Zoe put her head down on the table.

Hamid raised an eyebrow at her. "And surviving isn't enough of a challenge for you?"

"Not when all I have to do is sit around and wait for the next piece of news to trickle in. I need a purpose beyond surviving."

"You'll find it again. We won't be stuck in this trailer forever. Once things settle down out in the world, we'll be able to find a place to start over. Then you'll have all the challenges you want. Until then, can I suggest some reading?" Hamid leaned over and grabbed a book off the shelf behind him.

Zoe took it and smiled as she looked over the cover: *Frontier Farming Techniques*. "You think I should take up farming?"

"It can't hurt," Hamid said with a shrug.

"What are you reading?" Zoe eyed the book sitting on the table in front of him.

"James Patterson," Hamid said with a smirk.

Blake burst into the trailer. "Someone triggered the perimeter alarm."

"We have a perimeter alarm?" Zoe shifted in her chair. Ian and Iris followed Blake inside, everyone suddenly on high alert.

"A basic one. It just tells us if anyone is driving on the road here. It can't stop them or anything," Ian said.

"That's too bad," Zoe said under her breath.

"Do you think it's the Arrows?" Iris looked to each of them. The fear in her eyes shook Zoe to her core.

"Who else would it be?" Ian pulled out his gun and made sure it was loaded.

"We need to go," Hamid said, getting to his feet.

Blake shook his head as he looked at the computer in his hand. "I don't think there's time." He turned the computer to show a security feed from outside the trailer as two black Cadillacs came into view.

Zoe sucked in a breath. That was Gordon's car.

"How did they find us?" Iris asked.

"It doesn't matter. We'll slip out the back and hide until they've left, then we'll make a run for it." Ian started to remove a wall panel next to the kitchen cabinets.

"They'll see us." Zoe peeked out the window. Someone was getting out of the cars, but it wasn't Gordon. He was younger. "I'll go out and see if I can buy you some time to get away. I'm pretty sure they're here for me anyway."

Ian gently grabbed her arm and pulled her away from the window. "I can't let you do that."

"I'm not asking permission." Zoe pulled her arm away and limped over to the door. "I'll only slow you down if I try to run now. Let me do this. It'll be all right."

Ian sighed but nodded.

"Stay out of sight until I'm out there, then go." Zoe tried to give them a reassuring smile; this would likely be the last time she saw them. There would be no getting away from the Arrows once they had her.

Ian came over and took both of her hands in his and squeezed them gently. Their eyes locked, but Zoe couldn't find the right words to express what she was feeling. She bit her lower lip and nodded. Ian squeezed her hands one more time before releasing them, and everyone moved to the side so they wouldn't be seen when she opened the door.

With one last look at them, Zoe opened the door and stepped out to face the Arrows on her own.

"Jackson?" she exclaimed as her eyes adjusted to the dim evening light.

"Zoe, you're all right." Jackson rushed forward to give her a hug, but Zoe stepped back and held her hand out in front of her. She had no idea if she could trust him or not.

"How did you find me?" Her eyes scanned the two cars parked in front of the trailer. Could Cole be in one of them? If he was here, he would have made his presence known the moment she stepped outside.

"Someone told Dad where to find you. I'm not sure who. We're to bring you home." Jackson looked over his shoulder at the car. "Things are really messed up."

"I know. How's Cole?" This was the real reason she had volunteered to come out here. She needed to know what had happened to Cole after the press conference. She no longer believed that being a Wilborn would be enough to keep him safe.

"He's safe, but he's a mess. He needs you."

Zoe sighed. Her gaze shifted from Jackson to the tinted windows of the car. "Then help him get away from your parents."

Jackson shook his head. "They aren't going to let him go, but if you come with me, then maybe we can find a way to move past this as a family."

Zoe let out a deranged laugh. "Your mom shot me in the leg because I tried to stop her. I very much doubt she thinks of me as family."

"That's not true."

"Jackson, stop doing your parents' dirty work. I'm not going willingly with you just to have the Arrows kill me once I get there."

"Mom and Dad won't let that happen. You know them. You know they would do anything to keep their family safe."

"You are aware that they developed and released a toxin that is currently killing billions of people around the globe?" Zoe crossed her arms. Jackson had always been a little clueless when it came to the big picture.

"Look." Jackson glanced over his shoulder. "Dad's not going to give me much more time to convince you to come willingly. I don't know what kind of force he'll use if you refuse."

"Like the force they used to drag Cole off the stage at the press conference?"

Jackson smirked. "Cole will be happy to hear that you saw the live version and not the edited replays."

"If your parents are fine with having armed guards pull their own son off the stage for speaking out, what makes you think I'll be safe?"

"We can keep you safe—Cole, Victoria, and I."

"Here's your chance to prove it." Zoe nodded to the car where Gordon was getting out with two armed men Zoe didn't recognize.

"Is there a problem here?" Gordon walked over to them. Zoe took a step back, fighting the urge to run. She needed to buy the others as much time to get away as she could. She would make this sacrifice for them.

Jackson stepped between Zoe and Gordon. "Nope, no problems." He turned his head to look at her. "Right, Zoe?" Jackson's eyes bore into her as if he was trying to tell her something, but with fear threatening to overtake her at any moment, she had no idea what it was.

"Good," Gordon said with a smile that did nothing to calm her fear. "Now, Zoe, why don't you tell me where your friends are? And then I can take you to Cole."

"I don't know what you're talking about." Zoe's words tumbled over each other.

"You're a terrible liar," Gordon said. "This will be easier for everyone if you cooperate."

"Who says I want to make anything easier for you?" Zoe said, finally finding a shred of confidence.

"It really didn't have to be this way." Gordon nodded to the armed men, who rushed forward and grabbed her. Zoe used all the strength she had to fight them off. One of the guards pulled her arms behind her back while the other punched her in the stomach. She buckled over and gasped for air. She had almost recovered when the guard brought the grip of his gun down on her injured thigh. She screamed in pain, her legs buckling under her. The guard holding her arms released her as she fell to the ground. She tried to get back up, but one of the guards slapped her across the face.

"Stop!" Jackson rushed forward, once again putting himself between Zoe and Gordon. "How could you do this? Zoe's family!"

"I gave you a chance to convince her to come willingly. You failed. This was the only alternative we had," Gordon said calmly. "Get her in the car."

One of the guards reached down and grabbed Zoe by the forearm, but Jackson pushed him away. "I'll do it." He gently helped Zoe to her feet. "Please, trust me," he whispered as he draped one of her arms around his shoulder.

Zoe nodded—what else could she do? She leaned into him, allowing him to take some of the weight off her freshly reinjured leg as they slowly made their way toward the car.

"Let her go, Gordon."

Zoe turned her head, stunned to see Hamid standing outside of the trailer. Why didn't he run with the others? Had any of them managed to get away, or had she given herself up for nothing?

"Hamid Sami, is that really you?" Shock radiated in Gordon's voice. "How are you still alive?"

"Your assassins aren't as reliable as you think they are. Now let Zoe go, and leave us in peace."

"I should have suspected you were still alive after your nephew broke into Green Tech," Gordon said, once again ignoring Hamid's demand. "I'm actually glad you're still alive to see everything we've accomplished. You could have been a part of it if you hadn't turned your back on the Arrows all those years ago."

"The Arrow Equilibrium isn't what we dreamed it would be. We spoke of environmental justice, not genocide."

"It was the only way."

"There's always another way," Hamid said, taking a step forward. "Bring Zoe here." He held his hand out.

"I don't think so." Gordon turned to one of the guards, who aimed their gun at Hamid's chest and fired twice.

Zoe gasped as Hamid fell to the ground, the sound of the gunshots echoing in her ears. How could Gordon have done that?

Jackson eased his grip on Zoe as he looked at his dad in horror. If she was ever going to get away, it had to be now. Hamid had given his life to try to save her—she wouldn't let it go to waste.

She slipped out of Jackson's hold completely and limped rapidly toward the tree line.

"Search the trailer for the others," Gordon said. Zoe didn't stop to see what was happening. She had to hope that the others had gotten out.

"Zoe, wait," Jackson called behind her, but she didn't stop. A second later, he touched her shoulder.

"Don't you see why I can't go back with you? I won't live if I do," Zoe pleaded. "Please, Jackson, let me go."

Jackson ran a hand through his hair. "How will you get away? You can barely walk."

"With my help." Blake emerged from the tree line with a gun fixed on Jackson.

"Don't shoot him," Zoe said as she limped to Blake's side.

"He deserves it," Blake said through gritted teeth. "Hamid is dead."

"Jackson didn't do that."

"I'll try to buy you some time," Jackson said to Zoe. "Make them think you fought your way free and send them off in the wrong direction."

"Thank you," Zoe said with a sigh. "Please tell Cole that I love him and I'm sorry I can't come back to him."

"He'll understand." Jackson gave her a weak smile before turning his gaze to Blake. "You're going to have to make it look believable."

"Gladly." Blake handed Zoe the gun, strode over to Jackson, and punched him once in the face and once in the stomach. Jackson fell to a ball on the ground. "That should do it."

A moment later, the trailer erupted in flames.

"That's our cue." Blake scoped Zoe up and ran to the truck they had hidden in the trees. Ian and Iris were already there, climbing into the back seat. Tears stood out in Iris's eyes as Blake helped Zoe into the front seat. He ran around to the driver side, jumped in, and pulled away.

Ian tapped Zoe on the shoulder. "Here." He held up an ice pack. "For your cheek."

"Thanks." Zoe gingerly held it to her swollen face. "Where are we going?" she whispered to Blake, not wanting to intrude on Ian and Iris's grief. "Is there another safe house?"

"No. I have no idea where we're going. There was no plan past the trailer." Blake glanced over at Zoe, his eyes glistening with tears and an underlying fear Zoe was sure was echoed in her own.

She closed her eyes as she tried to process everything that had happened. The truck felt empty without Hamid's presence. In the back seat, Ian was holding Iris as she sobbed into his chest. Zoe had no words to try to comfort either of them. She wondered what would become of Hamid's body. Maybe they could come back once it was safe and give him a proper burial, though she knew deep down that wasn't possible. He deserved so much better.

Zoe said a silent prayer as they drove into the darkness.

««Chapter 9»»

Cole wasn't left alone for a moment the whole time they traveled from Detroit to Washington DC. He even had a guard standing outside the stall door while he used the bathroom before boarding Wilborn Holdings' company jet. He had feigned having to stop as an excuse to sneak away, which Alana had clearly suspected. He was beginning to lose hope that he would ever be able to escape her grasp.

The airport had been eerily empty. There was no one there other than their pilots, and they saw no one when they landed a few hours later. It felt like they were the only ones left on the planet, but he knew that couldn't be true. Zoe was out there somewhere, and he needed to believe that she was still alive.

It was late when they finally arrived at the White House, and his guards took him directly to a bedroom. Cole fully expected the door to be locked when he woke up the next morning, but he was pleasantly surprised to find that it wasn't.

He wandered around the residential wing. The former president's personal belongings seemed to have disappeared, along with the rest of the first family. Cole wondered if they had died from the toxin or if the Arrows had them removed by some other means to clear the way for Alana to take over.

He found Victoria sitting alone in some kind of living space. "Where is everyone?" Cole asked as he made his way over to her.

Victoria looked up from the book in her hand. "Still sleeping, I guess."

Cole sat down across from her. "Any word on where Jackson and Dad went?"

"No. I tried to get it out of Trevor, but he's keeping his mouth shut. I wonder if divorce is still a thing?" Victoria glared at the door as if she expected her husband to be there.

"That's the least of my concerns at the moment. I think Dad might have an idea where Zoe is, and I'm afraid of what he'll do if he finds her," Cole confessed.

"You don't really think he would hurt her, do you?"

"I wouldn't put it past him at this point."

Victoria slid over and took his hands in hers. "Dad won't kill her. Despite everything, I'm sure he still loves her and wants to keep her safe."

At that moment, Jackson walked into the room with a black eye, looking completely shell-shocked. He plopped down in a chair and stared at the wall without acknowledging them. Cole shot Victoria a look before getting up and heading over to him. "What happened?"

"Dad had someone killed. One second, they were talking, and the next, he ordered one of the guards to shoot him point blank. He never even gave it a second thought."

"He wouldn't do that," Victoria said, looking between Cole and Jackson.

"I was there. I saw it all happen," Jackson said without looking at them.

Cole knelt down in front of his older brother so that he was in Jackson's direct line of sight. "Who did Dad kill?"

"I don't know his name. An older Middle Eastern man." Jackson's gaze shifted to meet Cole's. "He was with Zoe."

Cole had to catch himself as Jackson's words washed over him. Jackson had seen Zoe. Cole was terrified to ask what had happened to her, so instead he chose an easier topic to handle first. "It must have been Dr. Hamid Sami, Ian Sutton's uncle."

"Why do I recognize that name?" Victoria said.

"He was Dad's friend when we were little. They started Green Tech together, but when Dr. Sami realized what the Arrows were planning, he tried to leave. The Arrows thought they had killed him years ago, but he survived and went into hiding."

"How do you know all this?"

"I met him. He was in Zoe's apartment with us when the Arrows burned it down." It was the first time Cole had admitted that his parents were responsible for the fire that almost killed him. He remembered his parents' surprise to see him there. They had only meant to kill Zoe. Cole turned to Jackson. "How was Zoe?"

"She looked good. She stood up to Dad, which I wouldn't have been able to do if I was in her place," Jackson said with a smile. "She cut her hair and dyed it red."

Cole let out a sigh of relief. "And her leg where Mom

shot her?"

"It must be healing fine. She was standing and walking a little," Jackson's eyes dropped back to his lap. "At least, when we first got there."

"What happened?" Victoria asked.

"I asked Dad to let me talk to Zoe alone. I thought I could convince her to come with us willingly. I figured that would be easier than whatever Dad was planning. She wouldn't listen. That's when Dad told the guards to take her. She fought back, but there were two of them. Dad just stood there and watched while they attacked her."

All the air rushed out of Cole's body. Time slowed as he waited for Jackson to finish. Had they killed Zoe? Was that what Jackson was trying to tell him?

"Is she all right?" Victoria asked the question Cole couldn't seem to voice.

"I think so, but they hit her in the leg where she was shot. She could barely stand after that. I got them to stop. That's when Hamid came out. I helped Zoe escape with one of the guys who was at Wilborn Holdings the day this all started. They got away."

Cole leaned back against the couch and let out a breath. Zoe was still out there. There was still hope.

"Did Dad give you the black eye?" Victoria asked.

"No. I told the guy with Zoe to do it. I wanted it to look like I fought them so Dad would still trust me. I think it worked, but who knows?" Jackson looked Cole straight in the eye. "He's not the man I thought he was."

Cole swallowed hard and nodded. He had been trying to tell them that for weeks, but it sounded like this was the wake-up call Jackson needed. Hopefully now they could stop waiting for the right time and come up with a real plan to get away from their lunatic parents.

«‹›»

They drove through the night in silence. They were all processing the loss of Hamid, and Zoe felt like an intruder on their grief. She had liked Hamid, and her heart ached that he was gone, but she hardly knew him. He was the only parental figure the others had in their lives. Even Blake had looked at Hamid as a parent.

Zoe tried to pay attention to where they were going, but her mind kept drifting back to Gordon and Jackson. A small part of her had wanted to go with them so she could see Cole again. It had all sounded so perfect: be with Cole under the Wilborns' protection. Try to find a way to rebuild their life together. But it wouldn't have been that easy. There was no way she would be welcomed back after what she did. They were using her love for Cole to manipulate her into handing herself over.

She had been right to resist them; she just wished it hadn't cost so much. If she had gone with Jackson like he asked, Hamid would probably still be alive.

As the sun came up, Zoe started to pay better attention to their surroundings. They hadn't seen another car on the road all night, and now that it was morning, she expected to see at least a few people, but there was no one. They were coming up on a town, and the streets were completely empty except for a few cars parked on the side of the road.

Zoe looked closer at one to see a body slumped over the steering wheel. She quickly sat back and locked her eyes on the road. She doubted it would be the last dead body they came across.

"We're getting low on gas. Do you want to see if we

can get more or find a place to lay low for a while?" Blake's voice was flat, lacking the normal, happy tone Zoe was used to hearing from him.

"Let's stop." Ian sighed. "We could all use some rest, and I want to make sure those assholes didn't hurt you too badly," he said to Zoe.

"I'm fine, really," Zoe said, though her leg throbbed in protest. She couldn't believe with everything that had happened, Ian was concerned about her.

"Still, I saw what Gordon let those guards do to you. I'd feel better if you'd let me check you out."

"Sure," Zoe said softly.

"Then we'll stop." Blake slowed the truck down and pulled into a hotel parking lot. It was a risk — they would want to see ID and credit cards to book a room, and that would make it incredibly easy for the Arrows to find them — but no one else said anything as they got out of the car. Blake handed Zoe a gun while Ian and Iris grabbed two duffel bags from the truck. They must have had time to pack a few things up while she was busy with Jackson.

"You ready?" Blake asked.

"I guess."

Zoe limped after him into the hotel lobby. There was no one around. She held out the gun as Blake went to check the office behind the front desk.

"It's clear." He put his gun back in his belt and walked over to the computer behind the front desk.

"You think there's still guests here?" Iris asked. Zoe hadn't heard her talk since they left the trailer.

"It's possible. We should try to avoid people. There's a good chance we'll be recognized even with the makeovers," Ian said.

"It looks like there's a suite free on the top floor,"

Blake said.

"How do you know?" Zoe asked.

"I worked at a hotel for a little while. All their systems are basically the same." Blake activated some key cards and handed them out. It almost felt normal.

Ian pulled out a gun. "Everyone, stay quiet."

They followed him down the hall and up a flight of stairs. Zoe struggled to keep up on the stairs, but Iris hung back to help her. At least it was only three flights; she wasn't sure how much more she could do. The Arrows had really done a number on her leg. She wondered if they had managed to grab any of the painkillers when they were making their escape.

At the top of the stairs, Ian glanced over his shoulder at them. There was no telling what they would see once they opened the door to the hallway.

They all nodded.

He pulled the door open with the gun drawn and waited. Zoe listened hard for any signs of life, but everything was silent. Ian took a few steps into the hall and stopped as if he expected someone to jump out at them.

"I think it's okay," he whispered when nothing happened.

They slowly made their way down the hall. A few doors were left open, and Zoe spotted unmade beds and abandoned luggage in the rooms. Thankfully, she didn't see any more bodies. It felt eerie, like they shouldn't be there.

The door to the suite was closed. Blake pulled out a key card and inserted it in the lock. It gave off the loudest beep Zoe had ever heard, but the lights on the lock turned green, and the door unlocked.

Blake looked at Ian before opening the door. Ian

went in with his gun drawn. "All clear."

They all filed in, and Zoe closed the door and secured the latch behind her. They couldn't be too careful at this point. The room was huge, with a small sitting area, kitchenette, and two bedrooms, each with their own bathroom. It was a lot more comfortable than the trailer they had been living in.

Zoe collapsed on the couch and rubbed her leg. Ian stood at the window, peeking through the gap in the closed curtains.

"What are you doing?" Zoe asked.

"Making sure we weren't followed," Ian mumbled. He stood there for a few more minutes before collapsing in a chair.

"Did you see anything?"

"No. There's no one out there . . . and I mean no one," Ian said. "I never imagined it would be like this."

"There have to be survivors out there somewhere," Iris said. "They're all probably in hiding too. No one knows how to handle this."

"At least no one saw us come in," Blake said. "We'll probably be safe here for a few days."

"That's it?" Zoe hated the idea of having to move every few days.

"We can't stay in one place for too long. The trailer was supposed to be impossible to find, and the Arrows still got to us there. The only way we can ensure they don't find us again is to keep moving," Ian said.

Zoe nodded and picked up the remote off the table next to her. She turned the TV on out of habit, not expecting anything to be there except static. She was shocked to see an image of the Oval Office and a countdown in the middle of the screen. Apparently, something was going to happen in less than a minute.

Everyone's eyes were glued to the screen.

Zoe couldn't believe what she was seeing as people started to file into the room with Alana leading the way. The Wilborns were in the White House. This couldn't be good.

Zoe searched the screen for Cole. He was standing between Jackson and Victoria, with two armed men behind him. She doubted they would let him speak again, but at least she could see he was still alive.

"It's nice to see the black eye I gave that asshole stuck," Blake said.

"Jackson let us go," Zoe said, but there were no feelings in her words. He had tried to get her to go back with him. She wondered if he would have let her go if Gordon hadn't ordered Hamid to be killed.

"They're swearing her in," Iris said in disbelief. Zoe was so focused on Cole that she wasn't paying attention to what was happening on the screen.

"They're what?" Zoe picked up the remote and turned the volume up.

"Not too loud, in case someone else is in the building," Ian said sternly.

Zoe set the remote back down and held her hands up. She gave the TV her full attention.

Alana had her hand on a Bible and was repeating the presidential oath.

"How is this happening? They can't just make her president!"

"I guess they can," Blake said.

"Do laws even matter anymore? The Arrows are doing whatever they want anyway. This is just a ploy to get what's left of the country to fall in line. The last thing they want is people to challenge them. This is all for show," Ian said.

He was right. Zoe hadn't fallen in line, and they were out to kill her. She could never go back, no matter how much they tried to reassure her that she would be safe; she only wished her safety hadn't cost her Cole.

When they were done swearing Alana in, she sat down at the desk. The camera zoomed in on her.

"Hello, my fellow Americans. I know this is a difficult time. We have suffered immeasurable losses thanks to Zoe Antos and her group of terrorists. It would be easy to give up now, but America doesn't give up. We are a strong, resilient nation, and we are being called to pull ourselves up and start to rebuild. I have a plan for that. We are going to rebuild a better, stronger nation together. One where we aren't divided by our differences, where we don't destroy our beautiful planet in the name of progress. We are in the process of setting up colonies across the country where we will be able to maintain utilities. We are asking everyone to begin making their way to the one closest to them. The rest of the country will be allowed to return to its natural state as we work to remediate the damage humans have caused the planet. This horrific tragedy has given us a unique opportunity to reverse the negative effects human have had on the planet and build a future where humans and nature live in perfect balance. The relocation details will be broadcasted on all channels soon. Anyone found not complying with these plans will be seen as an enemy of that state and will be dealt with accordingly."

"That went dark fast," Blake said.

"Here's our list of places to avoid," Ian said. A list of cities appeared on the screen. "Where exactly are we?"

"Somewhere in Indiana. I wasn't paying real close attention last night," Blake said.

"We should be all right then. There doesn't appear to be a relocation camp in Indiana," Iris said.

"But it looks like we can't go home." Zoe nodded to the screen.

"It's not surprising they would put a settlement in Detroit. They probably have all kinds of resources already staged there," Ian said.

"What matters is we're safe for now. I'm going to see if this place still has water to shower and then go to bed." Iris got up and walked over to one of the bedrooms without waiting for a response.

"What if someone hears the water running and comes to investigate?" Ian called after her.

"Then I guess you'll have to deal with it." Iris closed the door behind her, making it clear that the conversation was over.

«‹›»

They didn't leave the room for two days. They ate the beef jerky and trail mix they brought from the trailer and drank the overpriced pop from the mini bar. They took turns standing watch from the crack in the curtain but had yet to see another person. Zoe was sitting in the chair they had stationed near the window as the sun was setting on their third night there and nearly jumped out of her skin when she saw two deer walking down the middle of the street.

They kept the television off and only spoke to one another when it was absolutely necessary. They were all grieving with no idea how to handle it in this new world. She wished there was some way to give them some sense of closure for Hamid.

"I can't sit here anymore," Zoe finally said. She

couldn't take the silence and boredom; she needed to do something useful. "I'm going to look around the hotel and see if there is anything we can use."

"I'm not sure that's a good idea," Ian said.

"We haven't seen anyone since we got here. If there was anyone else in the building, they would have heard us by now." Zoe waved her arm toward the window. "I'm going crazy sitting here waiting for something to happen."

"I don't think it's smart for any of us to be alone right now," Ian said, though lacking some of the conviction that was normally in his voice.

"I'll go with her," Blake said, jumping to his feet.

Ian sighed. "Take your guns, just in case."

They both nodded and took a handgun from the counter. Zoe wasn't used to carrying it; the only time she had used one had resulted in Alana triggering the end of the world. Still, she understood why they needed them. There was no telling how people were going to react, especially since everyone thought she was responsible for the toxin. She needed a way to protect herself.

"Where do you want to start?" Blake said once they were out in the hall.

"I guess the open room down the hall," Zoe whispered, though she wasn't sure why. She had been the one to say there was no one else in the building, but being out in the hall, exposed, changed things.

They walked down the hall in silence until they got to the open room. Blake went in first, with Zoe close behind. She braced herself in case there was a body in the room, but thankfully it was empty.

Blake put his gun away and turned toward her. "What are we looking for?"

Zoe shrugged. "I didn't really have a plan. I just had

to get out of that room."

"I get it. That's how I ended up spending so much time at Ian's house growing up."

Zoe picked up the suitcase and put it on the bed. Maybe there would be something they could use in there. "What do you mean?"

"My parents weren't really up to the job. They drank a lot, would disappear for days at a time. I figured out how to take care of myself pretty quickly. A lot of my childhood was spent waiting alone in an empty house for them to come back. That is, until Ian and Iris moved in with Hamid and I finally had somewhere to go."

Zoe looked down at the open suitcase. It was full of business shirts and a pair of dress shoes. Nothing they could use. "Do you still see your parents?"

Blake shook his head and crouched down to go through the mini fridge. "I haven't spoken to them in years. They could be dead for all I know . . . hell, they probably are at this point. They weren't big on drinking things that didn't get them buzzed."

"I'm sorry," Zoe said.

"Don't be, it was a long time ago."

Zoe turned away from the open suitcase. "What do you think happened to this guy?" she asked, hoping to steer the conversation in a different direction. At least five times a day, she had to stop herself from wondering what had happened to her own parents. They had probably drunk enough RiverLife water at the events the Wilborns had invited them to over the years to be safe from the toxin, but that alone didn't guarantee their survival. Zoe wouldn't put it past the Arrows to make her parents pay for her actions. She could only hope that by distancing herself, she could protect them.

"Maybe he survived." Blake stood up and showed

her an unopened bottle of RiverLife.

"You think he's still here?" Zoe looked around the room, wondering if someone was going to jump out of the closet and attack her at any moment.

"If someone was here, we'd know it by now." Blake walked over and peeked out the window at the empty parking lot below. "He probably didn't want to waste time packing before he left."

Zoe nodded and turned her attention back to the suitcase. She riffled through the rest of the clothes but didn't find anything they could use. She turned away from the bed and spotted a backpack sitting on the floor next to the desk. She grabbed it, quickly discarding the computer, cords, and files inside. "This would be much easier to carry than the duffel bags." She tossed it to Blake. "Put the water and any food you find in there."

They slowly worked their way from room to room. Most were empty, though they did find a few more backpacks, bottles of water, and some snacks they took with them. The small breakfast area off the lobby offered some fruit that didn't look too bad, and Zoe even found a pack of frozen precooked sausage patties. The only protein they had eaten since leaving the trailer was beef jerky, and she was over it.

Zoe went back to the lobby where Blake was standing guard. They were much easier to spot on the first floor. "I found some real food . . . we can warm it up in the room. We should probably head back." Zoe adjusted the now-overstuffed backpack on her shoulders.

"Sure." Blake turned to face her, his arms weighed down with flowers and candles he had pilfered from behind the front desk.

"What are those for?"

"I thought we could have a little memorial service for Hamid," Blake said with a shrug.

"I think that's an excellent idea."

They made their way upstairs. When they got back to their room, Blake inserted the key card and opened the door. Ian was standing on the other side with a gun pointed at them.

"Easy there, killer, it's just us," Blake said as he entered the room.

"Sorry." Ian put the gun away.

Zoe took a deep breath to calm her nerves before entering the room. Would there ever be a time when she didn't panic seeing a gun in Ian's hand?

"I found some food," she said in what she hoped was a normal voice, dumping the backpack out on the counter by the small kitchenette.

Blake was in the process of spreading the flowers and candles out on the coffee table in the sitting area. "I thought we could do something to honor Hamid," he said, looking from Ian to Iris, who had emerged from the bedroom.

Iris came over and kissed him on the cheek. "Thank you," she said softly as she began to help him arrange the flowers.

«Chapter 10»»

Zoe jerked awake at the sound of the door opening. Her first thought was that the Arrows had managed to find them again. She nearly screamed when she saw a man standing over Iris's bed, but through the sliver of light coming in from the crack in the curtains, she was able to make out a partially shaved head and a hint of faded blue hair. It was Blake.

"Hey, wake up and get dressed. Quick." Blake gently shook Iris's shoulder and then glanced at Zoe.

"What's going on?" Zoe asked while pulling on her shoes. She had been sleeping in her clothes for this very reason. Not that she had pajamas to change into even if she wanted to. At least she found a clean shirt to wear while going through the rooms yesterday.

"There're people outside." Fear hung heavy in Blake's voice.

She looked at Iris, her eyes wide. Were the people outside Arrows or other survivors?

They made their way to the main room, where Ian was standing by the window just out of sight. He had cracked open the window so they could hear what was happening down below. Zoe peeked outside; there was a group of six people standing in the middle of the street in front of the hotel. In the darkness, it was impossible to tell whom they were.

"Did you find anyone?" one of the men on the street said.

"Not yet, but we saw lights turning on and off in the hotel earlier," another said.

"What do you think are the chances they'll want to avoid coming in here?" Iris asked, her voice so soft Zoe barely heard it.

"Not good," Ian said as they watched the group approach the hotel. "Grab what you can. We need to go. Now."

They quickly gathered their weapons and newfound backpacks. Ian cracked the door and listened while Blake looked out the window.

"I don't see them anymore," Blake whispered.

"I can't hear anything, but if we stay here, we're sitting ducks. Let's go." Ian led them out into the hall. Zoe looked back. She would miss this place. It was more comfortable than the trailer, and who knew where they would end up next?

Ian took them down the hall to a back set of stairs. The door creaked when it opened, and Zoe cringed. Everything sounded so much louder now.

At the other end of the hall, a door flew open, and two people ran out. They were also armed. "Stop!" one of them yelled.

"I don't think so," Ian said under his breath, and he pushed them into the stairwell as the other survivors rushed down the hall toward them. Ian tried to jam the door shut behind them, and they ran down the stairs. There was no point being quiet now.

The stairwell let them out at the back of the hotel. "Which way should we go?" Zoe asked.

"We need a car," Ian said as he scanned their surroundings. "You won't be able to run for long." He was right, Zoe's leg was already sore from her explorations with Blake yesterday; the run down the stairs had kicked the throbbing into overdrive.

"This way," Blake said as he led them around the back of the building. There weren't any cars in the hotel parking lot, but there was a store across the street with a few vehicles outside. They just had to find one they could get into.

They were almost out of the hotel parking lot when one of the survivors burst out of the lobby. "Hold it right there!" He aimed his gun at them.

Zoe, Ian, Blake, and Iris all turned to face him with their own guns out. This was a showdown.

"Who are you?" Ian yelled.

"Why should I tell you?" the man yelled back.

"Look, we don't want any trouble," Zoe said. "We're just trying to survive the same as you. We can all go our separate ways. No one has to get hurt." She held up her hand to show that she wasn't a threat.

"Wait a second," he said. "I recognize you. You're the one who started all of this. My family is dead because of you!"

"I didn't do this," Zoe said as the stranger closed in on them.

"We're done talking." Ian grabbed her hand and pulled her into a run. It was hard to see where they were going. They didn't make it far before the first gunshot rang out behind them. Zoe flinched, but nothing hit her. She looked to Ian, who was still pulling her behind him, and Blake, who was running at her other side, but Iris was gone.

"Iris," Zoe said in desperation.

Ian stopped instantly and spun around, looking for his twin. She was on the ground, but she was getting up. Ian released Zoe's hand and sprinted to Iris. Zoe and Blake followed, but they weren't the first to reach her. One of the attackers pulled Iris up by her hair and held his gun to her head.

"Are you hurt?" Ian never took his eyes off Iris.

"No," Iris said as she struggled against the man holding her.

"If you keep fighting me, you will be," the man said.

"Let her go," Ian growled, placing his finger on the trigger.

"Easy there, pretty boy, unless you'd like me to scatter her brains all over the pavement."

"No one has to get hurt here," Zoe said slowly. "Just let her go."

"I can't do that," the man said. "You're the ones the people in charge are looking for. If we turn you in, we'll be rewarded."

"The people in power are the ones who really caused all of this. They'll kill you the moment you hand us over."

"You're just saying that so I let her go. I saw the security footage. I saw you trigger this." The man pressed his gun harder against Iris's temple. "So unless you want me to kill her, I suggest you put your weapons down."

Ian lunged forward, but Zoe threw a hand out to stop him. If he wasn't careful, he would get his sister killed. "If I was the one who started this, do you really think I'd be on the run right now, or would I be sitting pretty in the White House with the power to do whatever I wanted? They manipulated the security footage to make it look like I did this. I was there to stop them. I failed, but I won't let you take another life because of Alana Wilborn's lies. So how about we make a deal? You can have me, but you have to let the rest of them go. I'm the one Alana really wants anyway."

"No," Iris said.

"It's okay," Zoe said. She didn't know how to tell them that she had a plan. She had no idea if it would work, but she had to try something. She set her gun down and held up her hands. "Do we have a deal?" Zoe didn't take her eyes off the man holding Iris.

"All right."

He let Iris go as Zoe slowly made her way over to him. Zoe glanced back at Ian and mouthed "Get ready."

His finger moved to the trigger.

The man pushed Iris forward as Zoe neared. He reached out to grab Zoe, but instead she fell to the ground, pulling Iris down with her. A moment later, a gunshot rang out, and the man fell to the ground.

"Go!" Zoe yelled. Blake and Ian rushed forward and helped them to their feet.

Blake handed Zoe back her gun and put an arm around her waist to help her run. "His friends would have heard that. They'll be here soon."

"In here." Ian and Iris were a few feet ahead of them and had opened the door to an abandoned store. Blake and Zoe ducked in after them, pulling the door closed behind them. They all crouched down and listened.

It wasn't long before they heard voices outside, gathered around the man who Ian had shot. His scream of pain let Zoe know that wherever Ian had shot him, it hadn't been fatal. She was glad; they had enough blood on their hands.

Zoe slumped to the floor. They would have to wait for the coast to be clear before they could do anything, but at least, for the moment, they were safe.

«‹«›»»

It had been a few days since Alana had taken over the White House. Cole had full access to the residential wing, but he couldn't go beyond that. It seemed Jackson and Victoria were in a similar situation. The only people the guards seemed to let pass were their parents and Victoria's husband. Unlike his siblings, Cole hadn't wasted the time sitting around complaining; he was busy memorizing the guard schedules and scouting out all the exits he could find.

He was done waiting for the right time to act. He would do whatever he needed to get away. The only thing he still had to figure out was how to find Zoe once he broke free. She could be anywhere at this point, and it wasn't like he could call her.

Cole had been slowly stashing away food and supplies. He was in his room taking inventory when Jackson and Victoria came in.

"What's all that for?" Jackson asked as he sat down on the bed.

"I'm leaving," Cole said as he carefully packed everything in the pink backpack he had found in the back of his closet. He assumed it belonged to the first daughter, but he tried not to think about that. No one would tell him exactly what had happened to the president's family. He suspected the Arrows had taken them out.

"When?" Jackson asked as he fiddled with the flashlight lying on the bed.

Cole took the flashlight from Jackson. "As soon as I can figure out how I'm going to find Zoe."

"She could be anywhere," Victoria said.

"I know. Have either of you heard if the Arrows have any credible leads on her location?"

Victoria shook her head. "It's not like they would share that information with us if they had."

"I hate thinking of her out there on the run while the public thinks she's the one responsible for this whole mess. I wish there was a way to get the target off her back."

"Zoe can handle herself," Jackson said with a smirk. "She certainly put up a fight when Dad had the guards try to take her."

Cole's insides turned to ice as he imagined what the guards had done to her. She shouldn't have to deal with any of this. She always wanted a quiet, normal life. "She shouldn't have to worry about being hunted in the streets. Dad's guards were trying to take her alive . . . what if the next people she comes across decide to take a different approach? Mom did say they would pay for confirmation of her death."

"That's a bit of a leap, isn't it?" Victoria said.

"I don't think so. She's not safe out there on her own."

"She's not on her own," Jackson said. "She's got the Suttons and that Blake guy looking out for her."

Cole shot Jackson a look. "They won't be able to keep Mom and Dad from killing her. I will."

Jackson let out a laugh. "How, exactly? It's not like you can single-handedly take out their army."

"No, but I'm good at getting people to do what I need them to do. Why do you think Dad put me in charge of operations instead of you? Once I find Zoe, I'll convince Mom and Dad that she isn't a threat."

"As long as someone else doesn't kill her first," Jackson said.

Victoria smacked Jackson in the back of his head. "Are you deliberately trying to make things worse?"

"I'm trying to get him to see reason. You can't just go out there and hope to run into her. You need a plan. Maybe there's a way we can get a message to her. Tell her where to meet you."

"That would lead everyone right to her," Victoria said in frustration.

"Not if I'm smart about it. It will have to be something just the two of us will understand." A smile started to form on Cole's lips. This could work. Things were finally starting to come together.

He would get out of here and get Zoe back; all he needed to do was come up with the right place for them to meet.

«‹Chapter 11›»

Cole sat alone in the library, tapping his pen against the table. He had been trying to come up with the perfect message to tell Zoe where to meet him without putting her in more danger than she was already in. So far, the only thing he had accomplished was creating a mountain of crumpled paper in the wastebasket. Normally he would go to Jackson for help, but something was holding him back. This message had to come from him; it had to be in his own words. Part of him knew this could be the last thing Zoe ever heard him say, and it had to be perfect.

"How's it going?" Victoria asked as she entered the room with Jackson.

Cole covered the notepad with his hand. "Slowly."

"Well, I've figured out how we're going to clear Zoe's name," Victoria said with a wicked grin.

"You did? How?"

"With this." She pulled out a laptop and set it on the

table in front of him. "This is Trevor's computer, and it has the unedited security footage from the control room the day the toxin was released."

"He just left that lying around?" Jackson said as he leaned on the empty chair next to Cole.

"I'm sure he didn't think anything of it. He's still under the illusion that we're a happily married couple and I'm on board with the Arrows' plan. Trevor thinks the only reason I'm mad at him is because he didn't tell me he was an Arrow from the beginning." Victoria rolled her eyes as she pulled up the security footage and hit play.

"This is it," Cole said as he watched the video play on the computer.

"Now we need your message to go along with it," Jackson said. "Do you want me to take a look at what you've put together?" He reached for the notepad, but Cole slid it out of reach.

"No, that's okay. I want to do this myself," Cole said as he gripped the notepad tighter.

Jackson held up his hands. "Fair enough. You can use the computer to record it, and then I'll piece it all together into a package we can broadcast."

"Do you really think you'll be able to get it on the air?" Victoria asked.

Jackson nodded. "Mom and Dad brought the PR team from Wilborn Holdings here. These guys have worked for me for years. They'll give me access if I ask."

"We'll want to leave as soon as it goes live," Cole said. "There's no telling how Mom will react when she finds out." The others nodded in agreement. "Good, then I'll go record my message." Cole stood up and grabbed the laptop. "I'll bring this to you when I'm done." With one last look at his siblings, Cole left the room.

«‹›»

They sat in the dark for hours. None of them spoke, fearing they would give their location away. They hadn't heard any voices outside in a long time, but it was impossible to say if their attackers had moved on or if they were trying to wait them out. No one wanted to risk finding out.

Zoe wondered if this was how it was going to be to be from now on. Would their lives be in danger anytime they came across another survivor? She desperately wanted to believe that there was a way to live peacefully, but she wasn't sure if that was true. Maybe peace was only possible in Alana's designated resettlement locations where they would never be welcomed.

The sun was starting to rise, and they still hadn't heard anything outside. "We can't sit here forever," Iris said in a harsh whisper as she readjusted her position on the floor. "Those people could be back at any time. We need to get out of here."

Ian peeked out of the store window. "You're right. Blake and I will go out and see if the coast is clear. You two wait here."

"I'm not some helpless woman you need to protect," Iris said.

"I know that."

"Good, then I'm coming with you." Iris moved to get to her feet.

"Please, Iris, just stay here and wait 'til it's safe."

Iris crossed her arms. "Give me one good reason why I should stay."

"Because I can't risk anything happening to you!" Ian said harshly. He let out a breath and looked down at the floor for a moment before looking back at Iris. "I wanted to tear that man to shreds when he held that gun to your head. I've never felt rage like that before. We already lost Uncle; I can't handle the idea of losing you too. I'd do anything to keep you safe."

"And you think I'm okay with you going out there and risking your life?" Iris said, though her voice was lacking its normal bite.

Ian ran his hand over his shaved scalp. "What do you want me to do here, Iris?"

"Why don't you two stay here, and Blake and I will go," Zoe suggested.

"No way," Ian said. "Your leg still isn't fully healed. I'm not willing to risk you going out there either."

"Why not? We've only known each other for a month, it's not like you have some deep lifelong attachment to me. If things go bad, it wouldn't be that big of a loss for you. In fact, it would probably take the target off your back," Zoe said.

"Why would you think that?" Ian looked genuinely hurt, and it threw Zoe off. She had assumed she was just a necessary annoyance to him. That he felt responsible for her safety because he had dragged her into this in the first place. It never occurred to her that he might actually care about her.

"We're wasting time," Blake said. Zoe wasn't used to hearing him take charge. "Ian and I will go get a car because he's the best shot out of all of us, and I'm especially skilled at hot-wiring cars."

"Fine," Iris said with a roll of her eyes. "But you better be quick about it, or Zoe and I will come find you."

Ian's whole posture relaxed. "Thank you." He tapped Blake on the shoulder, and the two of them left the building with their guns in their hands.

Zoe held her breath and listened. She expected to hear gunshots the moment they stepped outside, but thankfully, everything stayed silent. She exchanged a look with Iris as they waited, neither of them risking talking, fearing they might miss what was happening outside. Zoe inched closer to the door, as if that would make it easier to hear.

It felt like hours passed, but every time Zoe glanced down at her watch, the hands had barely moved. How long would it take Ian and Blake to secure a car and come back for them? At what point should they go out and make sure the others were all right? Zoe's nerves grew with every passing second to the point that she had to stifle a scream with her hand when the door finally opened.

Ian popped his head in. "It's clear. Blake's got us a car."

They followed Ian out of the building and across two parking lots, where Blake had secured them a brand-new Cadillac from a car dealership. Zoe hesitated. It looked too much like the cars the Wilborns drove. Like the cars that had shown up at the trailer to take her back to the Arrows.

"Figured we could ride in style," Blake said. Ian was already in the driver seat, with Iris taking the passenger seat. Blake held open the back door for Zoe, but she didn't move.

Ian stuck his head out the front window. "What's the holdup?"

Zoe shook her head. "Nothing, sorry." She climbed in the back seat, silently scolding herself for her irrational fears.

Ian pulled out the moment they were inside. He sped

down the street, swerving to miss a car parked in the middle of the road. He clearly wanted to put as much distance between them and this town as he could.

Zoe knew better than to ask where they were going. Blake had already told her there wasn't a plan after the trailer. They were truly on the run now.

««»»

"I hate that you aren't coming with us," Cole said as he checked the contents of his backpack for the tenth time.

"I can't, not with the baby. Besides, you need someone here to keep Mom and Dad from noticing that you hijacked their feed," Victoria said. "I'll do everything I can to make sure it plays for as long as possible."

"Do you think Zoe will see it?" Jackson zipped up his backpack and slung it over his shoulder.

"I don't know, but I hope she will." Cole looked in his backpack one last time. Two bottles of water, a handful of protein bars, a change of clothes, a bar of soap, and a package of beef jerky. It wouldn't last them long, but it was the best he could find. They would need to find more supplies as they made their way north.

"How are you going to get back to Michigan?" Victoria asked.

"We're starting out on foot," Jackson said. "But we'll try to find a car or something to get us there faster. I really don't want to have to walk that whole way, that would take forever."

"And you know how to get out of the White House without Mom or Dad finding out?"

Cole took his older sister's hand. "V, we've been over

and over it. We know what we have to do."

"I'm just worried about what will happen if something goes wrong." Victoria brushed a tear from her cheek.

"We'll be all right." Jackson got up and put his arm around Victoria. "I'm more worried about you staying here."

"I'll be safe here," Victoria said with a nod as she swallowed back her tears.

"We'll come back for you and the boys once we've found a safe place to settle," Cole said.

"You two be careful, and give Zoe my love when you find her—because you will find her, Cole."

"I will." He gave Victoria a quick hug and grabbed his bag.

"Now, go. And take care of one another."

Cole and Jackson slipped out of the bedroom and started to make their way toward one of the exits. Gordon was out of town, and Alana was so busy taking over the world that they rarely saw her anymore; they wouldn't get a better opportunity. It would be easier to try leaving in the middle of the day when everyone was busy than in the middle of the night when the guards would be on high alert.

"Won't it look suspicious that we're carrying bags?" Cole asked as they neared the door.

"Act normal, and no one will question it. The guards here are different from the ones at the safe house in Michigan. There's a chance they don't know we're under house arrest," Jackson whispered. He flashed the guard at the door a smile and went to open it.

The guard stepped in front of the handle. "Where are you two going?"

Cole took a deep breath. They had planned for this.

All he had to do was not give them away, and it would be fine. Jackson had assured him that he would be able to handle the guard.

"Our mom, Alana Wilborn, the president . . ." Jackson started.

"I know who she is," the guard snapped.

"Right. Anyway, she wants us to film some footage of what's happening around the White House to use in her next address to the survivors." Jackson pulled a small video camera out of his backpack to show the guard. "She thinks it will help calm people to know that everything is under control here and that it's safe to start proceeding to the resettlement locations."

"You need an exit pass." The guard eyed them suspiciously.

They were done for. In all their planning, they hadn't discussed an exit pass. In all the time he studied the guards, he had never seen anyone produce any kind of pass to get out of the building.

Jackson didn't appear to be fazed by the request. "Right, of course." Jackson made a show of searching his pockets. He turned to Cole. "Did I give it to you?"

"Let me check," Cole said carefully. He quickly checked his pockets, which he knew were empty, and then pulled off his backpack. Careful not to let the guard see what was inside, he opened the front pocket and found a folded piece of paper he hadn't seen before.

It was an exit pass signed by Tyrone Roberts, the director of the RiverLife bottling plant. Cole had always liked the man, but at that moment, he was overwhelmed with gratitude. Whether Tyrone had been an Arrow all along or if he was just going along with them to protect himself, it was a risk for him to put his name on this pass. "Here," Cole said as he flashed the paper to the guard.

The guard snatched it from his hand and read it carefully. Cole shot Jackson a look, but Jackson ignored him. He seemed completely at ease, but he was clenching his hands. After several long seconds, the guard handed the note back to Cole. "You're free to go."

Jackson flashed Cole a smile. They calmly walked through the door.

"That wasn't so hard, was it?" Jackson clapped Cole's back.

"Don't celebrate yet. We're outside the building, but we're still on the property."

"You have the exit pass, we'll be fine," Jackson said, but Cole could tell from the hesitancy in his voice that he didn't fully believe it.

Cole tried to maintain a normal pace as they neared the main gate. Part of him wanted to try to catch the guards by surprise and make a run for it, but the size of the automatic weapons they were holding held him back. He wasn't entirely convinced they wouldn't shoot him if he tried to make a break for it.

"Good morning," Cole said as they approached.

"Exit pass," the guard said without any kind of greeting. These men weren't going to be easily charmed. They meant business.

"Sure." Cole pulled the piece of paper out again and handed it to the guard. It had worked once, hopefully it would be enough to get them to the other side of the fence. Then he would be free to start making his way to Zoe.

The guard pulled out a tablet. "This exit pass hasn't been registered. I'm going to have to call it in to get authorization."

Cole looked at Jackson, panicked. If the guard called

it in, they were done for.

Jackson took a deep breath. "Can I see that for a second?" He rushed at the guard, knocking him to the ground. "Run!" Jackson said as he scrambled to his feet.

Cole took off, trying and failing to knock the second guard over as he ran past. Gunshots rang out behind him. The guards were firing at them. Cole pushed himself to run harder, all while praying that Jackson was close behind him.

Cole turned down an alley and paused for a moment to catch his breath. He didn't hear any footsteps behind him. Maybe they wouldn't come after him.

He knew he couldn't stay here for long. Even if the guards didn't chase after him, it wouldn't be long before Alana realized he was gone and sent a team out to find him.

He slowly made his way to the corner of the building and peered around to see if Jackson was anywhere in sight, but the street was deserted.

A knot formed in the pit of his stomach. If anything had happened to Jackson, it would be his fault. Maybe he should go back for him . . . but if he went back, he'd be trapped there forever. He needed to keep going. He needed to find Zoe.

Cole turned away from the street and started to make his way back down the alley. He was on his own. They had mapped out a route to take through the city before they left. Cole had done his best to memorize it, but now that he was out here, nothing looked familiar. He wished he hadn't let Jackson convince him that carrying the map would be too suspicious. He was pretty sure he was heading north at least, which was a start.

He was making pretty good progress until he turned down a side street to see it completely blocked by soldiers, with Alana standing in the middle of the road. Cole turned to run the other way, only to find another group of soldiers closing in on him from behind.

He was trapped.

Alana stepped forward. "I'm very disappointed in you, Cole. Did you really think your silly message would be enough to distract me from what your real goal was?"

"It was worth a shot," Cole said with a shrug. He needed to stay calm, even though he had never been more afraid in his life.

"And to drag Jackson into this with you. I thought you cared about the safety of your family." Alana shook her head and tutted.

"Is Jackson all right?" The panic he had been keeping at bay rose to the surface.

"He will be," Alana said in a matter-of-fact tone. "The real question you should be asking is if *you're* going to be all right."

Cole looked at his mother, fear pounding in his chest. No emotions showed on her face. Was this really the same woman who had raised him? Alana nodded to one of the soldiers, and they started to move toward him in unison. Cole spun, looking for a weak spot, an opening he could use to break away, but there was none. A second later, hands pulled at him, throwing him to the ground; he barely dodged a boot coming toward his face. He scrambled to his feet, but every time he got more than a foot off the ground, they kicked him back down. He was trapped in a ring of punches and kicks that he couldn't protect himself from.

"This is for your own good, Cole." He heard Alana's voice despite the onslaught of pain the soldiers were inflicting on him. "You need to learn to respect your place in this family and start doing as you're told. Once you do, your life will be so much easier."

Cole could almost feel his body turning black and blue. How much longer would Alana let this go on? "Mom, help me." A choked cry left his lips as the assault continued. He was losing strength. The pain was overwhelming. He collapsed to the ground.

"That's enough," Alana said, and the assault stopped instantly. "Take him back to the White House and lock him up with his brother."

Cole didn't fight as two men grabbed him by his arms and dragged him over to one of the waiting cars. A man was waiting there with a syringe in his hand. He barely looked at Cole as he plunged the needle into his neck.

««Chapter 12»»

It was an odd feeling, being the only ones on the highway, though it allowed them to travel at high speeds to the point that Zoe couldn't read the road signs. She had no idea where they were going, but she was pretty sure they were heading south. When Ian finally pulled off the highway, Zoe assumed they were getting low on gas.

Eventually, the car petered to a stop in a middle-class neighborhood. Zoe looked over the street with its overgrown lawns and houses with dark windows. They got out with their guns already in their hands. It felt weird to be walking down the middle of the empty street.

"That one looks as good as any." Iris nodded to a pale blue colonial up ahead.

"Do you want the honors?" Ian asked.

"Sure." Iris shrugged out of her backpack. "Hold this for me." She handed it to Ian and walked up to the front door.

Iris knocked on the door while the rest of them looked over the house for signs of life. No one answered, so Iris knocked again, waiting only a few seconds before trying the handle. The door swung open.

Iris nodded to the others, and they quickly joined her on the porch. It was almost like they had done this before and weren't just making it up as they went. Iris stuck her head into the house.

"Hello?" she called. They held their breath while they waited for a response. "Is anyone here? We don't want any trouble."

There was no answer.

Iris stepped inside with her gun in front of her. Zoe half expected someone to jump out and attack them the moment they were inside, but no one did.

Zoe glanced around the foyer. There were small pink and orange tennis shoes by the front door and a discarded soccer ball in the corner. "There could be kids here," Zoe whispered, putting her gun away. Reluctantly, the others did the same. They moved through the house as a group searching for any signs that someone had been there recently. There was a sippy cup lying on the table in the family room. Zoe picked it up and saw the milk inside had curdled. "I don't think anyone's been here for a while."

They moved to the back of the house where the kitchen was. The blinds over the sliding glass door were open, and out back were three mounds of freshly turned dirt.

"Graves," Ian said reading Zoe's mind.

"What do you think happened to the person who dug them?" Blake moved to the door and checked the lock.

"There." Zoe pointed to a mound on the grass next to the graves. It was hard to make out, but she was certain it was the remains of an adult male.

Ian pulled the blinds shut. "We should be safe here for a while. Let's see if we can find anything to make a decent meal for a change." He moved to the kitchen with Iris.

Zoe went to the family room, trying not to look at the family pictures on the mantel. It was possible to block out the ramifications of what Alana had done while they were staying in the hotel, but not here. Not when the evidence was staring her in the face.

She picked a stuffed animal up off the couch and sat down. Tears started to run down her cheeks, and there was nothing she could do to stop them. Why had she survived when this family hadn't? Why couldn't she have saved them? What made the child who owned this toy such a threat to Alana's new world? Why couldn't there have been a place for them?

Blake sat down next to her and handed her a box of tissues. "They still have power here. Want to watch a movie or something? Try to take our mind off things for a bit."

"Pick out something light, okay," Zoe said as she wiped away her tears.

Blake nodded and went to search the stand of movies next to the television.

Zoe picked up the remote and turned on the TV. She expected to see the same relocation orders that had been playing nonstop since Alana took over the White House, but that's not what was on the screen.

Instead, she saw Cole talking.

She fumbled with the remote as she turned up the volume. In a trance, she slid off the couch and inched closer to the man she loved, desperately wishing she could reach through the TV and bring him to her side.

"I want to set the record straight," Cole was saying. Zoe had no idea where he was or how he had managed to get onto the Arrows' broadcast, but she didn't care. The only thing that mattered was that he was safe. "Zoe Antos had nothing to do with the release of the toxin that killed billions of people across the globe. It was developed and released by the Arrow Equilibrium with the sole purpose of reducing the global population so they could take control without protest. Zoe tried to stop them. That's what you saw her doing on the security video my mother manipulated to place the blame on her. I have the full, unedited footage, and I'll play it for you in a minute. But first, I want to warn you not to trust my mother or the Arrows. They are only out for themselves and will kill anyone who gets in their way without hesitation. We need to band together to stop them. They made this world, but that doesn't give them the right to run it." Cole looked directly at the camera. "Zoe, if you're watching, stay fired up . . . it's the only way we'll be able to survive this. There is power out there, power you helped to create. Find that power. We can move forward as long as we're fired up."

The image on the screen changed, and they were now watching the unedited version of the security tape from the moment Zoe entered the control room, to Alana releasing the toxin, to her shooting Zoe in the leg.

Zoe turned away from the screen. She didn't need to see any reminders of that day.

It was only then that she realized the others were watching the broadcast with her. She had no idea when they entered the room, but it didn't matter. Cole must have a plan, and it was up to her to figure out what he needed her to do.

"That was risky. I hope he managed to get away from the Arrows before that aired," Iris said.

"But what did he mean? He said fired up twice, that had to be on purpose, right?" Ian said.

Zoe spun around and looked at Ian, a smile forming on her face. She knew exactly what he was trying to tell her. It wasn't a plan so much as it was a location. A place where they had a chance to rebuild. "I know where we need to go."

"Where?" Blake asked.

"To college." A huge grin took over Zoe's face. It was brilliant. "*Fire up* is Central Michigan University's slogan. That's where Cole and I met."

"Okay, but why do we need to go there?" Ian crossed his arms. "What if the Arrows are using him to get to you? It could be a trap."

"I don't think so. Cole's parents weren't thrilled that he chose to go there when he could have easily gotten into a more prestigious school. They were never involved in the university. They wouldn't know the slogan."

"Okay, but that doesn't mean it's the best place for us to go," Iris argued.

"You don't understand. His parents weren't involved in the school, but Cole and I were. We donated a lot of money and resources to the environmental club. We helped them make a quad of dorms completely self-sustainable. There are state-of-the-art solar panels and mini wind turbines to power the building, a fully enclosed water system that treats and recycles the water. It's cleaner than typical city water. We could rebuild there. Maybe this is a sign that the tide is turning in our favor."

"Or it's about to crash down and drown us," Iris said under her breath.

"I don't know. It's dangerous to set up shop when the Arrows are hunting us," Ian said.

"How long do you want to keep running? Because they won't ever stop hunting us," Zoe said. She had to make them see that this was the best option. "I'm tired of just surviving, I want a chance to live. We could do that at Central."

"It would be nice to have a place where we could rebuild," Blake said with a shrug. "We could find a way to defend ourselves. Mount Pleasant is a smaller town, there's not a lot around it. We would be pretty isolated up there."

Finally, someone was starting to get it. If she could convince Blake, the others would get on board as well. "Did you go to Central?"

"Not officially, though I've spent my fair share of weekends up there." Blake turned to Ian. "I think it's worth a shot. It has to be better than what we're doing."

"Are you both forgetting it's November, and Central is pretty far north? The roads could be covered in snow, and if any of that state-of-the-art equipment isn't working, we could freeze to death before the Arrows ever find us," Iris said. "I think we should keep heading south."

"But what about long term? Do you really want to be moving from house to house every few days?"

Iris rolled her eyes and sighed.

"We could use the snow to our advantage," Zoe pressed. "It could stop the Arrows from getting to us. We would have time to set up our defenses. I think it's worth the risk." And there was a chance she would see Cole again. She looked at each of them. "You don't have to come if you don't want to, but I'm heading to Central. I'd like all of you to come with me, but I won't force you."

"We'll leave the day after tomorrow," Ian sighed. "We need to rest and restock our supplies before we go anywhere."

"Thank you." For the first time since she heard about the Arrow Equilibrium, Zoe felt a flicker of hope.

«‹›»

Zoe was at the sink cleaning up the dishes from their dinner when she saw someone in the backyard.

It was too dark to tell who it was. She had no idea where the others were, but she didn't think calling for help was a good idea in case whoever was outside heard her.

She pulled out her gun, which was always on her now, and headed toward the sliding door. She watched the figure for a minute; it was a man with a decent build, and he was carrying something.

Zoe glanced back into the house, hoping for some backup, but she was alone.

Carefully, she slid the door open without a sound. She took a deep breath before stepping outside. She aimed her gun and said with as much confidence as she could, "Drop your weapon, then turn around slowly with your hands up."

The man dropped what he was carrying and turned to face her with both hands up by his head. "It's okay, Zoe, it's just me," Ian said as he looked her straight in the eye.

"Ian?" Zoe lowered her gun. "I'm so sorry." She stumbled, and Ian rushed forward to catch her before she fell off the porch. "I'm shaking."

"It's the adrenaline." Ian pulled her close and held her against him. Zoe leaned her head on his chest and listened to his heartbeat as she willed hers to slow down. "Hey, it's all right," he said as he rubbed her back. "I should have told someone I was coming out here."

"I saw you out here and thought about the people who attacked us at the hotel."

"I know. I'm sorry. I never meant to scare you. You're pretty terrifying with a gun, by the way."

Zoe pulled her head off his chest and saw the trace of a smile on his lips. "I think *terrified* is a more accurate description." She gently extracted herself from Ian's arms and sat down on the edge of the deck. It was a nice evening, warmer than any November evening she could remember in Michigan. Maybe the others had a point about not traveling north until winter was over, but Zoe couldn't put off going to Central for that long. Not when Cole could be there waiting for her.

"Don't underestimate yourself." Ian sat down next to her. "You can hold your own just fine."

"What are you doing out here?"

Ian nodded to the body lying on the grass on the other side of the lawn. Zoe had forgotten it was there. "I thought he should be with his family."

Zoe rested her hand on Ian's knee. "That's really sweet of you."

Ian shrugged. "It's the least I can do." He looked at Zoe, his gaze piercing into her. Electricity passed between them. She wondered if he felt it too.

"I guess I should get started," he said, finally breaking eye contact.

"Okay." Zoe removed her hand and watched as Ian walked over to the line of graves in the back of the yard.

He started to dig with his back to her; Zoe watched him for a few minutes before returning to the house. There had to be something she could do to help, some way to honor the family whose house was providing them with a safe place to rest for a few days.

She found exactly what she needed hanging on the wall in the entryway, a hand-painted wooden sign that read *The Morse Family*. She took it to the attached garage, hoping to find something she could use as a stake. She was pleasantly surprised to find a beautifully organized work bench out there with scraps of wood neatly stacked under it. She found one the right length and took a few minutes to attach it to the back of the sign. On her way through the house, she spotted a family photo on the mantel. She had avoided looking at it before, but now she went straight to it and brought it with her to the backyard.

Ian was filling in the grave. Zoe stood on the deck, watching him until he finished. As Ian stood back to survey his work, Zoe joined him. She didn't say anything as she carefully hammered the newly made grave marker into the ground and placed the family picture next to it.

She went and stood by Ian when she was done. Ian took her hand in his, and Zoe said a silent prayer for the family and for all the families that had died because of the Arrows.

A chill overtook her. She ran her free hand over her arm as she continued to look at the line of graves.

"Let's go inside." Ian let go of her hand, sending an unexpected wave of disappointment through her. It was short-lived, though, as he wrapped his arm around her shoulders and pulled her close.

Zoe glanced back over her shoulder at the graves.

She doubted anyone would ever see them, but at least, on some level, this family would be remembered. They weren't some nameless bodies sacrificed for the Arrows' vision of a better world. They were the Morse family.

«‹›»

Every inch of Cole's body ached. He had no idea how Alana had known exactly where to ambush him. Had she just gotten lucky, or had someone told her where he was going? The drugs they had given him were making it hard to think clearly. Whatever it took to keep him under control.

He pulled himself up into a seated position and scanned his surroundings. The room was dimly lit, the floor under him was cold, and a musty smell hung in the air. Had Alana locked him in a basement?

"Hello?" Cole tentatively called. His mouth was so dry that the word hurt his throat on the way out.

"I'm glad you're finally waking up. I was getting worried."

That was Jackson's voice, but Cole couldn't tell where it was coming from. "Where are you? Are you hurt?" Cole clutched his side as he slowly got to his feet.

"I'm here." Jackson emerged from the back corner of the basement. "I was trying to see if there was a way out, but it doesn't look good."

Cole stumbled toward his brother. He braced himself against Jackson's shoulders as he looked him over for injuries. "Are you hurt?"

"No," Jackson said as he steadied Cole. "But you look like shit. Sit back down." Jackson helped Cole lower himself back to the floor.

"How long was I out?" Cole shifted positions so he

could lean against the cement wall with a minimal amount of pain.

"I don't know. It's hard to keep track of time in here. It could have been a few hours or maybe even a day or two. I had already been in here for a while when the soldiers threw you in. You were out cold."

Cole's hand went to his neck where the soldier had injected him. "They drugged me."

"Was that before or after they beat the shit out of you?"

"After."

"Shit," Jackson said as he slid down the wall next to Cole.

"How are we going to get out of here?"

"I don't think we are," Jackson said slowly. "I really thought the worst Mom would do was lock us in our rooms. I never imagined she'd throw us some place like this. Maybe it's time to fall in line with her. It's got to be better than this."

Cole turned his head to look at Jackson. "No. We can't."

"Come on, I mean, they already went through with their plan to restore balance, there's nothing we can do to change that now. It's not worth getting yourself killed over."

"You can't be serious!" This had to be some kind of trick. Maybe Jackson had found some kind of listening device, and this was a ploy to get their parents to think they've seen the error of their ways.

"It can't be that bad. It's not like we have to actually help the Arrows, just stop getting in their way, and in return we get a comfortable bed, warm clothes, food, and drinks. God, I could use a beer right now."

Cole scooted away from Jackson. "I'm never going to

fall in line. I'll never stop fighting her. She shot Zoe, she's held me against my will for weeks, there's no way I can get in line with her. Just look at what her soldiers did to me!"

"Mom's going to be pissed when she finds out how rough they were with you."

"Jackson, she was there. She ordered them to do it and then stood by and watched until I had nearly passed out."

"She wouldn't." Concern etched Jackson's face for the first time since Cole woke up.

"Why not? She's killed billions of people so she could get power, why would you think we're exempt from her cruelty?"

"Because she's our mom. Despite everything, I still believe she loves us."

"Alana Wilborn might have given birth to me, but she's not my mom. Not anymore. Now help me up. I'm going to find a way out of here." Cole clutched the wall as he pulled himself to his feet, ignoring the pain that shot through his body every time he moved.

"I've already looked, there's nothing to find," Jackson said from the floor.

Cole shook his head and slowly made his way around the room. Jackson might be ready to give in and be the perfect son, but he wasn't. He couldn't. Not while Zoe was still out there somewhere waiting for him.

«Chapter 13»»

Jackson was right, it was impossible to keep track of time in here. The only way Cole knew time was passing at all was that the swelling had gone down slightly on some of his bruises. The guards brought them food in sporadic intervals; they weren't getting the three square meals a day he was getting while locked in the bedroom. Cole would doze off occasionally but wouldn't stay asleep for long. It was a dreary existence that almost made him wish Alana had let the soldiers kill him.

Cole had gotten used to being his mom's prisoner, but Jackson wasn't holding up as well. He spent hours pacing around the small room. He couldn't sit still for more than a few minutes before getting up and starting again. If something didn't happen soon, Cole feared this would break his brother.

"How long do you think they're going to leave us in here?" Jackson asked for what had to be the hundredth time.

"I don't know," Cole said offhandedly. Maybe Alana was hoping they would drive each other insane until they were willing to do anything she wanted. Cole hated to admit it, but a few more days locked up with Jackson might actually get him to that point.

"Is there any more water?" Jackson stopped pacing and went over to the tray of food sitting in the corner of the room. Cole knew Jackson didn't expect him to answer; he leaned his head back against the wall and closed his eyes instead, hoping to block out some of Jackson's anxious energy.

In the distance, a door opened. Usually this meant a fresh tray of food was being brought down. Slowly, Cole opened his eyes and sat up straighter. At some point, they would have to try to take out the guard and make a run for it, but he was still in too much pain to try anything.

Cole didn't pay much attention when the door finally opened. Jackson was already standing. He could get the tray from the guard.

Except the man standing in the open doorway wasn't a guard; it was their father.

"Thank God I finally found you boys," Gordon said with relief.

"You didn't know Mom's been holding us down here for days?" Jackson said.

"No. I just got back this morning. Your mother left two days ago and didn't bother to tell anyone where you boys were," Gordon said. "Let's get you out of here."

He stepped away from the threshold, leaving the path to freedom clear. Jackson nearly ran out of the door, but Cole didn't move. Something about this didn't feel right. "I thought you and Mom were a team. Do you really expect me to believe that she kept you in the dark about where we were?"

"Your mother is very busy at the moment." Gordon chose his words carefully. "There isn't time to discuss every decision. Now, come on. I want to have a doctor look you over."

Cole scoffed. "You're concerned about my well-being now? Where were you when Mom had her soldiers beat the shit out of me in the first place?"

"I'm sure your mother didn't know how far they would take it. They must have gotten carried away. I'm sure they didn't mean to actually hurt you."

Cole pulled up his shirt to reveal his purpled chest and side. "Does this look like something that happens by accident?" Gordon's hands balled into fists as he looked at Cole's bruises. "Oh, and Mom was there the entire time. She could have stopped them at any point, but she didn't. I believe I heard her say it was *for my own good*, but it's hard to say for sure since I was a little focused on making sure I wasn't beaten to death in the middle of the street."

"She's under a lot of pressure," Gordon started.

"Don't try to justify her actions. She doesn't care about me. She only cares about preserving her power. It doesn't matter who she has to take out along the way, even if it's her own flesh and blood."

"How can you say that?"

"Maybe it's a side effect of whatever they injected me with before throwing me in here."

"You were drugged?"

"Sure was."

Gordon ran a hand through his hair. "Cole, I'm so sorry. None of this was supposed to happen."

"Maybe you and Mom aren't the team you think you are. She seems to have no problem making unilateral decisions without your input."

"We can discuss that later," Gordon said tensely. "Now, would you prefer to stay locked up in this basement, or would you like to come with me?"

Cole winced as he got to his feet, his muscles tight from inactivity. Gordon extended his hand, and begrudgingly, Cole took it and let his father lead him over to the door.

It wasn't like he had any chance of getting away if he stayed down here. This was just a step closer to finding Zoe. It didn't mean he was falling in line with his parents.

«‹‹›»»

After a solid day and a half of driving, they finally arrived in Mount Pleasant, Michigan. It was weird being back at her alma mater, especially given the current circumstances. Zoe had so many happy memories here, so many memories of Cole, but everything felt different now. The college town that was always so full of life was now deserted.

They parked the truck at what used to be a dance club just off campus. Zoe got out of the truck, looking for any signs of life as she stretched out her legs. The wind sliced through the sweater she was wearing. She had forgotten how cold it could get up here; they would have to find some real winter clothes soon.

"We need to go to Beddow Hall," Zoe said as they gathered a few things from the truck. "It's a little less than a mile down this road."

"I think we should leave the truck here and go on foot. That way, if it's a trap, they won't hear us coming," Ian said as he checked his weapon.

"I'm pretty sure if this was a trap, the Arrows would already know we're here," Blake said, handing Zoe a backpack and gun.

"Thanks." Zoe put the handgun in the holster on her hip. Though the others weren't completely on board with her plan to rebuild here, she appreciated their support.

"Lead the way," Iris said as she pulled on another sweater.

Zoe started to walk down the street across from the dorm. She hoped they would be able to tell if anyone was there before they actually went into the building. If something went wrong, it would be her fault, and she already had enough blood on her hands.

The sun was starting to set as they made their way past the football stadium and athletic center in silence. Zoe kept waiting for cars to drive by on what was once a busy street into campus, or to hear the laughter of a group of students coming up behind them, but there was nothing.

No one said anything until they stopped, a four-lane road separating them from what Zoe hoped would be their new home. "That's it." She nodded across the street.

"I don't see any signs of life," Blake said. "Are you sure there's power there?"

"There should be." Zoe pointed to the roof. "The solar panels and mini turbine are still there. We might have to get them up and running again, though. Cole and I donated the equipment and the money to have it installed, but we didn't keep up with the maintenance after that."

"As long as it's not damaged, I should be able to get it running," Iris said.

"Then let's go see if anyone is home." Ian adjusted his grip on the gun and led them across the street.

Zoe tightened the straps on her backpack, pulled out her own gun, and followed. Her nerves grew with ever step they took.

Blake reached the front door first and tentatively pulled the handle. Zoe was surprised it was unlocked. Did that mean someone had beaten them here, or had everyone simply forgotten to lock up when the government ordered the schools to shut down?

Ian went in first. The building was dark, but they didn't attempt to turn the lights on, at least not yet. Zoe closed her eyes and tried to imagine what it had looked like when she lived here. The U-shaped desk directly across from the front door. To the right was a hall that led to the joint dining room for the four dorms that made up the quad. To the left was a common room and a hall to the dorms.

Zoe pointed to the left, and Ian headed in that direction.

They had only taken two steps into the common room when Zoe sensed a presence in the room. She aimed her gun in front of her. "I think someone's here," she whispered to Ian, who nodded.

They moved farther into the room, everyone with their guns in front of them. "Don't move," Ian said as the shadowy figure emerged in front of them.

"Don't shoot." The shadow held up their hands. Zoe recognized the voice, but she couldn't place it. All she knew for sure was that it didn't belong to Cole.

Blake pulled out a flashlight and trained it on the man's face.

"Do you mind?" he said as he tried to block the light from blinding him.

"Detective Pearson?" Zoe said as she slowly lowered her gun.

"Ms. Antos." Pearson nodded to her but kept his hands in the air. "Can you ask your friends to put their weapons down?"

"You first," Ian growled.

Zoe shot him a look. Pearson didn't have a weapon in his hands.

"I have a gun under my shirt. Let me take it out and set it on the table," Pearson said slowly. He sounded like he had complete control of the situation, even though there were still three guns pointed at him. Zoe wondered if he had ever been in this type of situation before.

"Slowly," Ian said.

Pearson locked eyes with Ian while he pulled his gun out by the grip, making sure to keep his fingers away from the trigger, and set it down on the table next to him. "Now, your turn."

Reluctantly, Ian lowered his gun and placed it back in the holster on his hip. Iris and Blake followed suit.

"Why are you here?" Ian's hand hovered over his gun as he talked. He was being ridiculous, but Zoe kept that thought to herself.

"I saw Cole's message and figured out where he was telling you to meet him. I'm a detective after all," Pearson said with a smirk.

"So you came here hoping to find Zoe? Why? I won't let you turn her over to the Arrows." Ian took a step closer to Pearson.

"I did come here to find Zoe, but I have no intention of turning her over to anyone. I thought we could work together. I can't keep running with my family, and I won't take them to live under Alana Wilborn's authority at one of the resettlement locations. I need a third option, and I figured you would be in a similar situation. We can help each other. There's safety in numbers."

"You want to work together?" Iris said.

"Yes."

"To do what?"

"To figure out a way forward. To give my kids some sense of a normal life again."

"Your family's here? They're alive?" Zoe asked, her brain trying to keep up with all the new information Pearson was giving them.

"Yes, thanks to you." Pearson turned around and called, "It's all right, you can come out."

Zoe looked toward the hallway where a group of people were coming out of the first dorm room. There was a man around the same age as Pearson, an older couple, and two young girls. "This is my husband, Shane, our girls, Nina and Gemma, and my parents, Floyd and Dottie. They're all here because you told me about RiverLife."

Zoe cocked a smile. Somehow, in all the insanity, she had managed to do something right. She had managed to save this family, and for now, that was enough. "Is anyone else here?" Zoe tried to look past the Pearson family down the hall of dorms.

"No. I swept the whole building," Pearson said. Zoe tried not to let the disappointment show on her face.

"How long have you been here?" Ian asked.

"We got here this morning."

"Did you find any bodies?" Iris asked, her voice quiet.

Shane nodded. "One. We buried her outside."

Ian pulled a set of keys out of his pocket and tossed them to Blake. "Can you go get the truck?"

Ian sat down on one of the couches in the common

room. Zoe was glad he was all right with the recent development. It would be nice to have a few more people around for protection, but she wasn't sure how Ian and Pearson would get along. He had been the one to throw Ian in jail for kidnapping her. The Arrows had tried to kill him while he was in there, before Zoe bailed him out.

"Sure thing," Blake said, twirling the keys on his finger.

"Wait, is it safe for you to go by yourself?" Iris asked with a hint of fear in her voice. They had already lost so much. The idea of losing Blake was unbearable.

Blake put his arm around Iris's shoulders. "If you're so worried, you're more than welcome to come with me. It's been a while since we had some alone time." Blake kissed her cheek, and Iris pushed him away in disgust. Blake put both hands on his heart and bowed his way out of the building.

Ian chuckled from his place on the couch. "So, was Cole right? Is there power here, or are we going to have to rebuild society in the dark?"

"We haven't tried it yet, though the heat is clearly still working." Pearson came over and sat down in a chair across from Ian, who shifted slightly on the couch, his muscles tensing.

Zoe went to sit next to him. She trusted Pearson, but it would take a bit longer for Ian to be completely at ease around him.

"There's only one way to find out." Iris walked over to the switch on the wall. Zoe found herself holding her breath as Iris flipped it.

The room flooded with light.

Zoe let out her breath. "That's something, at least."

Ian turned to tuck a stray strand of hair behind her

ear. "We might attract attention with it, though."

"I agree," Pearson said. Ian turned and gave him a weird look. Zoe guessed he was surprised that Pearson agreed with them. Pearson shot Ian a questioning glance in return while reaching for his gun on the table; Ian nodded, and Pearson picked it up and returned it to his holster.

"Is anyone hungry?" Dottie asked.

"We had some granola bars before we got here," Iris said, sitting down next to Zoe.

"That's not a meal. We found a hot plate in one of the dorms. Let me get you something real to eat." Dottie left without waiting for an answer.

"There's no point trying to stop her," Shane said, taking a seat across from Zoe.

"How old are your girls?" Zoe watched the two girls huddled up with their grandfather on the other side of the room. Things would be different now that there were kids they needed to keep safe. It wouldn't be easy to run—though the whole point of coming here was so that they wouldn't have to run anymore.

Zoe couldn't help but wonder if they were in more danger now that she was here. The Arrows would find them at some point. When they did, Zoe would do everything she could to keep those girls out of the crossfire.

"Nina is ten, and Gemma is six," Shane said.

"How are they handling all of this?" Ian stretched his arm out along the back of the couch so it was around Zoe's shoulders.

Pearson looked over his shoulder at the girls. "As good as can be expected."

"Honestly, they're dealing with it better than Toby is," Shane said with a smile.

"Your first name's Toby?" Iris laughed.

"You got a problem with that?" Pearson said.

"Nope, but I get why you like *Detective* better."

"Tobias is a family name."

"I think it's cute." Shane leaned over and gave Pearson a chaste kiss.

Pearson turned to Zoe. "So, tell me what happened. The last time we spoke, I told you to let me handle it."

Zoe blushed. "I didn't listen."

"Clearly," Pearson smirked.

"That seems to be a common problem with you," Ian said.

Zoe playfully backhanded his chest before answering Pearson's question. "I found out that the Arrows were planning on controlling the release of the toxin from Wilborn Holdings Headquarters, and I thought I could stop them, but I failed."

She wondered what would have happened if she had listened to Pearson and let him handle it. Would he have been able to stop the Arrows if she hadn't interfered?

"It doesn't matter," Pearson said gently. "I asked every judge in the state to give me a warrant to search Wilborn Holdings, and every one of them turned me down."

"Most of them are probably Arrows, or too afraid of the Arrows to risk going against them," Iris said. "They've killed people for a lot less."

A car pulled up out front, and they all reached for their guns. Ian and Pearson got to their feet and stood in front of the group as the front door opened.

"It's just me," Blake said as he walked in, his arms loaded down with bottles.

"What's all that?" Ian asked as he put away his gun.

"I figured we could take one night off from surviving

and actually celebrate the fact that we made it through the damned apocalypse." Blake lined the bottles up on the front desk, setting up a makeshift bar.

"Where did you find all of this?" Zoe examined the selection of spirits and wine. A drink didn't sound so bad at the moment.

"I went to The Store," Blake said with a wink. It took Zoe a minute to remember that was the name of a popular liquor store around the corner. "I have some more stuff out in the truck, and then we can party."

"There are kids here," Iris scolded.

"I didn't forget about the kids." Blake started to empty his pockets, which were loaded with king-size candy bars. "There are also a few cases of pop out in the truck."

Ian shook his head and followed Blake out to get the rest of their supplies.

"I'm sorry about him," Zoe said to Pearson.

"Don't be," Pearson said. "He's right, we could all use a night to unwind." He grabbed a handful of candy and a bottle of whiskey before making his way back to his family.

"I guess he doesn't care." Iris grabbed a bottle of wine and went back to the common room. Zoe sighed and followed suit, grabbing an expensive bottle of red wine that Cole always had stocked for her at his house.

Zoe retook her seat on the couch, and Iris tossed her a pocketknife with a corkscrew. Zoe removed the cork and took a sip. This wasn't a time for glasses.

She held the wine in her mouth for moment, savoring the flavor. If she closed her eyes, she could almost imagine she was back at Cole's house, snuggled up on the couch with him. Some cheesy romantic comedy playing on the TV that neither of them was really paying attention to. What she wouldn't give for one more night like that.

She felt someone sit down next to her. Zoe opened her eyes to see Ian reclaim his spot next to her. "Cheers." He held up a bottle of whiskey.

"To surviving the end of the world." Zoe held up her bottle. Everyone followed suit.

They drank and joked the rest of the night. At some point, Floyd and Dottie took the girls to one of the rooms to try to sleep. They would have to figure out the living arrangements at some point, but for now, Zoe was comfortable on the couch. She felt safe for the first time in weeks surrounded by these people, though part of that might've been the full bottle of wine she had consumed.

Ian and Pearson were in a heated debate about something — she had stopped listening a while ago. She had never seen Ian this animated before. On the edge of drifting off, Zoe leaned her head on Ian's shoulder and closed her eyes. He stiffened for a moment before adjusting his position so he could put his arm around her.

She let herself relax against him. All she wanted was to feel safe, and at that moment, she did.

«‹‹›»

Gordon had convinced Alana that Cole didn't need to be locked up. Instead, he had a soldier following him around anytime he stepped out of his bedroom.

Honestly, Cole wasn't sure which was worse.

He was more determined than ever to get away from his parents, but with his new shadow, he couldn't even begin to come up with a plan. Besides, the ever present throbbing from his bruised ribs and the black eye that wouldn't go away were a constant reminder of the extremes Alana was willing to take to keep him here.

Cole's stomach grumbled. He had skipped family dinner last night, not wanting to be in Alana's presence. If he was going to get out of here, he would need to keep his strength up, or at the very least get it back to what it once was. The lack of food while they were locked in the basement had taken a bigger toll on him than he'd realized.

He rolled off the bed and opened the door, where he found the same soldier who had been guarding him the last few days waiting for him.

"Good morning," Cole said to the soldier, who followed him in silence to the dining room. Thankfully, Victoria was the only one there when he arrived. "Where's Jackson?" Cole had barely seen him since Gordon had let them out of the basement.

"I haven't seen him today. That's why I'm hanging out in here. I'm worried about him. He's pulling away from everyone."

"Being locked up was really hard on him, but I'm sure he'll bounce back. He has to, right?" Cole picked up a piece of peanut butter toast from the table.

"I hope so," Victoria said as she sipped her coffee. "How much longer do you think this is going to go on?" Her eyes shot to the door where Cole's guard was waiting silently.

"I can't see Mom trusting me anytime soon. I'm open to suggestions if you can think of a way to shake him." Cole picked up the plate of toast from the center of the table and turned around in his seat. "Hungry?" He offered the plate to the soldier, who didn't even acknowledge him. Cole shook his head and turned back to Victoria.

"Maybe I can try talking to Mom," Victoria offered.

"I wouldn't. I don't want her to think I've corrupted you like I did Jackson. Who knows what she'd do then?"

"It can't be much worse than what she's doing now."

"I don't know. I'm pretty sure the next time I step out of line, she's going to have me killed. Which, honestly, wouldn't be the worst thing to happen," Cole said offhandedly.

"Don't say that," Victoria whispered harshly. "Your message played for ten hours before they were able to shut it down. There's a chance Zoe saw it."

"What does it matter if the only way I'm getting out of here is in a body bag? Face it, V, Mom's snapped . . . even Dad thinks so, but he won't admit it. He was pissed when he found Jackson and me locked in the basement. Mom never bothered to tell him what she did to us. The Arrows are the only thing that matters to her now, and if we challenge that, then we're the enemy. It's that simple."

"There has to be a way to bring her back. I know she still loves us."

"Sometimes love isn't enough." Cole got up and walked back to the door. "Come on, soldier boy, let's go for a walk."

He left the dining room, and as expected, the guard followed behind him with his weapon in his hand. They walked to the back door and out onto the lawn. Every day, Cole had been seeing how far he was able to get before he was stopped. It seemed he was fine as long as he didn't go within fifteen feet of the fence line. They really overestimated his abilities if they thought he could scale the black metal bars that divided the White House from the rest of the world.

"Do you really believe all of this nonsense about Alana wanting to build a better world?" Cole asked the guard as they walked. "You know she killed billions of people to get her power, right? She probably killed your family, and you still do what she tells you to do."

The guard didn't say anything. He never said anything, but Cole couldn't stand the silence, so he kept talking. Maybe something would get through to him. "Is this what you wanted to be doing with your life? Holding people prisoner for an insane dictator? I bet you thought joining the military would mean serving your country, helping its citizens, and now here you are, nothing more than a babysitter with a gun."

The guard's mouth twitched, but he remained silent. His eyes fixed on the path in front of them.

"I guess there are worse things that you could be doing. At least you have food and shelter. How many people out there don't have that right now, do you think? People terrified to venture out because they don't know what waits for them. People like my fiancée, who is being hunted and for what? For standing up against the Arrows. For trying to stop them from creating this nightmare in the first place. Somehow, that makes her the biggest threat to the world." Cole rolled his eyes.

"Do you ever stop talking?" the guard finally said.

"If I'm bothering you, feel free to leave at any time," Cole said with a smirk.

"We both know I can't do that."

"Then how about you participate in the conversation so I'm not talking to myself? I have a feeling we're going to be together for a long time. Might as well make it as enjoyable as possible. Or are you not allowed to talk to me?"

"I was never told I couldn't talk to you," the soldier

said through gritted teeth.

"Perfect," Cole said, keeping his tone friendlier than it had been before. If he could befriend his guard, maybe he would take sympathy on Cole and help him get out of here. It was the best shot he had at the moment. "Let's start with something simple. What's your name?"

"Private Griffin."

"Good. Is there a first name that goes with that?" Cole paused, looking his guard over for the first time. He was young, significantly younger than Cole. He was probably fresh out of boot camp when the world flipped upside down. Cole wanted to blame him for going along with the Arrows, but really, what else could the kid do? He was only following orders, trying to figure out what was happening, just like the rest of them.

Griffin's shoulders sagged. Cole was wearing him down. "It's Adam."

"I'm Cole." He held his hand out to Adam, who hesitated a moment before shifting the gun he was carrying to shake Cole's hand. For a second, Cole thought about trying to grab the gun, but even though he easily had fifteen years on the kid, it was clear Adam hadn't been skipping out on the gym. There was no way Cole would be able to overpower him. He'd have to charm him instead, a skill he had honed while overseeing all the manufacturing plants for Wilborn Holdings. He never thought he'd have to use it to get away from his family.

Cole turned and started to head back inside. "Do you know if any of your family survived the toxin?"

Adam sighed. "I wish I knew. I'm hoping we can get access to the survivor list from the resettlements soon."

"Maybe I can help," Cole offered.

Adam laughed, but there was no malice in it. "I

know everything you do at this point."

"I'm still a Wilborn," Cole said with a small laugh of his own. "Albeit the black sheep of the family. There might still be a few people out there willing to help me or, at the very least, a few who don't know I'm at the top of Alana's shit list."

Adam stopped. "You would really do that for me, even though my job is to keep you here against your will?"

"You're only following orders. Despite what you've probably been told, I'm not the bad guy here. My fiancée is out there somewhere, and I'd give anything to know where she is, even if it's bad news. The not knowing is the worst part. If I can make it easier for you, I will."

"You don't seem like much of an anarchist," Adam said as he held the door open.

"Is that what they're calling me? I guess I should be flattered Alana thinks so highly of me. I assure you, the only thing I want is to find Zoe. There's no grand plan beside that." Cole stepped past Adam and made his way back to his room.

«‹Chapter 14›»

Zoe's head was pounding, and her neck was stiff. She opened her eyes to see the lobby of her old college dorm, and for a second, she thought she was still dreaming.

That is, until she saw Detective Pearson and his husband lying together on the floor in front of her.

She glanced up to see Ian still sleeping, his arm wrapped tightly around her. She carefully extracted herself so she wouldn't wake him and made her way to the front desk. She needed water and maybe some aspirin. She couldn't remember the last time she had drunk that much.

"You look like you could use this." Blake emerged from the hallway leading to the dorms and tossed her a bottle of aspirin.

"Thanks." Zoe opened the bottle and popped two in her mouth. She grabbed a bottle of water from the desk and forced the pills down. "Where did you find these?"

Blake hopped onto the desk. "I got up early and started looking through a few of the rooms."

"I guess we'll have to clean all of them out at some point." Zoe gently messaged her neck. "We can't keep sleeping in the lobby."

Blake nudged her with his shoulder. "I don't know, you and Ian looked pretty cozy last night."

"Shut up." A blush started to cross her cheeks. "Nothing happened. It was completely innocent."

"You keep telling yourself that."

"We were drunk. That was it."

"I would have thought a Central girl would be able to handle her alcohol better." Blake smirked.

"I graduated twelve years ago. My tolerance is significantly lower now."

"We'll have to work on building it back up."

Zoe shook her head but regretted it instantly. "We aren't here to party. We need to make this place feel like home and not just another place to crash for a few days."

"So, we're staying here? This is our home now?" a small voice asked.

Zoe looked over to see Gemma and Nina standing with their grandparents next to the desk. She had no idea how to answer them. What could she say to kids who had already lost everything?

"Yes, baby," Shane said as he picked up Gemma, his other arm wrapped around Pearson's waist. "We're going to make this the best home ever." He kissed his daughter's cheek.

"That's right." Pearson looked down at Nina with a warm smile. "We have our new friends here, and we'll work together to keep everyone safe."

"Well, now that's settled," Dottie said. "If someone can point me in the direction of an actual kitchen, I can try to come up with something for breakfast."

"The cafeteria is down there." Zoe pointed to the dark hall behind her. "It connects the four dorms in the quad."

"Have you checked to make sure the other buildings are empty?" Ian joined them at the front desk, and Zoe tossed him the bottle of aspirin. He caught it and smiled, causing her heart to skip a few beats. Blake nudged her again with his shoulder, but she wouldn't look at him; if she did, she would start blushing again, and she didn't want Ian to question it.

"Not yet," Pearson said as he pulled out his gun. "Anyone care to join me?"

"Sure," Zoe said, though she really didn't want to.

"Might as well." Ian walked back to the common room to grab their guns, which had been left on table the night before. He handed one to her, his fingers brushing against her palm as he did.

"Let's go." Zoe led the way down the dark hallway toward the cafeteria, her gun out in front of her.

"Later, I'm going to have to teach you how to properly use that." Pearson nodded toward her gun.

"I'm hoping I won't need it for much longer," Zoe whispered back.

"We'll take whatever pointers you can give," Ian said. "I think we're going to need to be able to protect ourselves for the foreseeable future. I know I'd feel better if everyone was proficient with a gun."

Zoe paused outside of a set of glass doors. "This is it. The hallway keeps going and connects to Thorpe Hall. Merrill and Sweeney Halls have the same configuration on the other side."

"That's a lot of entry points. We won't be able to cover them all." Pearson stared into the dark cafeteria.

"I'll keep going and check out the other dorm on this side. You two go make sure there's no sign of anyone on the other side," Ian said.

Pearson nodded and pulled open the glass door.

"Be safe," Zoe said to Ian.

"You too." Ian took off down the dark hallway toward Thorpe while Zoe followed Pearson into the dining commons. There was one emergency light shining over the sea of tables. Zoe remembered cutting through here late at night to get back to her dorm. It was much creepier now.

"The dining room looks clear," Pearson said, and Zoe nearly jumped out of her skin. She really shouldn't have volunteered for this. "Let's go check the hallway and see if there's anything there before we bring the others in."

"Yeah, okay." She followed Pearson to the other side of the dining room and out to the hallway connecting Merrill and Sweeney to the cafeteria. Pearson went one way, and Zoe went the other. It was the first time she had been alone in weeks, and it made her feel uneasy. The hallway to Sweeney felt much longer than she remembered. She peered through the glass door into the darkness to try to see if anyone was moving around. Carefully, she cracked open the door and listened intently. If there was someone in there, she would be more likely to hear them than see them.

"It looks like we're alone."

Zoe spun around and pointed her gun.

"Relax, it's just me," Ian said as he held up his hands.

"If people keep sneaking up on me, I'm going to accidently shoot someone," Zoe said as she lowered the gun and took a few deep breaths to calm her nerves.

"Sorry." Ian put his hands on her shoulders and looked her over with concern in his eyes. "Are you all right?"

Zoe took one last deep breath and put her gun away. "Yeah, I'm good. I promise."

"Pearson sent me to come check on you while he went to get the others," Ian said as if he was talking to a child. Zoe just nodded. She really needed to get her heart rate back to normal. "You know, at this point I think you've pointed a gun at me more times than I've pointed one at you."

A laugh escaped Zoe's lips, and she started to relax.

"Let's go see if there's anything to eat in the kitchen." Ian put his arm around her and guided her back toward the dining commons. Zoe found herself leaning into him. When had she gone from fearing him to finding comfort in his touch? Was it because of the underlying fear she constantly felt, or was there more to it? And what about Cole? Was this betraying him? Was she using Ian as a substitute for him? And why wasn't Cole here yet? Zoe couldn't bear the idea that something had happened to him while he tried to get to her.

As they neared the kitchen, she gently shrugged Ian's arm off her. It was all just too confusing to deal with, especially given the hangover headache that had taken up residence behind her eyes.

The others were standing around in the kitchen while Dottie and Floyd went through the walk-in fridge. "There's a decent amount of food in here, but a lot of it probably isn't good anymore. I'll go through it later to see what can be salvaged," Dottie said.

"Remember, we aren't trying to meet the health code like at the diner," Pearson said. "Anything that won't kill us to eat, we should keep."

Dottie waved him away. "You go set a table and leave the cooking to us." She shooed them all out of the kitchen.

Zoe grabbed a stack of plates from behind one of the serving stations and brought it out to the long table in the middle of the room. "Your mom's right. We're going to need to go through everything in this place to see what we can use." Zoe placed a plate in front of each of the maroon-and-gold plaid chairs.

"That's going to take forever," Blake complained. "Do you know how much stuff college kids manage to cram into those rooms?"

"So we start small," Shane said as he settled the girls into their chairs. "Take a couple of dorms and start converting them to living spaces for us."

Pearson emerged from the kitchen with a stack of plastic cups and a jug of orange juice. "We should think about getting some supplies from outside of here too. Maybe hit up a few stores and see if we can find anything useful. I doubt the college kids here were well stocked on essentials, and they certainly won't have any clothes for the girls."

"We need warmer clothes too." Iris sat down at the table. "The stuff we took from that house in Missouri isn't going to cut it here."

"Missouri? You guys really have been all over," Pearson said.

Zoe nodded. "There's a Target not far from here," she said as she tried to remember the location of all the stores in town. She went over to the hostess stand where she used to have to swipe her card to count her meal credits and pulled out a pencil and some paper. Back at the table, she started to draw a map. "We're here. The Target it here," she said, making Xs on the map as she talked. "There's a Walmart and Sam's Club over here. A local grocery store in the middle of town and a Meijer at the other end of town."

Ian leaned over her chair and looked at the map. "There are typically pharmacies at all of them. I want to get some medications to have on hand."

"That's smart," Pearson said as he poured juice for everyone. "We don't want to be out trying to find something in an emergency."

"Let's go to the Sam's Club after breakfast," Zoe suggested. "We might have better odds of finding what we need at a bulk store. We can load up the truck."

Iris turned to Pearson and Shane. "What did you guys come here in?"

"An old Tempo. It's parked out back," Shane said. "It's not going to hold much."

"I'll try to hot-wire something bigger while we're there. It couldn't hurt to have some extra vehicles lined up, just in case," Blake said with a shrug. Dottie emerged from the kitchen with a huge plate of scrambled eggs and sausage links.

"This looks amazing." They had been living on junk food for so long that Zoe had forgotten how good a home-cooked meal could be.

"Well, I hope you enjoy it. That was the last of the eggs," Floyd said as he sat down. They passed the plate of food around, everyone taking a small amount to make sure there was enough to go around. Zoe looked down at the end of the table where Nina and Gemma were scarfing down their food and wondered when was the last time they'd had a decent meal. Kids shouldn't have to be dealing with this. How many more were out there trying to find food? At least Nina and Gemma had their dads—how many kids were left to survive on their own? That had to be worse than dying from the toxin.

«‹◊›»

An hour later Zoe, Blake, Ian, Iris, Pearson, and Shane piled into the truck and took off for the Sam's Club a few miles away. Ian and Pearson were in the bed of the truck with their guns out. Zoe was amazed at how well they worked together given that the last time they had been together, Pearson had arrested Ian.

The parking lot was empty when they arrived, though there was a delivery truck parked off to the side. "That would make it easier to get things back to the dorm." Iris nodded to the box truck as she got out.

"I'm sure, between the two of us, we can get it working again." Blake offered Iris his arm.

"Be careful." Ian gave them a stern look.

"You too." Iris kissed Ian on the cheek and grabbed a toolbox out of the back of their truck. She smacked Blake's arm down as she started toward the truck.

The rest of them headed to the store's entrance. "Any idea how we get the door opened?" Zoe stepped up to the automatic door to see if it would open on its own, but it didn't budge. She peered through the window. The inside of the store was pitch black. This part of town had lost power.

"One." Ian bent down and picked up a large metal cigarette holder and threw it at the door. The glass shattered and rained down on the cement. Ian reached in, unlocked the door, and pushed it open.

"So, how do we want to do this?" Shane tiptoed over the broken glass into the store.

Zoe looked around to where the carts and flatbeds were lined up, as if the end of the world hadn't happened. "Everyone take a cart and spread out. Grab anything you think could be of use . . . soaps, clothes, food with a decent shelf life." Zoe looked into the dark store. The sunlight only penetrated a few feet into the building. "Flashlights."

"We can stage everything up here for Iris and Blake to load once they get the truck started," Ian said.

"I don't want anyone in there alone," Pearson said. "Shane and I will start in clothing, try to find some winter jackets for you guys, and then head to the food."

Ian nodded. "I want to try to get into the pharmacy first, stock up on some basics." He turned to Zoe. "That work for you?"

"Yeah. I can grab some health care items while you do that, and then we'll start working through the food and meet you in the middle."

"Let's try to be quick about this, though. I don't like my parents and the girls being alone with no one to protect them," Pearson said.

"I thought you gave your dad a gun?" Shane asked. The concern was clear on his face despite the lack of light.

"I did, but I don't think he'll use it." Pearson grabbed a few carts and took off into the store. Shane grabbed a flatbed and followed after him.

Zoe and Ian each took a cart and headed into the store in search of the pharmacy. Zoe had a general idea of the store's layout from shopping at similar places in the past, but it was impossible to see anything in the pitch black. How were they going to be able to find what they needed?

"Hey!"

Zoe's blood turned to ice at the shout. Had someone seen them come in? Were Blake and Iris safe? Where were Pearson and Shane? Through the dark, Zoe could make out the shadow of a man jogging toward them. She started to reach for her gun when the figure turned on a flashlight and she saw it was Shane; Zoe took a deep breath and pulled her hand away from the gun on her hip.

"We found these near the entrance, thought you could use them," Shane said once he reached them. "Toby is loading them up and all the batteries we can manage."

"Thanks," Zoe said as she took the flashlight, her heart rate still slightly elevated.

"Just be careful. The light will give you away if anyone else is in here." Shane handed one to Ian before turning and jogging back into the darkness.

The beam of light only made the whole place feel creepier. She tried to push her fear from her mind as she followed Ian through the store. The lack of power made it easy for him to open the security gate to access the pharmacy; he headed back with his cart, and Zoe went over to the personal care items, making sure that she could still hear Ian if he ran into trouble. She began to stack cases of shampoo and soap into her cart. She worked as fast as she could, and soon the cart was overflowing with everything from toothbrushes to hair ties.

Ian came out of the pharmacy pushing two shopping carts loaded down with medications. "I got everything I could. I really hope Iris got that delivery truck running. There's no way this will all fit in the pickup."

Zoe struggled to maneuver her overloaded cart over to Ian. "Should we take these to the front and come back for another load?"

"Sounds good. Though, you take one of my carts, they aren't as heavy. You really should still be taking it easy on that leg of yours." Ian's hand brushed against hers as he took the cart from her. Her breath caught in her throat.

"Thanks," she said softly as she stepped away.

This couldn't keep happening. She loved Cole. She needed to be faithful to Cole, though she had no idea if they would ever see each other again. Should she really be denying herself a chance at happiness when there was no guarantee that Cole would ever find his way back to her? If he had gotten away when he put out his message, he should be here by now. Zoe didn't like to think about what it meant that he wasn't here yet. Was it wrong to try to grab whatever sliver of happiness she could out of this new world the Arrows had forced them to live in?

She had no idea what the right answer was. She sighed and started to push the cart of medication after Ian.

Pearson and Shane were already at the entrance helping Iris and Blake load items into the box truck. "Here, these should keep you warmer." Shane handed Zoe and Ian new winter coats and took their carts from them. Zoe didn't realize how cold she was until she put the coat on.

"We grabbed as much produce as we could find. Figured we better eat it while we still can." Pearson handed Blake a box of potatoes. "With the power out, I'm not sure if we should trust any of the food in the coolers and freezers."

"I agree. It's not worth the risk of food poisoning," Ian said as he began to unload the cases of shampoo.

"Hopefully the power is still on in another part of town so we can get some meat and frozen vegetables." Zoe pulled the jacket tighter around her body, relishing the warmth.

"Zoe and I will go see what kind of protein we can

find in the packaged foods." Ian grabbed a few empty carts.

Zoe let him handle the carts while she held the light out in front of them, scanning the shelves they passed for anything that might be useful.

Zoe paused at an endcap filled with dolls; she wanted to get something fun for Nina and Gemma. She was about to ask Ian his opinion when she heard someone cough. She whipped around to look at Ian, but he shook his head. His gun was already in his hand.

Zoe went to his side. "Could it have been one of the others?" Her voice was so quiet, she wasn't even sure he would hear her.

"They're all still up at the entrance. Someone else is in here." Ian stepped in front of her with his gun out in front of them. Slowly they moved forward, listening closely for any other sounds.

"Over there," Zoe said as she pointed her flashlight down one of the aisles. She had seen a shadow move between the boxes on the shelves.

Ian rounded the corner and pointed his gun down the center while Zoe used the flashlight to search for the person.

A young man was standing at the other end of the aisle. His eyes locked on the gun. "Don't shoot. I'm not armed." He dropped the box he was holding and put his hands over his head.

"What are you doing here?" Ian didn't lower his gun as they closed the distance between them and the young man.

"Just trying to get supplies, same as you," the man said with a tremble in his voice.

Zoe looked around. They were in the baby aisle. A box of newborn diapers lay at the man's feet. Zoe reached out and put her hand on Ian's arm, slowly lowering the gun for him. "I'm Zoe, this is Ian. What's your name?"

"Mark. My name's Mark." The young man lowered his arms.

"Keep your hands where I can see them," Ian said with a growl she hadn't heard from him since he had kidnapped her.

Mark quickly put his hands in front of him. "Yeah, of course. Look, I don't want any trouble. I promise."

Zoe shot Ian a look and walked over to Mark. She picked up the box of diapers and handed it to him. "You're looking for diapers. You're not alone."

Mark swallowed hard. "My girlfriend's waiting for me back at our apartment. I wouldn't let her come with me. I didn't know if it was safe."

"She's pregnant, isn't she?" Zoe couldn't imagine the fear this young couple must be feeling.

Mark nodded. "She's due in a couple of weeks, I think. We've lost track of the days with everything happening." He glanced at the diapers in his hand. "I wanted to get ready for the baby, try to keep Allissa's stress down, but I don't know what we're going to do when she goes into labor."

Zoe turned to look at Ian for help, but he just shrugged.

"You should come stay with us," Zoe offered. "We're at Beddow Hall. There's electricity, heat, food, clean water. We can help you, if you want."

"I don't know. I don't know if I can trust anyone right now." Mark's expression was apologetic, and Zoe's heart went out to him.

"I get it, and honestly, it's smart. With the way things are now, it's impossible to know who to trust. But I think

I can take a chance on you. You know where we are. You're the one who holds all the cards. If you want to join us, you're more than welcome. If not, that's okay too." Zoe tried to keep her voice calm. The last thing she wanted to do was put more pressure on the kid.

"All right," Mark said, though he still seemed unsure.

"You don't have to decide now. We aren't going anywhere. Get what you need, and go talk it over with your girlfriend."

Ian gave him one of their flatbeds. "Use this. You're going to need more than one box of diapers." He started to load the flatbed up with diapers and wipes.

"Thanks," Mark said as he watched Ian get the baby supplies they would need for a newborn.

When Ian was done, he handed the cart over to Mark. "We'll walk you out. We have some people at the entrance. We'll make sure they don't give you a hard time."

"Do you really think we'll be safer together?" Mark asked as they made their way back to the front of the store.

"I do," Zoe said. "We can all help take care of one another."

They reached the front of the store. Iris and Blake were still loading their supplies, but they froze as they saw them approach. Ian didn't acknowledge them as he walked Mark out of the building.

"You know where to find us," Zoe said. "I promise, we can help. With a baby coming, you're going to need all the help you can get."

"I'll think about it." Mark gave them a weary smile and began to push the flatbed across the parking lot.

Blake came over and leaned on Zoe's shoulder. "Who

was that?"

"He was in the store. He's scared," Zoe said as she watched him walk away.

"Zoe invited him to come stay with us," Ian said. "Him and his pregnant girlfriend."

Zoe turned to Ian. "What else could I do? We have the resources now to build a new community. A community needs people. Besides, what do you think that baby's odds are without some help? He couldn't have been more than twenty years old."

"I know," Ian said with a sigh. "I just hope we can trust him."

"Do you really think the Arrows would have one of their assassins stalking the diaper aisle of a bulk food store in the middle of Michigan on the off chance we stop by?"

"No, I guess not," Iris said.

"At some point, we're going to have to start trusting people again," Zoe said.

"Let's go get the rest of the stuff we need before you find any more strays to take in," Ian said with a smirk, and he led them back inside.

«‹‹›»»

Cole sat on a couch in the living space, absentmindedly running his finger over the seams in the cushions. Jackson and Victoria were sitting across from him, discussing some unimportant topic he wasn't interested in, while the boys played on the other side of the room. Adam was standing inside the doorway, watching and listening.

Cole wondered if Adam was as bored with this as he was. He felt like he was making some headway befriending the kid, but it was a slow process. At least Adam had stopped getting his weapon out whenever Cole was nearby. For now, he would count that as a win.

Gordon brushed past Adam and plopped down on the couch next to Cole. He loosened his tie as he leaned back into the cushion. Cole looked at Jackson and Victoria; they hadn't seen either of their parents in days.

"Everything all right?" Cole asked tentatively. He had no idea where he stood with his dad these days.

"Yes," Gordon said, but the way he squeezed the bridge of his nose made it clear he was lying. "We've been dealing with some issues at the resettlement locations. Your mother has gone out to try to ease some of the tension."

Alana was out of the White House again. Cole's heart leaped in his chest. Could this be the chance he was looking for? She would have taken some of the security detail with her.

He stole a glance at Adam and the automatic rifle on his back. He wasn't going anywhere until he could shake his guard.

"What's happening at the camps?" Victoria asked.

"They aren't camps, they're towns we're trying to create," Gordon bit out. Cole wondered how many times a day he had to clarify this point.

"Sorry," Victoria said, holding up her hands. "What's happening at the *new towns* you're creating?"

"People are stressed. They don't want to leave their homes behind, which is understandable, but we can only support utilities in certain areas."

"You can't really be surprised by that," Cole said.

"No, but the amount of resistance we are facing is more than we anticipated. We didn't think people would attack our relocation teams. We've lost some good people this week." Gordon sighed.

"Were they better than the billions of people you killed with the toxin?"

"Cole," Gordon said sternly, "it's time for you to move past that. I'm never going to be able to convince your mother that you shouldn't be locked up for good if you keep making comments like that."

Cole shifted in his seat. "That's what she wants, isn't it? To hold me prisoner here forever. To punish me for not blindly following her while she takes over the world."

Gordon didn't answer, which told Cole everything he needed to know. His parents were divided on the best way to deal with him. He would have to see if there was a way to use that to his advantage.

"Have you thought about making the relocations voluntary instead of mandating that everyone moves away from everything they know?" Victoria asked.

"It was discussed, but if we really want to achieve our remediation and restoration goals, we need to consolidate man power and resources." Gordon got up and went over to the drink cart in the corner of the room.

"Do you have a list of people who have arrived at the resettlement locations yet?" Cole asked.

"Names are starting to come in," Gordon said as he focused on fixing himself a drink.

"Any chance I can see those names?"

Gordon turned back to face Cole. "Zoe's not on there, if that's what you're looking for."

"It's not. I know she wouldn't be stupid enough to go anywhere near the Arrows."

Gordon sighed. "Then why do you want to see it?"

Cole turned to look at Adam standing at the door. He was paying much closer attention than he had been a few minutes ago. "Because there are other people here who don't know what happened to their loved ones."

Gordon's eyes shifted to Adam. "Of course. I'm sorry, Private Griffin." Gordon walked over to him. "I'm supposed to get an update later this evening. I'll bring you the list to look over once I have it."

"Thank you, sir," Adam said. "That would mean a lot to me."

"What are these resettlement locations like?" Jackson asked as he fixed himself a drink.

Gordon retook his seat on the couch. "We're housing people in apartments and condos where we can. The goal is to get the remaining population centralized to a few locations and build a community around that."

"What's going to happen to them once they're there?" Victoria asked.

"They'll be interviewed to assess what kind of training they need, and then they'll be assigned new jobs. The focus is going to be on remediation. We want to restore the natural environment as much as possible. If we can build that mindset into everything we do, it will carry on for generations, and we won't find ourselves in a mess like this again."

Cole scoffed. "It's that simple, huh?" Gordon was talking like this whole thing was some tragic incident that couldn't be prevented, not something that he personally caused.

"It's not simple at all. That's why your mother is on the other side of the country trying to keep the survivors from turning against us. The last thing we want is to create rogue groups that go around causing further destruction." Gordon drained the rest of his drink in one swallow. "In fact, I should go see if she's sent an update." He left the room without looking at any of them.

"I've never seen Dad that stressed before," Victoria said, her eyes trailing after Gordon.

"He should be stressed. This is all his fault. He can't really expect people to fall in line with whatever the Arrows say just because they created this new world." Cole got up and walked to the door. "Come on, Adam. Let's go see if we can find out if your family is at one of the resettlement locations."

«Chapter 15»

It took them two hours to gather all the items they wanted from the store, load them, and get back to the dorm. It was a massive amount of stuff, but it wasn't like they could get more whenever they wanted. At some point, there would be nothing left. If they were really going to make this place their home, they needed to be prepared.

"Where are we going to put all of this?" Iris asked as she handed down the last of the boxes from the truck. The lobby was packed with piles of food, medical supplies, clothing, and health care items.

"We should be able to get all of the food in the kitchen," Dottie said, scanning over the items they had found. "I've started to set up the back dining room as a pantry so we can easily see what we have to work with."

"Perfect." Pearson pushed an empty flatbed cart they had taken from the store over to the nearest pile of food and started to fill it with cases of spaghetti sauce.

"I guess we can use some of the dorms for storage. Maybe the lower level can be like our store," Zoe suggested as she sorted through the mountain of clothing falling off the front desk.

"We haven't cleaned out any of the rooms down there yet," Floyd said.

"That's okay. There's another common room down there that we can stage things in while we get organized."

"Have you cleaned out any of the rooms yet?" Blake asked as he jumped down from the back of the truck and turned to help Iris down.

"We have four rooms ready for us to move into. People will have to double up, though," Dottie said.

"I'm not sure I'm ready to be in a room alone yet anyway," Iris said. She was probably remembering the man who had held a gun to her head when they were trying to make their escape from the hotel.

"Agreed," Zoe said. "Safety in numbers, right?"

"Can we join those numbers?"

Zoe whipped around to see Mark standing in the open doorway with a very pregnant young woman beside him. The flatbed cart Ian had given him was loaded with suitcases and the diapers Ian had helped him get at the store.

"Of course," Zoe said without waiting for the others to weigh in. "Come in out of the cold."

Pearson stepped over to Zoe and whispered, "Are you sure about this?"

"Yes, I am." Zoe stepped past him and helped the pregnant girl to the common room. Everyone else followed. "What's your name?"

"Allissa," she said as she slowly lowered herself to the couch.

"I'm Zoe." She sat down across from them. "I'm glad you decided to come."

Ian helped Mark push the cart over to the common room. "Were you students here?" He sat down on the arm of Zoe's chair.

"Yeah." Mark sat down next to Allissa and took her hand. "We shared an apartment off campus, over in Franklin Village."

"I never heard of that one," Blake said.

"That's because it's not a big party place. I actually lived there for two years when I went here." Zoe had a lot of good memories in that apartment—most of which involved Cole.

She snuck a glance at Ian who was so close, she could feel the energy radiating from his body.

"Why didn't you go home when the school closed down?" Pearson stood in the gap between the armchairs with his arms folded, staring down Mark and Allissa. Zoe almost reminded him that this wasn't an interrogation, but she thought better of it.

"We weren't welcome. Our parents weren't thrilled with our current situation." Allissa rubbed her hand over her belly. "And between the baby and the toxin, we didn't know if it was safe to travel, so we just stayed here until it felt like we were the only ones left on the whole planet."

"When was the last time you had a decent meal?" Dottie asked.

"Three or four days," Allissa said.

"Our apartment lost power a few days ago. Since then, we've been getting by on what we didn't have to cook. I thought the whole town had lost power, but I didn't really investigate. I didn't want to leave Allissa alone for too long." Mark took her hand and kissed it.

"This dorm was retrofitted two years ago to be self-sustaining. We have solar and wind power, and clean water. As long as we can maintain the equipment, we'll be good," Zoe assured him. "You did the right thing coming here."

"I'm going to start fixing something for dinner," Dottie said. "Floyd, come help me."

Floyd grabbed the flatbed cart Pearson had been loading with food and pushed it after Dottie to the dining commons.

"How have you been feeling?" Ian asked as he looked over Allissa.

"All right, all things considered," she said awkwardly. "Are you a doctor?"

"No, but I did go to medical school for a few years, so I'm the best we got. If you're comfortable with it, I'd like to do a simple checkup, make sure your vitals are normal at least."

Allissa looked at Mark with concern in her eyes before finally agreeing.

"Why don't we go to one of the rooms for some privacy?" Ian stood up.

"The first door on your left is open," Shane said as he came back from checking on the girls.

"Thanks." Ian ushered them back to the room, stopping by one of the stacks of boxes on his way.

"What are you looking for?" Blake asked.

"I picked up a basic doctor's bag from the pharmacy."

"I'll find it and bring it to you."

Ian nodded and patted him on the back, then went to join Allissa and Mark.

Zoe leaned back into the chair. She knew she should start bringing the items they had picked up to the right places, but she was drained.

"Are you sure inviting them to stay was the best idea?" Iris asked.

"What else could we do? She's about to pop. If she went into labor out there on her own, they both would have probably died," Zoe said.

"I want to ask them some questions," Pearson said, his arms still crossed — a stance he'd perfected after years on the police force. "See if I can get a good sense if they're telling the truth."

"I guess it can't hurt, but do you really think there's a chance they're working for the Arrows? I mean, she's pregnant."

"You can't be too careful. I'm not willing to risk my girls' lives on it."

"You're the detective. I leave it in your hands," Zoe said. "Maybe we should come up with a system for how we're going to handle it when more people show up."

Iris rolled her eyes. "Are we running a bed-and-breakfast now?"

Zoe shrugged. "We're rebuilding the world. We're going to need people to do that."

"And where are these people going to come from?"

Zoe ignored the fact that Iris was looking at her like she had grown a second head. "I don't know. There could be more people alive in this town who we haven't run across yet. At some point, they're bound to notice that we have power and come to check it out."

"There's always the possibility that other people saw Cole's message and figured out what it meant." Pearson finally uncrossed his arms and took seat in the empty chair next to Zoe. "It's impossible to know who is making their way here. We just have to hope they're willing to work with us and not coming here to take us out."

"He's got a point," Iris said. "We need to be careful about who we let into this new world we're building."

Zoe sighed and nodded. "I want to build a community that helps take care of one another. Anyone who shows up and wants to be a part of that should be allowed to stay."

"And if someone shows up who wants to cause trouble?" Pearson said.

"We'll deal with it then. I'm going to go start putting some of our supplies away." Zoe got up and walked over to the lobby. She didn't want to focus on the negative, it had consumed too much of her life already. This was supposed to be their fresh start, and she was determined to make it a good one.

«<‹›»»

Cole and Adam walked through the White House toward the Oval Office. Alana still hadn't returned, which meant Cole had slightly more freedom than when she was here. They had just finished checking the lists of people who had arrived at the resettlement locations; Adam hadn't found his family on any of the lists, and it was clearly starting to wear on him. Cole wanted to talk to Gordon and see if maybe he could get a little more information that might help ease Adam's growing stress.

There were guards outside of the Oval Office, but they didn't move to stop him as he stepped forward to knock on the door.

"Enter." Gordon's voice rang through the door.

Cole opened the door slowly. It was weird seeing his dad sitting at the president's desk. "Hi, Dad," Cole said as he stepped into the room. "Can we talk?"

This was the first time he had sought out either of his parents since Zoe had told him about the Arrows, and he fidgeted waiting to see how Gordon would react. This nervousness was a new sensation for him.

Gordon looked up from what he was working on, shock clear on his face. "Cole, of course." He got up and motioned for Cole to join him on the couches.

Cole turned to Adam. "Would you mind waiting for me outside?" It was a risk asking Adam to leave; Cole had begun to build a relationship with the kid, and he was afraid this could ruin it, but he'd get more out of Gordon if they were alone.

Adam looked from Cole to Gordon.

"It's all right," Gordon said with a smile.

"Yes, sir." Adam left the room, shutting the door behind him.

"I'm surprised you came to see me," Gordon said as Cole sat down.

"I hope it's okay that I did," Cole said carefully. There was something that had been bothering him the last few days, and he wasn't sure how his dad would take him asking.

"Of course. No matter what happens, you're still my son, and I love you, Cole. Even when we don't see eye to eye on things."

Cole fought back the urge to laugh—as if killing billions of people to further your own rise to power was simply a difference of opinion. "Right. Thanks for setting it up so that I can help Adam review the survivor lists from the resettlement locations."

"Has he found his family yet?"

"Not yet. He's not giving up hope yet, though."

"Good. It's taking longer than we expected to get the survivor lists, people are reluctant to report in."

Can you blame them? Cole wanted to say, but he held his tongue. "About that . . . what I really wanted to ask you is if there was any word on where Zoe's parents are? I'm sure they had enough of the vaccine in them to survive the toxin, but I haven't seen their names on any of the survivor lists either."

Gordon sighed, but he didn't seem angry. "We had some transports in Southeast Michigan picking up survivors and taking them to the Detroit-area resettlement. Max and Gloria were picked up, but their transport hit a patch of ice, and they crashed. It took us a few days to find them, and by then there were no survivors."

Cole took a deep breath and nodded. It was what he had expected, though he didn't believe for a second it was an accident. He was certain Alana had arranged for it to happen as a way to hurt Zoe. "All right," he said, fighting to keep all his emotions inside. "I guess I'll let you get back to whatever it is Mom has you doing these days." He slowly rose to his feet.

"Cole," Gordon said, standing as well. "I'm sorry about Zoe's parents. They were good people, and I know they loved you."

"They were family," Cole said, "and like you always taught us, family comes above everything else. It would have been nice to have seen them again." Cole made his way over to the door, then stopped and turned around. "Why didn't you tell me when you found out?"

"I wanted to, but your mother thought . . ." Gordon's voice trailed off.

"Thought that it would make me fight back harder," Cole finished for him. Gordon gave him a weak smile, and Cole shrugged. "She's probably right."

«‹«›»»

"Oh my God, a salad," Iris said as she sat down at the table they had been using for their meals in the dining commons. "This looks amazing, Dottie."

"Thank you, dear. I figured we'd better use the fresh produce while we can." Dottie set two bowls of spaghetti down on the table while Floyd brought out a basket full of garlic toast.

"You're going to spoil us," Iris said as she loaded her plate with food.

"Enjoy it now because the longer we're here, the more meager the food is going to get." Floyd sat down next to Allissa and handed her a bowl of pasta.

"Are you sure you want to share all of this with us?" Allissa asked.

"Of course." Floyd spooned some onto her plate to drive his point home.

"But we haven't done anything to help," Mark said.

"You will. We're all going to have to work together. I'm sure you'll more than earn your keep," Ian said as he passed around the plate of toast.

"We'll try," Mark said as he accepted the plate.

"We should start thinking about what we're going to do for food long term," Shane said. "What we found today won't last forever. We're going to have to find our own food sources if we want this to be a long-term solution."

"There's a greenhouse on campus. Maybe we could start growing crops in there?" Zoe had never been in the greenhouse, but she'd walked by it every day while going between the science buildings for class.

"Do you think they're already growing food?" Blake asked with a piece of garlic bread hanging out of his mouth.

"I don't really know what they used it for, but it's worth checking out," Zoe said. "At the very least, it's a place where we might be able to grow things year round."

Ian looked around the table. "Any chance anyone knows anything about farming?" Everyone shook their heads.

"So, we'll learn," Shane said. "This is a college, right? There's got to be books about agriculture in the school's library."

"What about protein?" Floyd asked.

"I can hunt," Mark offered through a mouthful of pasta.

"That's a good start," Pearson said.

"I don't have my shotgun, though, or even a bow."

"We'll find something. We can check the evidence locker at the police station. There's a decent chance they've confiscated something we can use to hunt."

"There are farms all around this town. Think we might be able to get some livestock from there? Maybe pigs or cows? Set up a chicken coop?" Blake asked.

"I can see you as pig farmer," Ian said with a huge grin. "They're on the same wavelength as you."

"Hey, pigs are majestic, intelligent creatures," Blake said as he pointed his butter knife across the table at Ian. "And they taste delicious. In fact, I don't think I can live in a world without bacon, so I'm making it my mission to ensure that doesn't happen."

"Figures it would take the end of the world for you to find your purpose in life," Iris teased.

"What can I say, I'm a complicated man." Blake leaned back in his chair.

Next to Zoe, Ian chuckled. "I like seeing you like

this," she said softly so none of the others heard her.

Ian turned and smiled at her. "Like what?"

"Happy, relaxed. I don't know, you just seem freer today. It's nice."

Ian's smiled faltered for a moment. "I've known what the Arrows were planning for years. I guess when you know the end of the world is coming, it's hard to truly let yourself be happy. But for the first time in a long time, I actually feel like there's a chance for a future. I have hope again . . . and that's because of you."

«‹Chapter 16›»

Zoe stood looking out the window in the common room. The sun was just starting to rise as she watched the road. She caught herself gazing out the window with greater frequency every day, but she never saw the one thing she was looking for. She was starting to think she never would.

"Enjoying the view?" Blake nudged her with his shoulder. She hadn't even heard him come over to her.

"Not as much as I'd like to." She rubbed her hands over her arms and turned away from the window.

Blake turned and leaned his back against the window as he watched her. "What are you hoping to see?"

Zoe shot him a look. "You know very well who I'm looking for."

"Give him time."

"How much time? It's been, what, two, three weeks since Cole's message went out? Even if he had to walk the whole way from DC to Mount Pleasant, he should be here by now."

Blake pushed off the window and went over to her. He put an arm around her shoulder and guided her to a chair. "There are plenty of reasonable explanations as to why he hasn't shown up yet."

Zoe's eyes locked on Blake's. "Like he's dead." She said the words she feared the most, hoping that by saying them out loud, they would lose some of their power over her.

Blake crouched down in front of her. "Maybe he got lost, or the Arrows caught him trying to escape."

Zoe took a deep breath. "If he didn't get away when that message aired, he's as good as dead."

"Alana wouldn't kill her own son."

"You don't know that. And even if she didn't kill him, she'll make sure he doesn't have another chance to get away. She knows keeping him away will hurt me." Zoe got up and walked back to this window. "I stand here every day waiting for some sign that he's coming, but there's never one. How long am I supposed to wait for something that will likely never happen?" She glanced over her shoulder at Blake. "We came here to rebuild our lives, to start over, but I feel like I'm stuck in limbo with no way forward."

Blake watched her from his spot on the floor. "Is that what you want? To move forward?"

Zoe shrugged. "I feel terrible about it. I don't want to lose Cole, but . . ." Tears choked out the rest of her words. She couldn't help but feel like she was betraying Cole anytime she found a moment of happiness without him.

"But it's not fair for you to waste your second chance at a happy life either."

"Maybe I don't deserve to be happy. Maybe this is

my punishment for failing to stop Alana."

"That might be the stupidest thing I've heard anyone say, ever. If life punished people who deserved it, Alana Wilborn wouldn't be running the world right now." Blake got to his feet. "Zoe, you're allowed to be happy, and there's no set definition on what that has to look like. Maybe Cole is out there making his way here, and maybe he's not . . . you don't have any control over that. What you do have control over is what you do today. Now, you can stand at this window wasting time waiting for him to show up — which you're right, might not ever happen — or you can look around and appreciate what you do have." Blake draped his arm around her shoulder again. "Mainly me and my exceedingly charming personality."

Zoe covered her mouth with her hand as a laugh burst from her lips. It was still early, and she didn't want to wake anyone up. "Thank you, Blake." She laid her head on his shoulder, her gaze still fixed on the road in front of the dorm.

"You two are up early," Ian said behind them.

Blake let go of Zoe and turned toward him. "Just making the most of the day." He winked at Zoe and picked up his coat from the back of one of the couches.

"Where are you guys off to?" Zoe wiped a stray tear off her cheek and smiled at Ian.

"The police station," Pearson called from the front desk where he was busy checking his weapon. "I'm hoping we can find some radios and weapons there. I don't like that we have no way of communicating when someone leaves."

"Agreed," Zoe said.

"Want to join us?" Ian asked.

Zoe shook her head. "I'm good. I'll stay here and

help Iris and Shane clean out the dorms." She was far too distracted to be helpful on a supply run right now.

Ian gently grabbed her arm and guided her farther into the common room, away from Blake and Pearson. "What's going on? You seem off this morning."

"It's nothing." Tears started to bubble in her eyes again. She didn't need to burden Ian with this.

"Tell me," Ian urged, his eyes filled with concern that raised Zoe's guilt to a new level.

She sighed. "Just thinking about Cole."

Ian bit his lip and nodded. She was grateful that he didn't offer any explanations or excuses for why Cole wasn't there. "I can stay."

"No. What you're doing is more important. I'll be fine. I promise."

"Ian, are you ready?" Pearson called.

Ian didn't move.

"Go. I'm good," Zoe said.

He reached up and wiped away a tear from her cheek. "I hate leaving you like this."

"Don't worry about me. My mind just needs something to occupy itself. I'll get started on something soon, and then I'll be good." Zoe nodded to try to emphasize her point. There was no telling what they would run into once they left the relative safety of the dorms, and she didn't want Ian to be distracted worrying about her.

"Ian, hurry up." Blake stood in the entrance to the common room. "Pearson's already in the truck and he's getting anxious."

"I'll be right there," Ian called without taking his eyes off Zoe. "We'll only be gone a few hours," he said to her.

"Be safe," she said, giving him what she hoped was a

convincing smile. Ian squeezed her hand, then followed Blake out of the building.

«‹«‹›»›

Zoe sat alone in the lobby for a while after they left. The days were starting to blend together. Every few days, they would plan a supply run somewhere in town. The far side of town still had power, and they had been able to get some frozen meats and vegetables that would last for a while. During a trip to the hardware store, Ian had found packs of seeds they could use to start growing their own produce. Allissa turned out to be a natural green thumb and had taken over management of the greenhouse, though the trip across campus was starting to become too much for her.

When they weren't out on a supply run, they spent their time sorting through the items left in the dorms as they tried to make them into comfortable living spaces. The dorms were fairly spacious, each with two bedrooms connected by a living space and private bathroom. The furniture looked like it hadn't been updated since Zoe lived there, but it was sturdy. The room Zoe was sharing with Iris had a nice rug covering the cold tile floor in the main room and a futon with a dark blue mattress. Zoe's first thought upon seeing it was to take it outside and burn it—she had sworn to never sit on a futon again after being handcuffed to one for four days—but since they couldn't exactly order new furniture, she was stuck with it for now.

"How's it going in here?" Shane walked into the room Iris and Zoe were trying to clean out with an empty garbage bin. They were trying to limit the things they disposed of since the only option they had was to burn it, which might attract unwanted attention, but some things simply weren't worth saving.

"Since when are crop tops back in style?" Iris said as she held a cutoff CMU T-shirt up to her chest.

Zoe laughed. "Maybe Gemma could wear it."

Iris tossed the shirt to Shane. "It might be more useful as a rag," he said as he looked it over.

Zoe opened the desk drawer and shook her head. "I found more alcohol for Blake's ever-growing bar at the front desk."

"Anything decent this time?" Iris walked over to the desk.

Zoe pulled out a bottle. "Burnett's cherry-flavored vodka. A CMU special. College kids lived here. If you want anything of quality, you'll have to break into Blake's private stash."

"I already have." Iris picked up a decorative box from the shelf over the desk. "This is cute." She opened it and rolled her eyes. "And of course, it's full of condoms."

"I don't think anyone has a use for those at the moment," Zoe said with a laugh.

"Not even you and Ian?" Shane raised an eyebrow at Zoe.

Her cheeks grew hot. "There's nothing going on between Ian and me," she said quickly.

"Right." Shane took the condoms from Iris and tossed them to Zoe. "Still, you might want to hang on to them, just in case."

Iris burst out laughing. "I like you more and more every day, Shane."

"Help!"

Zoe, Iris, and Shane exchanged a look before rushing into the hall. Mark ran over to them.

"What's going on?" Zoe asked.

"I think Allissa is in labor," Mark said, panic clear in his eyes.

"Shit." Iris looked to Zoe. "Where's Ian?"

"How the hell should I know? Can't you use your twin connection to like, summon him here or something?"

Iris looked at her with disgust. "Aren't you a scientist?"

"Where's Allissa now?" Shane asked, his voice completely calm. Thank God someone was keeping it together, because Zoe had no idea what to do.

"I'm here." Allissa slowly made her way down the hall. "The contraction's over. It's fine."

Mark rushed over to her and took her hand. "You should go lie down."

"Let me move around while I can. The contractions are like eight minutes apart. We have a long way to go."

"Is that safe?" Iris asked Zoe.

"Why do you keep asking me? I studied chemistry, not biology!"

"Didn't you tell me you had nephews?" Iris said.

"They're Cole's nephews, and it's not like I delivered them."

"Everyone needs to relax," Shane said. "Toby, Blake, and Ian are still at the police station. I'm sure they'll be back soon. Until then, we need to keep Allissa calm." He put a hand on Allissa's back and led her toward her room. They made it a few steps before he stopped abruptly. "Does anyone else hear that?" Concern etched his face for the first time.

Zoe strained to pick up the distant sounds of an approaching car. "Could it be the guys coming back?"

Iris shook her head and pulled out her gun. "It

sounds too big to be one of our trucks."

"We really don't need this right now," Zoe muttered as she pulled out her own gun.

"You two, go wait in our room with Floyd, Dottie, and the girls. We'll call you when it's safe," Shane said. Mark nodded and ushered Allissa away.

"Let's go see what we're dealing with." Zoe led the way to the lobby. She needed to protect these people from whatever threat was coming their way, but she had no idea if she would be able to do it. She peered out the window. A flash of bright yellow through the pine trees caught her eye. "Is that a school bus?"

"Maybe they'll drive by without realizing we're here." Shane looked even less comfortable with a gun than Zoe was. If whoever was on that bus had come to hurt them, they were screwed.

"Doesn't look like it." The bus turned into the driveway, and Zoe tensed. She never thought she'd be scared of a school bus, but given the number of people that it could hold, it was easily the most terrifying thing she had seen in a long time.

The bus stopped right in front of the dorm, and a man stepped off. He looked vaguely familiar, but Zoe couldn't place him. At least he didn't appear to be armed.

Next to her, Iris lowered her gun in disbelief. "Dillion?" Iris ran from the building to meet the man.

"Do we follow her?" Shane asked as they watched the man run forward and swoop Iris up in his arms. He swung her around in a circle before putting her back down on her feet.

"I guess." Zoe slowly made her way outside. As Iris and the man walked over to them hand in hand, Zoe finally recognized him as the doctor who had patched her up after Alana shot her. She lowered her gun.

"Do you know him?" Shane's gun was still pointed toward the bus.

"Yeah, it's all right," Zoe said, putting her gun away. "He's friends with Ian and Iris. He's a doctor."

"It's good to see you on your feet," Dillion said to Zoe with a huge smile.

"Good to see you too, Doc."

"Call me Dillion. There's no reason for you not to know my name at this point."

"Who's with you?" Zoe nodded toward the bus, where faces had appeared in the windows.

"People I picked up while making my way here. They didn't want to live under the Arrows' laws and had nowhere else to go."

"Can we trust them?" Shane asked.

"I wouldn't have brought them here if I thought they would be a threat to any of you," Dillion insisted.

Zoe ran her hand through her hair. These people were looking for a safe place to rebuild, just like them. She couldn't turn them away — especially since they now knew where to find them — but letting them in was a risk. It had been different with Mark and Allissa, since it was clear they were just scared kids on their own, but Zoe had no way of knowing who was on that bus.

She glanced at Iris, who was still tucked under Dillion's arm. Ian and Iris trusted Dillion, so if he said these people weren't a threat, she would have to trust him on that too. He had saved her life when he didn't have to, after all.

"All right. Let's get everyone out of the cold. We'll take them to the dining commons and get them some food and go from there." Zoe really hoped she was making the right call.

"Toby is going to want to question them," Shane said.

"That's fine. We'll keep them in the dining commons until he gets back. In the meantime, Doc, have you ever delivered a baby?"

Dillion looked from Iris to Zoe. "No. Why?"

"There's a young woman in there who just went into labor." Shane pointed to the building behind him.

"Is Ian with her?" Dillion asked, his voice now serious.

"No," Iris said as their truck pulled in behind the school bus. "He's there." Iris nodded to the truck.

Blake, Ian, and Pearson jumped out of the truck and ran over to them, cutting through the sea of people coming off the bus. "What's going on?" Pearson asked as he looked over the people with concern.

"New arrivals." Zoe shrugged.

"Dillion," Ian said, embracing him. "How did you know where we were?"

"I saw her fiancé's message and knew enough people who went to CMU to figure out that you were likely heading here . . . but we can catch up later. We have a baby to deliver."

Ian turned to Zoe. "Allissa went into labor?"

"Yeah, maybe twenty minutes ago. She's inside with Mark, Dottie, Floyd, and the girls."

"You should get in there. Mark was pretty freaked out," Iris said.

"And I'm sure you handled it perfectly," Ian teased.

"I have a medical bag on the bus, let me grab it and then we can go see the patient." Dillion finally released Iris and ran over to the bus.

"What about all these people?" Ian looked over the crowd lingering outside the bus.

"I have it under control," Zoe assured him, even though she felt that the exact opposite was true. She reached out and gently squeezed his hand. "Go deliver a healthy baby."

Ian nodded, his eyes locked on Zoe's. He squeezed her hand back, then took Dillion inside.

Zoe let out a breath and turned to the people who had come with Dillion. "I'm Zoe. If you want to come in, we have heat and food. You'll be safe here." She prayed she wasn't lying to them.

««Chapter 17»»

Cole was spending less and less time with his family. Victoria was busy taking care of the boys, trying her hand at the whole homeschooling thing. Whenever she wasn't with the kids, she was complaining about her husband, and Cole couldn't take much more of it. At least she knew where the person she loved was. Cole didn't even know if Zoe was alive. On the other end of the spectrum was Jackson, who did nothing but sulk whenever Cole saw him.

When Cole wasn't helping Adam search the lists from the resettlements, he spent his time reading. He had to do something to keep from going crazy while he waited for a chance to escape. Besides, the library was almost always empty.

Movement at the library door drew Cole's eyes away from the book he was reading. Adam was still sitting in his chair next to the door with a book of his own in his hands. Jackson stood outside the door, looking up and down the hall.

"Everything all right?" Cole called as he watched his older brother.

Jackson whipped around. "I've been looking all over for you," he said as he made his way into the room and plopped down in the chair across from Cole. "For a second, I thought you had found a way out of here for good." Jackson stole a glance over his shoulder at Adam, who appeared to be reading again, but Cole didn't know for sure.

"Nope, I'm still here, unfortunately." Cole looked back down at his book.

"Is that your plan, then—to just stay here? Have you given up trying to find Zoe?"

Cole shot Jackson a look. Adam might be friendlier than when he first started guarding Cole, but he still worked for Alana. "Lower your voice," Cole said harshly. "And no, I haven't given up. But I don't have any idea how I can get out of here, so for now I'm trying to lie low."

"Sounds awful."

Cole rolled his eyes. "It's not great."

Jackson shifted in his seat, glancing over at Adam again. "Mom's back. She seems distracted. I don't think things are going the way she wants them to."

"I'm happy to hear it."

Jackson leaned forward. "I heard her arguing with William Conner this morning. I think he wants to take over."

Cole put his book down. It was clear Jackson wasn't going to leave him alone. "Mom will have him killed before she lets that happen."

"Do you think she's capable of that?"

Cole laughed. "Of course she is."

Jackson slumped back in his chair. "I really wish I didn't agree with you."

"It's about time you started paying attention. Even Dad is concerned about her."

That got Jackson's attention. "Did he say something to you?"

"Not directly, but he's let slip a few times how she's not sharing information with him and that he doesn't agree with all of her decisions. At least that was the impression I got when I went to see him the other day."

"Why did you go see him?"

"To find out what happened to Zoe's parents. He told me they were dead, a car accident, but I know Mom had them killed. She didn't want to risk them finding Zoe."

Jackson shifted in his seat. "Why, though?"

"Because the more support Zoe has, the bigger threat she is."

"Then we need to get out of here and find her before Mom does."

Cole stole a glance at Adam, who seemed to be concentrating incredibly hard on the page he was reading. "How? I can't even go to the bathroom without Mom knowing about it."

"I'll try to come up with a plan," Jackson said.

"Something better than your last one?" Cole raised an eyebrow at him.

"Hopefully, because I'm sure you don't want another run-in with Mom's army, and I really can't handle being locked up in that basement again."

"After a while, you get used to it," Cole said with a shrug.

"Let me do some digging and see what I can find. With Mom and Dad so distracted these days, it might be easier." Jackson got to his feet.

"Well, you know where to find me." Cole opened his book. He didn't really think Jackson could do anything to help him break free. He didn't want to get his hopes up; he wasn't sure he could handle the disappointment when they failed again.

«‹›»

It took hours to screen all the new arrivals. Zoe felt bad keeping them in the dining commons as Pearson slowly questioned them, but no one really seemed to mind. Floyd and Dottie kept bringing out food and water until no one could eat anymore, and Zoe moved from table to table introducing herself. She tried to listen to everyone's stories, but she couldn't stop wondering what was happening with Allissa and the baby. Childbirth could be dangerous, especially when they didn't have any equipment here. She prayed that Dillion and Ian knew what they were doing.

After Pearson screened the new arrivals, Zoe took them to the common room, where Iris and Blake were trying to sort out rooms. It seemed like almost everyone knew at least one other person there, so it made pairing people up easier — though they didn't have nearly enough rooms cleaned out yet to hold everyone who had been on the bus. Slowly, the common room cleared out as people got settled in.

Zoe was exhausted as she made her way to the front desk, where Pearson was sorting through a pile of weapons. "Did you get all of these from the police station?" she said as she looked over the guns laid out on the counter.

"Most of it, though a few weapons came from our

new arrivals," Pearson said.

"They just handed over their weapons?" Zoe wasn't sure she would have been willing to do the same if she was in their position. As much as she didn't like carrying a weapon, it was necessary. No matter what happened, she wasn't powerless. As long as she had her gun, she could protect herself and those around her. She had even gotten pretty good at using it, thanks to Pearson's help.

"I made it clear it was that or leave. Seemed they were happy to exchange their weapons for food and shelter."

"You think we can trust them?" Zoe asked as she looked over the people still lingering around the common room.

"I think so. We'll need to get to know them a little better before I'll be comfortable giving them weapons, though."

Zoe nodded, but she wasn't really listening anymore. Her eyes were fixed on a little boy sitting alone in the corner of the room. He looked to be about twelve and didn't appear to belong to anyone. "What's his story?"

Pearson turned to see who she was looking at. "I don't know. I couldn't get more than a name out of him. I didn't press him. I doubt he's any kind of risk."

"He looks terrified. I'm going to go talk to him." Zoe went behind the desk and grabbed a candy bar from the stash back there.

She went over to the boy and sat down on the floor next to him. "Here." She handed the candy bar to him.

"Thanks," he said as he took it tentatively.

"I'm Zoe. What's your name?"

"Andre." He ran his fingers over the wrapper slowly. "My mom never let me have a king-size candy bar. She said it was too much sugar to have at one time."

"Is your mom here?" Zoe looked over the women in the lobby.

Andre shook his head. "She's dead. They all are."

"I'm so sorry."

"They got sick so fast." Andre turned and looked at Zoe, guilt bright in his eyes. "I didn't know what to do. I just left them there."

"It's all right," Zoe said as she reached out and gently rubbed his back. "You did the right thing. I know your mom would be proud that you've survived on your own for so long."

"I heard people saying that we didn't get sick because we drank RiverLife water. I only ever had it at my friend's house, so I went there thinking they would be there, but they were gone too. I didn't know what do to. I just started walking, trying to figure out where to go. That's when Dr. Dillion found me."

"I'm glad he did."

Andre leaned into Zoe and started to cry.

"Hey, it's okay." Zoe wrapped her arms around him. "You don't have to do this on your own anymore. There are lots of people here to help take care of you. We're all going to look after one another now. You'll be safe here."

She looked up to see Ian watching her from across the room with a small smile on his face.

"Hey, Nina," Zoe said, waving the girl over. "Why don't you take Andre to the kitchen? I think your grandma was making cookies. Maybe you two can help her."

"Sure thing, Zoe," Nina said with a smile. "My grandma makes the best cookies. Come on." Reluctantly, Andre got up and took Nina's hand. He looked back at Zoe, who gave him what she hoped was a reassuring smile and shooed them away.

The moment they were out of sight, she let out a deep breath and put her face in her hands. She couldn't imagine going through what that kid had. To watch your whole family die and have nowhere left to go.

Someone's arm settled around her shoulders. She didn't need to open her eyes to know it was Ian. He pulled her close and held her tight.

"I know this isn't easy, but you're handling it amazingly well," Ian said.

Zoe looked up at him. "I don't have any idea what I'm doing."

"You're leading, bringing all these people together. You're making this a community. You're the heart of this place, the only reason we're going to be able to make any of this work."

Tears started to run down Zoe's face, and she quickly wiped them away. She didn't want anyone to see her breaking down. "How's Allissa?" she asked, changing the subject.

"She's doing good. She's strong. It really shouldn't be much longer."

"Good." Zoe nodded. "I've been thinking, though, there's no way to know if the Arrows' toxin is still in the air. What if it infects the baby?"

"Dillion and I were talking about that. I asked Blake and Iris to get some powdered baby formula that we can mix with RiverLife. I remember you saying Cole's sister gave it to her baby, so it's probably safe, and it'll make sure any toxin left in the atmosphere doesn't affect the baby."

"Thank you. I know it seems silly, but I feel like it's my job to keep everyone here safe, and I don't know if I can, and that terrifies me." Zoe turned to look at Ian, no longer trying to hold back her tears.

"Hey," Ian said, wiping her tears away with his thumb, "you're not alone in this. You have people here who care about you."

"I know. We're a team, and you have my back." Zoe gently bit her lip in an effort to stem the tears flowing from her eyes.

Ian moved his thumb from her cheek to her lip, freeing it from between her teeth. "It's more than that. I care about you, Zoe, you have to know that. I'll do anything for you."

He slowly leaned down and kissed her.

Zoe's breath caught in her throat. For a second, she thought about pulling away, but deep down, she didn't want to. Instead, she gave in to her desire and deepened the kiss. She was breathless when he finally pulled away. Ian's eyes, filled with desire and disbelief, locked on hers. She did not look away.

"Ian!" Dillion came running into the common room, breaking the moment between them. "It's time. I'm going to need your help." He turned and ran back toward the dorms without waiting for Ian's response.

"Go," Zoe said softly.

Ian didn't move. "Are you going to be all right?"

"Yes. Now go deliver that baby." Zoe put a smile on her face as she playfully pushed him away. Ian got up and ran after Dillion.

««Chapter 18»»

Zoe waited for news at the front desk with Iris, Pearson, and Shane, while Blake worked on setting up an elaborate bar behind them. He had declared the new arrivals and the baby a reason to celebrate, but Zoe wasn't going to celebrate anything until they got news that Allissa and the baby were all right. It had been almost an hour since Dillion had come to get Ian, which was for the best; Zoe had no idea how she felt about what had happened with Ian, and she was grateful for the time to figure it out.

Zoe ran her hands over her arms as she walked between the front desk and the common room for what had to be the hundredth time. It was weird seeing it full of strangers when she was just getting used to the little group they had put together. Mark, Allissa, and the Pearsons had become her family. Would she start to feel the same way about the new arrivals soon?

There was a group of kids playing in the corner with

Nina leading the charge, even though several of the kids appeared to be older than her. Zoe spotted Andre in the middle of them with a smile on his face. Kids were so much stronger than adults gave them credit for.

Zoe went back to the front desk. "How many kids do we have here now?"

"Fifteen," Shane said. "Ranging in age from three to twelve, and then another seven teenagers."

"You can add one more to that."

Zoe whipped around to see Mark coming toward them with a huge smile plastered on his face. His newborn was wrapped in blankets in his arms. "This is my daughter, Ariel."

"She's beautiful," Zoe said as she looked down at baby Ariel in awe. She was perfect. Zoe's heart swelled as she looked at the newest addition to their strange little family. "How's Allissa?"

"Tired, but good. The doctor and Ian are with her now, but I knew you would be waiting to meet this little princess." Mark's eyes lit up as he gazed at his daughter.

"Can I hold her?" Iris asked. Zoe had never imagined Iris as a baby person, but she seemed to know exactly what she was doing as she carefully took Ariel from Mark. "She's amazing."

"She's our future," Blake said as he leaned over the desk to get a better look. "Proof that life goes on."

Zoe gave him an odd look. "That's a little profound for you."

Blake held up an empty shot glass. "Just because you wanted to wait to get the party started, doesn't mean that everyone chose to wait."

They burst out laughing. Blake was right—now they really could celebrate. This was the best thing that had happened to any of them in a long time, with Ian kissing her being a close second.

Zoe quickly dashed the thought from her mind. She couldn't think that way, could she?

"Is the baby here?" Dottie came rushing over from the dining commons.

"Here she is." Iris handed Ariel to Dottie.

"What a blessing." Dottie gave Ariel a small kiss on the head and passed her back to Mark. "Ian asked that I fix her bottle with RiverLife. I'll bring it back to you in a few minutes."

"Thank you. I guess I should get this little one back to her mother."

Blake emerged from behind the desk carrying a red tray from the dining commons, loaded with plastic cups of champagne. He passed them out to everyone, then headed to the common room to start taking drink orders.

Zoe turned to Iris, who was staring down the hallway after Mark. "Is it the baby or the good doctor that you're trying to catch a glimpse of?"

"Let's just say the view has significantly improved with the arrival of the bus." Iris didn't look at Zoe while she answered.

Zoe pulled the condoms they had found out of her pocket and handed them to Iris. "I think you might have a use for these long before I do."

Iris turned to look at her and smirked. "You sure about that?"

Zoe felt her cheeks grow warm. "I don't know what you're talking about."

"I saw you and Ian kiss, so don't even try to pretend it didn't happen."

"I'm not sure if it should have happened, though. I mean, technically I'm engaged to Cole."

Iris laughed. "I'm not sure preapocalyptic

agreements matter much anymore."

"I still love him, though," Zoe said — trying to convince herself that was enough.

"I don't doubt that, but Cole's not here. And I'm sure you don't want to hear this, but if he hasn't made it by now, the chances of him getting away from the Arrows seems slim. I think we can all agree that life is unpredictable. I don't think you should put off a chance at happiness because of something that might never happen. The Arrows have shown us that we don't have that kind of time to waste. But that's just me."

"Thank you, Iris."

Iris split the sleeve of condoms in half. "You might want to hang on to some of these. I think I'm going to see if Dillion needs any help." Iris touched Zoe's arm and started to make her way down the hall toward the door. She stopped and turned back to Zoe. "And if you decide to use those, put a sock on the door or something. There are some things about my brother I don't want to know."

Zoe laughed as she watched Iris walk down the hall with a skip in her step. She swallowed the rest of her champagne and turned back to the desk to fix herself another drink . . . something a little stronger this time. Her mind kept wandering back to the kiss and how nice it had felt. Had Iris been right? Was it time to start letting Cole go and allow herself to be happy? What would Cole think if he knew? Was he even still alive? Was it fair to deny her growing feelings for Ian on the off chance Cole would find his way to her? Was it fair to Ian to give in to her feelings for him when part of her heart belonged to Cole?

She took a sip of her drink. She needed to get out of her head. Since she couldn't solve her own problems, she'd see if anyone else had any she could actually do something about.

She moved through the group of newcomers in the common room. They all seemed to be thrilled to have someplace to call home, which Zoe could appreciate. She had let her guard down since deciding to stay here. Was that when her feelings for Ian had really started to develop?

Zoe's eyes flicked to the hallway leading to the rooms. Ian still hadn't made an appearance since Ariel was born. Maybe he was avoiding her.

Zoe made her way back to the desk for another drink when she saw Ian finally emerge from the dorms. He plopped down on one of the couches and rested his head on the back of the couch. Zoe grabbed a clean cup and poured a glass of whiskey. She took a sip of her drink for an added boost of confidence before heading over to him.

"You look like you could use this." She held the drink out to him.

"Thanks." Ian's fingers brushed against her palm as he took the drink, sending a jolt of electricity through her.

Zoe took a deep breath and sat down next to him. She could do this. She *wanted* to do this. She had spent the last hour going over what she wanted to say, now she just needed to get the words from her brain to her mouth. "How are Allissa and the baby doing?"

She was a wimp.

"Good. Allissa handled it amazingly well. She was sleeping when I left."

Zoe shifted so she could see his face better. He hadn't shaved today, his cheeks covered in stubble. His hair had grown back, which she preferred to the shaved look he had sported while they were on the run. "It must feel amazing to have successfully delivered a baby."

"Amazing, yes, but also terrifying. I'm glad Dillion was here. I don't think I could have done that on my own." Ian took another sip of his drink.

Zoe put her hand on his arm. "I'm sure you would have done great. After everything we've been through, delivering a baby is a piece of cake."

"I'm glad you have faith in me." Ian brushed a strand of hair out of her face. The tips of his fingers lingered on her cheek. "We should talk about what happened earlier."

Zoe took a deep breath and nodded.

"I know you're with Cole, and he could still be out there somewhere. I never should have kissed you." Ian looked down at the drink in his hand. "I don't know what came over me."

"I could have stopped you, but the truth is, I wanted you to kiss me. I think I've wanted it for a while now." The alcohol in her system made it easier to speak freely, though she still felt a pang of guilt as the words left her mouth.

Ian's gaze met hers. Time seemed to stop as he looked at her. "What does this mean?" He gently took her hand in his.

"I don't know what it means." She looked at him, pain knifing through her chest. He deserved the truth from her, even if it was difficult. "I still love Cole." Ian started to pull his hand away, so she gripped it tighter. She had to make him see what she was struggling with. Then she would let him make up his mind about her; and if he decided she wasn't worth it, she would understand. She would be devastated, but she would understand. "I still love Cole, but I don't know if I'll ever see him again. I can't waste my life waiting for him to show up when I know there's a good chance he never will." She swallowed hard.

Zoe closed her eyes and tried to ignore the way Ian's thumb felt as he gently ran it over her knuckles. "Despite how I feel about Cole, I can't deny that there's something developing between us. I have feelings for you too, Ian. If things were normal, I wouldn't do anything about it, but nothing is normal anymore, and you're here. You're always here for me."

"And I always will be."

"I know. There's not much I can count on being true anymore, but I know, with absolute certainty, that is."

Ian gently tilted her chin up so her gaze met his. "So, what do we do?"

"Can we take it slow and let things develop naturally? I think we have enough to deal with at the moment without throwing a complicated romantic situation into the mix."

"That depends," Ian said, his voice laced with desire.

Zoe swallowed. "On what?"

"On if you'll let me kiss you again. We were interrupted the first time, you know."

Zoe smiled. "I'll allow it." She leaned in and kissed him.

«‹›»

Cole had given up hope that he would ever see Zoe again, which he was certain was his mother's plan. Not that she had come to see how he was doing. It seemed she had written him off completely, which didn't bother him—except she hadn't eased up with his security detail. Adam was still following him around wherever he went. At times, it almost felt like they were friends. Almost.

But the ever-present rifle slung on Adam's shoulder meant that the only time Cole was able to relax completely was when he was locked in his room, where he was spending more and more time.

He had retired to his room after a tense dinner with Jackson and Victoria's family, where he barely ate anything. What was the point? It was still light out when he crawled into bed, and for once, he didn't have any issues falling asleep. Giving up had calmed his mind to the point that there were no thoughts left to keep him awake most nights.

The door to his room burst open, jerking Cole from a dream of Zoe. He rolled over and looked at the clock. It was after midnight. Without warning, Adam switched on the lights, momentarily blinding him as his eyes were forced to adjust.

"What the hell is going on?" Cole sat up and tried to get his bearings.

"Get up, get dressed. I'll be back in five minutes. Be ready to go." There was a hardness in Adam's voice Cole hadn't heard before. Whatever was going on had to be serious.

"Where are we going?" Cole asked, but Adam was already leaving the room. The door locked behind him.

Cole scrambled out of bed and pulled on a pair of jeans, sweatshirt, and tennis shoes. He tried to come up with a logical explanation for what was happening, but his mind was blank.

The door to the room burst open again. "On your feet. Put your hands behind your back," Adam said.

"Are you serious?" Cole stared at Adam, who seemed like a completely different person than the soldier who had been his shadow for weeks. Jackson was in the hall with his hands secured behind his back.

What the hell was happening?

"Do it *now*." Adam grabbed his rifle and pointed it at him. Cole still didn't move.

"Do what he says, Cole, he's not messing around," Jackson said from the hallway.

"All right, all right." Cole slowly got to his feet and made a show of putting his hands behind his back.

Adam lowered the gun and came over to cuff Cole's hands. "Let's move." He pushed Cole toward the door.

"Do you have any idea what's happening?" Cole asked Jackson in a whisper once he was in the hall.

"No. He came and got me the same way he did you, only he punched me in the face when I didn't listen fast enough."

"No talking," Adam said as he followed them down the hall.

"Why are you doing this?" Cole asked despite Adam's warning.

"I have my orders." The lack of emotion in Adam's voice sent a chill down Cole's spine.

They walked through the residential wing in silence. Cole's nerves grew with every step they took. When they reached the door leading outside, a pair of guards stopped them.

"Where are you taking these two?"

"They have been found to be enemies of the country. I have orders from the president to dispatch with them," Adam said calmly.

Jackson shot Cole a look and mouthed the word *"dispatch."*

Cole shrugged. He really shouldn't be surprised Alana was ordering him to be killed after all the trouble he'd caused.

"They're the third ones this week," the guard said as

he pulled out a tablet. "What are their names?"

"Cole and Jackson Wilborn," Adam said as if they weren't there.

"I have the execution order for a Cole Wilborn, but nothing for a Jackson Wilborn."

"I knew there had been some kind of mistake. If you can uncuff me, I'll be on my way," Jackson said.

"Shut up," the guard at the door said.

"I caught him trying to help his brother escape," Adam said.

"He's lying! I was sleeping, and he dragged me out of bed at gunpoint." Jackson turned to Cole. "Look, man, I'm sorry, but there's no reason for both of us to die." Cole just shrugged. He didn't blame Jackson for trying to save himself. If Cole had anything left to live for, he might try doing the same thing. "Call my mother and I'm sure she'll clear this all up," Jackson said, looking between Adam and the other guard.

"I thought I told you to shut up." The guard smacked Jackson in the face. "I'll add his name to the execution order as a conspirator." He tapped the tablet in his hand before looking back at Adam. "Take them out the back entrance, and make sure no one sees you."

"Yes, sir." Adam pushed Jackson forward.

"You don't have to do this," Cole said once they were out of earshot of the other guard.

"Yes, I do. Keep your voice down, we're almost there." Cole detected a hint of nerves in Adam's voice now that they were outside of the White House. Was he nervous about having to kill him, or was there something else?

They walked through the darkness, weaving their way through abandoned streets. There were no lights on in this part of town, and Cole wondered if that was because there was no power or if there was no one left to use it.

"This is good enough." Adam's voice faltered as he spoke.

Cole stopped, but Jackson kept going.

"I said stop!"

Jackson started to run—albeit an awkward run with his hands still secured behind his back. "What the hell is wrong with your brother?" Adam said as he took off after Jackson. He caught him in a few seconds and pulled him to the ground.

"Fuck, fuck, fuck," Jackson muttered as he rolled to a seated position. Cole walked over to them.

"Just relax," Adam said, looking back and forth down the street. "I'm not going to kill you."

"Then what's with all the theatrics?" Cole asked as Adam removed his cuffs. Cole brought his hands in front of him and lightly rubbed his wrists.

"It was the only way I could get you both out of the White House without anyone being suspicious." Adam knelt to undo Jackson's cuffs.

"Really? Because no one would find you leading two people off into the night to be executed suspicious?" Jackson scrambled to his feet. Cole was a little surprised he didn't take off running again.

"At this point, no," Adam said calmly. "The execution order on Cole was real."

"You're lying," Jackson said.

"I wish I was."

"Thank you for not going through with it," Cole said. Adam nodded.

"That doesn't explain why I'm here," Jackson said.

"After I secured Cole in his room tonight, I was asked to report to the security office. That's when they gave me the execution order. I didn't know what to do. I knew I couldn't carry it out, but if I told my commander that, he would just have someone else do it. While I was there, they were reviewing what looked like a message you broadcasted," Adam said.

Jackson went over and stood next to Cole. "What about it?"

"I saw the unedited security footage. I know that Alana caused all this. I can't keep working for her. I certainly couldn't kill you for pushing back against her. I overheard the conversation the two of you had in library the other day. I knew you both wanted to get away from them. This seemed like the best opportunity to get you out of the White House safely."

"So you're letting us go?" Cole asked, hope returning for the first time in weeks.

Adam nodded. "I was hoping I could go with you. I heard your message to Zoe. You're going to Central Michigan University, aren't you?"

Cole looked at Jackson. He wanted to believe they could trust Adam, but at this point, Cole barely trusted himself.

"Maybe. Why do you want to know?" Jackson asked.

"My brother Mark goes — I mean went — there. If he survived, there's a chance he's still there."

"Wouldn't he have gone home when everything was closed?" Cole asked. They needed to move soon, before anyone realized that Adam hadn't gone through with his execution and came looking for them.

"My parents wouldn't let him come home after he got his girlfriend pregnant. They lived in an off-campus apartmcnt. I need to know if they're alive."

"You can come with us," Cole decided. "We need to go now, though. I want to put as much distance between us and my parents as we can."

Adam walked over to a metal trash can and pulled out three backpacks. He handed one to Jackson and Cole. "Some of my buddies mentioned they're monitoring the roads in this area. There are check points set up all over the place, so we'll need to travel on foot for a while to make sure we aren't caught."

"Lead the way." Cole didn't care if they had to walk all the way to Michigan if it meant that every step was finally getting him closer to Zoe.

«Chapter 19»»

Zoe had a spring in her step as she made her way to the dining commons. Things had been going amazingly well the past few weeks. The new arrivals had settled in and were going out of their way to help in whatever way they could. Baby Ariel was thriving, and Allissa and Mark were settling into their new role as parents with the help of everyone there. They had finished going through all the rooms in Beddow Hall, making them ready for new residents and inventorying whatever could be used. They had a nice shopping mall set up on the lower level of the building, where they were storing the items they gathered from the supply runs. Zoe had no idea how long an entire room stocked floor to ceiling with shampoo would last seventy-five people, but it should get them through winter at the very least.

"Good morning," Zoe called as she entered the dining commons. About half the residents were there already. Dottie and Floyd were still overseeing the kitchen, but they had a team of people helping them now. Preparing three meals a day for this many people was becoming more challenging every day. Zoe would be happy when their crops finally started to produce so they could have fresh vegetables again.

Zoe grabbed a plate of food and went to sit down with Ian, Blake, Iris, Mark, Allissa, and Ariel. Pearson and his family were having breakfast at the table behind them. She was still getting used to having people spread throughout the room instead of the large, single table they had been using before Dillion showed up with his bus full of refugees.

"Good morning." Ian leaned over and gave her a quick kiss. No one even batted an eye. It was amazing how comfortable Zoe had gotten with their strange new relationship over the last three weeks. Being with him was easy, which was a welcome change.

"Good morning," Zoe said.

"You're getting a late start this morning." Ian draped his arm around the back of her chair.

"She was up all night working on something," Iris said.

"You make it sound so scandalous," Zoe said with a laugh. She took a bite of her dry cereal. They had some evaporated milk they had been using, but Zoe didn't care for it. "People keep asking me what they can do, so I was trying to put together a work rotation."

"Speaking of jobs," Pearson said, leaning over from the other table. "I'm putting together a dedicated security team. I'll get you the names."

"See, that's what I'm talking about. Everyone here seems to think I'm in charge."

"You aren't?" Mark cocked an eyebrow at her.

"I never intended to be. I'm just doing what I can to

make sure everyone is taken care of and things run smoothly."

"I hate to break it to you," Blake said, "but that's called being in charge."

Zoe rolled her eyes. "Was there, like, an election I missed or something?"

"You brought us all here, convinced us to let everyone stay. Like it or not, you created this community," Iris said.

"Makes me miss my lab. Just me and my equipment, no one asking me for anything." Zoe sighed. "The worst that could happen if I failed was that I had to try something different. If I fail at this, people could get hurt."

Ian gently squeezed her shoulder. "Do you really think any of us would let that happen?" He pulled her close and kissed her temple.

Blake jumped out of his seat and stood on his chair. "That's right, Captain. We are at your disposal." He saluted her. "What are your orders?"

"You can start by getting down," Zoe said through her laughter. "What does everyone have planned for the day?" She wanted to get the attention off her long enough that she could actually finish eating her breakfast.

"Dillion and I are taking a group to the hospital to see what we can salvage from there," Ian said.

"Be careful. I'm sure there will be a lot of bodies there," Zoe said. The more often they ventured out, the more they tended to find. They tried their best to give them a proper burial, but it was quickly becoming impossible to keep up with it. At some point, they would have to consider a mass grave for all those who had been killed by the toxin.

"I'm not looking forward to it, but it's necessary."

"I'm going to head over to the greenhouse in a little bit and see how the seedlings are coming along, if anyone wants to come," Allissa said.

"Take it easy, though," Ian said. "You're still healing."

"I can handle a walk across campus. Besides, the fresh air will be good for us. Won't it, little miss?" she said to Ariel, who was happily drinking a bottle in her arms.

"How about you? Any big plans for the day?" Ian asked Zoe.

"I guess I'm going to make sure everyone has everything they need. That's what leaders do, right?"

"Hey Ian, Iris," Dillion called across the dining commons. "We're ready to go."

"You're going too?" Zoe asked. Iris and Dillion had been spending a lot of time together since he arrived. Most nights, Zoe had the dorm to herself.

Iris shrugged. "Just in case they can't figure out how to unhook any of the equipment."

"I'll see you later." Ian gave Zoe another kiss before leaving.

Zoe finished her breakfast and started to make her rounds to see if anyone needed anything—something she had done almost every day, but now that she knew everyone saw her as a leader, she felt a lot more pressure. She stopped by the common room, where people had taken to spending their free time. It seemed most of them didn't want to be alone. A group of kids were playing some kind of card game in the back corner of the room.

"Do you think the toxin killed Santa?" Zoe heard Gemma ask. It stopped her in her tracks.

"I don't know," Andre said. "But even if there aren't any presents, it's still going to be all right because we're all here and we're safe. We have people here to look out for us, and that's what matters." He caught Zoe's gaze and smiled at her.

"Still, if Santa is still alive, I really hope he knows where to find us. I miss the dollhouse my dads built me."

Zoe looked out the window as the snow fell outside, her mind racing as she formulated a plan. She had no idea what the actual date was—she had lost track back when they were at the trailer—but it had to be late December or maybe January. She wondered if they had missed Christmas altogether.

Zoe wandered over to the desk where Blake, Floyd, and Dottie were talking. "Hey, does anyone know what the date is?" She looked back at the kids still playing in the corner.

Floyd looked at his watch. "Oh, wow, it's December twenty-fourth."

"It's Christmas Eve!" Blake sat up straight in his chair. "How did we not realize that?"

"We've been a little busy," Dottie said as she put her hand on her head. "I wonder if we have the supplies to make pies or something."

"I think there are some turkeys in the freezer," Floyd offered.

"Would you have time to thaw them out and get them cooked for dinner tomorrow?" Zoe asked.

"We should be able to thaw them out in a water bath overnight," Dottie said.

Zoe motioned for the others to lean in. "I have a plan, but I'm going to need your help."

"We can handle the food," Dottie assured her.

"Blake, you care to do a little shopping?"

"Lead on, Captain," Blake said with a wicked grin.

"I'm going to grab the list of residents I've been working on. Can you get us one of the vehicles? Something with a lot of storage space."

"You got it." Blake vaulted over the desk and headed out the back door.

Zoe ran back to her room, found the notebook she was looking for, and headed out. The two box trucks they had found were gone, along with the pickup truck. "Is this enough space for you?" Blake asked, poking his head out the driver-side window of the school bus.

"It'll do." Zoe climbed on board and took a seat behind Blake. They should be able to fit everything she wanted in here.

"Where are we heading?"

"Let's start with Target."

Blake turned in his seat. "We already cleared out most of the stuff we could use from there."

"Yes, but that's not what we're after. We're going to give these people the best damned Christmas they've ever seen. I want decorations and piles of gifts. Fun, impractical things that have nothing to do with surviving."

"You're the boss." Blake pulled the bus out of the parking lot, and ten minutes later, they were parked in front of Target. They both pulled out their guns as they got off the bus. They had found a few more people on their supply runs, and while they had been grateful to join their community, it didn't hurt to be cautious.

Blake went in first, while Zoe stood watch outside. A few minutes later, he came back out. "It's all clear. Let's go shopping."

They grabbed a couple of shopping carts and headed

back to the toy section where they loaded the carts with everything from toy cars, to dolls, to Play-Doh and board games.

"This is what we need," Zoe said with a smile as she looked at the huge dollhouse on the shelf. "Blake, come help me with this."

Blake brought over an empty cart and helped Zoe lower the dollhouse into it. Then Zoe pulled out her list; she wanted to make sure they had something for everyone. "I think that should cover the kids."

"I just finished loading up the bus with all the baby gear I could find for Ariel."

"Great. Now, what about the teens?"

"I had some thoughts on that." Blake pushed his cart toward the video games. "I mean, we have power."

"Load them up," Zoe said. "Get a few more TVs too. I'm going to head to the beauty department for some makeup and things like that."

They worked for hours, gathering items for everyone back at the dorms. The bus was almost full by the time they were done.

"That just leaves decorations," Zoe said as she leaned against the side of the bus. "I didn't see anything out on the shelves. It was probably too early when this all started."

"We haven't checked the stock room yet. I bet they have stuff back there." Blake grabbed one of the empty carts and rode it into the store. Zoe followed, though in a less dramatic fashion. It took a while, but they eventually found where the Christmas decorations were stored.

"How many trees should we get?" Blake asked.

"At least two, maybe even three. I want the common room and lobby to look like a winter wonderland when everyone wakes up tomorrow."

"Winter wonderland. I think we can pull that off." Blake began loading up boxes of lights, ornaments, and decorations.

"I'm going to find some wrapping paper. I mean, what fun is Christmas without presents to open?"

The bus was packed floor to ceiling by the time they were done. There was barely enough room for Zoe to sit. She had to rest her feet on a case of champagne Blake had found in the stock room and insisted on taking with them. "Let's take this over to Merrill Hall. I don't think anyone is supposed to be in there today. We can start wrapping and then move everything over once everyone is asleep."

Blake drove the bus to the back side of the quad and parked in front of the door. It would take them hours to unload everything and get it wrapped, but it would all be worth it tomorrow when the kids woke up and saw that not only had the toxin not killed Santa, but he had brought them the best Christmas ever.

«‹›»

"Where have you two been all day?" Ian asked as Blake and Zoe sat down at their normal table in the dining commons. They had spent the last three hours wrapping presents and trying to get the decorations ready so they could get everything set up while everyone was sleeping.

"We were . . ." Zoe shot Blake a look. She didn't want to lie to Ian, but she couldn't risk ruining the surprise either.

"I whisked her away for a day of romance while you were off getting supplies," Blake said as he took a bite of macaroni and cheese.

"Oh, did you now?" Ian said with a smirk. He put his

hand on Zoe's knee.

"Yep. I figured what you two really needed was another layer of complication in whatever this whole thing is you have going on." Blake waved his hand between Ian and Zoe. "I wanted to see what all the fuss is about, and honestly, I'm not that impressed."

"Gee, thanks for that," Zoe said with a laugh. "How did things go at the hospital?" she asked, changing the subject.

"It was overwhelming." Ian's voice had a faraway quality to it. "Seeing all those people —" He stopped short. Zoe didn't need him to go into detail to understand how awful it must have been. "We were able to get a few things, though. Dillion and Iris are setting up the equipment in the rooms at the end of the first floor. We figured the back hall could be our medical wing. The Ramirez and Wells families agreed to relocate to the third floor. There was no way we could have gotten the equipment up to those empty rooms."

"I would have gladly moved," Zoe said.

"I know, but you weren't around to ask," Ian said with a raised eyebrow. "Besides, Dillion wanted a few rooms next to each other, and you and Iris are sandwiched between the Pearsons and Mark and Allissa. We didn't want to move either of them."

"That makes sense. I'll make sure the Ramirez and Wells families are settled in." Zoe started to get up, but Blake waved her back down.

"I can handle that." He winked at her as he left.

"So," Ian said, giving Zoe his full attention. "Are you going to tell me what you and Blake were really doing all day?"

"No. I am not," Zoe said with a wicked grin.

"Should I be concerned?"

"Only if you want to be." She probably shouldn't be enjoying this as much as she was.

"You are a woman of mystery, Zoe Antos. One of these days, I'm going to figure out all of your secrets."

"You'd better have a lot of time on your hands."

"For you, I have all the time in the world." Ian ran a finger over her cheek, and her insides melted.

Zoe leaned forward and kissed him. After a few seconds, she pulled away, breathless. Things were moving faster with Ian than she had intended, but it felt right. "I need to go," she whispered, her lips inches away from his.

"Are you sure?" Ian closed the distance between them and kissed her again.

"Yes," she said against his lips. "It's important."

"More important than this?" He trailed a line of soft kisses along her chin and down her neck.

"Yes," Zoe barely managed to say as her heart rate spiked. It would be so easy to go back to his room and let this play out. She had thought about it hundreds of times, though they hadn't taken that step yet. But there was a group of kids that needed her to prove that the Arrows hadn't taken out Santa, and she wasn't going to let them down. No matter what her hormones had to say.

Ian leaned back in his chair and put his hands over his heart. "I don't know how I'll ever recover."

Zoe laughed. "I'm sure you'll find a way." She got up, kissed him on the cheek, and left the dining commons. She needed to find Blake so they could get back to Operation Christmas Wonderland.

«Chapter 20»»

Blake and Zoe worked through the night bringing all the gifts over and setting up three Christmas trees in the common room. Zoe was antsy all night, sure someone was going to catch them, but no one did. By the time the sun was starting to come up, they had succeeded in turning the place into the winter wonderland she had imagined, sure to prove to all the kids that Santa was alive and well.

Zoe collapsed on one of the couches, too tired to go back to her room. "What are you doing over there?" she called to Blake, who was busy at the front desk.

"Setting up a mimosa bar," he said, as if it was the most logical thing in the world.

"Give me a second to rest my eyes, then I'll be over to help."

Blake chuckled as she closed her eyes.

"So, this is what you two were doing yesterday."

Zoe jerked awake at the sound of Ian's voice. She had

no idea how long she had been asleep, but it didn't feel nearly long enough.

"Fuck," Blake muttered from the front desk as the chair he must have fallen asleep in crashed to the ground. "Shit, wait. You need to get the full effect."

A second later, Christmas music filled the room.

Zoe sat up and watched as everyone slowly trickled in. Their wide eyes and dropped jaws made the lack of sleep and all the hard work worth it.

"Merry Christmas." Ian leaned down and kissed Zoe, then sat down next to her and put his arm around her. Zoe snuggled close, resting her head on his shoulder. "I can't believe you and Blake did all of this."

"I heard some of the kids talking about whether or not the toxin had killed Santa. They needed this." Zoe watched Gemma hugging the new baby doll she had just unwrapped.

"We all needed this." Ian kissed the top of her head.

Pearson came over carrying two cups of coffee. "Figured you could use this."

"Thank you." Zoe cupped her mug in both hands and took a sip.

"You're the one we should be thanking. I'll never be able to express how much this means to me. To my girls. Shane and I spent the last few days dodging Gemma's questions, thinking there was no way we'd be able to celebrate this year, but somehow you made it happen."

"It's easy when you don't have to pay for anything," Zoe said with a smile.

"It's not just the presents. It's the hope, magic, and most importantly, the sense of normalcy you brought to everyone here. That's what is going to keep us going." Pearson gave her a smile, then joined the rest of his family sitting on the floor near one of the trees. He picked up one of the dolls and started to play with Gemma. It was such a contrast to the hard-ass detective vibes he normally gave off.

Zoe leaned into Ian as she sipped her coffee and watched the families opening their gifts. This moment right here was perfect. After all the suffering and pain they had endured, they deserved to live in this perfect moment for as long as they could.

"Ian, Ian!" Gemma ran over to them carrying a large, wrapped box.

Ian leaned forward to give Gemma his full attention. "Yes, Queen Gemma, how might I be of service to you today?" he said in an extremely formal tone.

Gemma giggled. "I'm just me today, Ian."

Ian made a show of making sure no one else was watching before holding up his hand to cover his mouth and whispering, "You'll always be a queen to me."

Gemma giggled again. "This one has your name on it." She handed it to him and ran away in a fit of giggles.

"What was all that about?"

"Well, while you were off secretly putting all this together, I needed something to do to pass the time. Gemma is a very fair and just ruler . . . you might want to ask her for some pointers if you run into trouble."

Zoe's heart swelled as she imagined Ian playing make-believe with the kids. "Why don't you open your present?"

Ian raised an eyebrow at her and ripped off the paper, adding to the growing pile on the floor. He opened the box and gasped; he looked at Zoe and then back at the box. He pulled out the black leather jacket and held it up. "How did you know?"

"Blake found it, actually."

"My dad used to wear a jacket almost exactly like

this. It was the only thing I had of his, but it got left behind when we went on the run."

Zoe bit back tears; he'd had to leave his father's jacket behind because of her. Because she had been stupid enough to try to stop the Arrows on her own, and he had to come save her life. "See if it fits." She forced a smile so she wouldn't taint his excitement with her guilt.

Ian stood up and put it on as Blake came over with two glasses of mimosas in his hands. "Do you like it?" He handed Zoe one of the glasses.

Ian didn't say anything. He just pulled Blake into a huge hug, nearly spilling the drink in Blake's hand all over the back of the jacket. "Thank you," Ian said with a tear in his eye. He released Blake and quickly composed himself. "Any chance you were able to find what I asked you for last week?"

"Way ahead of you. Check the jacket pocket." Blake winked at Ian and left.

Ian sat back down, pulling a small, wrapped box from his pocket as he did. "For you." He held the box out to Zoe.

Zoe set her glass down and took the box. "And here I was thinking I actually surprised you with all of this."

"Oh, you did. I didn't even realize it was Christmas. It just worked out that Blake found it in time. But it seems right. You need something to open today too."

Zoe gave Ian a huge grin as she pulled the ribbon off the box and opened it. Inside was a necklace with two interlocking silver circles. It was simple, elegant, and absolutely perfect. "I love it." Zoe took it from the box and held it up. "Will you help me put it on?"

"Of course." Ian took the necklace from her and slowly brushed the hair off her neck. It was now just past her shoulders, and the top few inches were brown, fading into the red she had dyed it in trailer. Ian clasped the necklace around her neck, his fingers lingering on her skin as he did. "It looks stunning. Just like you."

"Thank you." Zoe kissed him, then leaned against his side as they watched everyone continue to open their gifts.

Eventually, Dottie and her kitchen team laid out a breakfast buffet on the front desk so everyone could eat when they wanted. They spent the rest of the day playing as if they were kids again. Iris put together the dollhouse and helped the girls fill each room with toy furniture; Blake hooked up the new TVs and video games. There was some kind of gaming tournament going on that Zoe didn't totally understand, but judging by the sounds coming from them, it must be getting pretty intense.

That evening, everyone gathered in the dining commons for the Christmas feast Dottie and Floyd had prepared. Zoe had no idea how they had managed to pull it off. There was ham and turkey, at least four different types of vegetables, and the biggest bowl of mashed potatoes Zoe had ever seen.

"This is the last of our fresh produce, but I think it's worth it." Floyd passed trays of food out to all the tables.

"Most of it was about to turn anyway." Dottie passed out plates with carved meat on them. "Everyone, eat up."

After dinner, they headed back to the common room where the party continued, especially as the kids started to fall asleep. Blake had his bar set up at the front desk again, and someone was playing piano.

"Care to dance?" Ian held his hand out to Zoe.

"I'd love to." Zoe smiled at the group of people she had been talking to as she took Ian's hand. People had been thanking her all day, and she was grateful for an excuse to escape for a few minutes. She hadn't done any of this for the praise. She simply wanted to keep everyone's spirits up.

Ian pulled her into his arms, and they started to sway in the middle of the room, where the furniture had been pushed aside to make a dance floor. "Has anyone told you how incredible you are, today?"

"Yes, repeatedly. It's getting a little annoying," she said with a smile.

"Well, get used to it. I am in awe of you, Zoe Antos."

"You're not so bad yourself," Zoe said, but Ian wasn't looking at her anymore. The next moment, he released her. He grabbed his gun and pulled her close to his side with his other hand.

Zoe's gaze followed the angle of the gun, where three new arrivals stood at the entrance of the common room.

"Cole." Zoe's voice was barely a whisper.

«‹«›»›

Cole was shocked by the number of people in the dorm's common room, but the moment his eyes locked on Zoe, they all seemed to melt away. She was here. She was safe. It didn't even matter that she was currently in Ian's arms. He couldn't believe that after nearly three months apart, they were in the same room again.

This wasn't a dream. He had really found her.

"Merry Christmas, beautiful."

The music stopped instantly. Every eye in the room fell on them, but Cole didn't care. All he could see was Zoe—though he wasn't sure what to make of the fact that Ian was still holding her tight while pointing his gun at them. He would have to worry later, as there were suddenly a lot more guns pointed at them.

Jackson leaned over and whispered, "Zoe and Sutton look awfully cozy, don't they?"

Cole ignored him. Through the crowd, he spotted Detective Pearson and thought he might step forward to take charge, but he was looking at Zoe for direction. Zoe nodded at Pearson, who then turned to Cole. "Everyone, take it easy," Pearson said to the group. "Cole, I need you to have your friend there carefully place his weapon on the ground, along with any other weapons you have."

"Adam, do it." Cole held up his hands to show them that he was unarmed. This was not the reception he had expected. "We didn't come here to cause any problems."

Cole shifted his gaze back to Zoe, who was finally removing herself from Ian's arms. She weaved through the crowd toward him, and Cole had to fight the urge to run to her, since there were still several guns pointed at him and he had no idea what these people would do if he tried it.

She had almost reached him when Pearson held out a hand to stop her. "Wait 'til my guys search them. Just to be safe."

"They aren't going to hurt us. We can trust them." Zoe's eyes were locked on him as she spoke. Cole's cheeks hurt from the smile on his face. She was so close . . . and she wanted him.

Pearson shot Cole a look before turning back to Zoe. "Don't you think you're a little too invested to make a rational call here?"

"Zoe, it's okay," Cole said. The faster they could get through this, the sooner she would be in his arms again.

"Please, let me do my job."

Zoe sighed and nodded. Pearson motioned for a few of his men to search their bags while he stepped forward to search them.

"Adam. Is that really you?" Cole turned his head to see a young man walking toward them with a baby in his arms. He had the same sharp chin and wide eyes as Adam. It had to be his brother. Cole couldn't wait to hear how all these people had come together.

Pearson stepped between Adam and the kid with the baby. "Mark, you know him?"

"Yeah, he's my brother."

Pearson looked Adam over once more, then nodded, allowing Mark and Adam to embrace. Pearson turned to Zoe. "They're clean. Do you want me to hold them until we can question them further?"

"There's no need for that. I told you, we can trust them." Zoe turned to the room. "You can lower your weapons."

Next to Cole, Jackson slowly lowered his hands. "Why is everyone doing what Zoe says?"

"Because she's in charge here," Pearson said. "You'd do well to remember that."

Zoe rolled her eyes. Cole knew how much she hated being the center of attention; he had to wonder how she came to be the leader. He had never really seen her take charge of a group of people before—she tended to hang back and work behind the scenes.

He pushed the thought from his mind. There was only one thing that mattered at the moment. "Can I say hello to my fiancée now?"

Pearson nodded, and a moment later, Zoe was in Cole's arms. He picked her up and swung her around before setting her back on her feet and kissing her.

"God, I missed you," he said against her lips. He felt alive for the first time in months.

"I missed you too." Zoe leaned against his chest. Her

tears soaked through his shirt, but he didn't care. Zoe was safe, and he had her back. Nothing else mattered.

«‹‹Chapter 21››»

The mattress in Zoe's dorm room wasn't nearly as comfortable as what he had back at the White House, but Cole couldn't remember ever having a better night's sleep. Zoe was stretched out on top of him, her head gently resting on his chest as she slept. He wanted to live in this moment forever. Everything he had been through had been worth it for this moment right here. Now that they were back together, nothing could pull them apart again.

Cole gently brushed a strand of hair out of Zoe's face as she started to stir. "Good morning," she mumbled against his skin.

"Good morning, beautiful." Cole kissed the top of her head, his hand running over her bare back. It had been so long since he touched her. He wanted to take the time to memorize every inch of her again.

"Did you sleep okay?"

"Of course I did, you're here. It's the best night of

sleep I've gotten in ages."

Zoe rolled onto her side. Cole shifted closer to the wall to give her some room. "Did you ever think we'd end up sleeping in the dorms again?" Her smile was dazzling.

Cole chuckled. "No, but it's fitting, isn't it? I mean, this is where we fell in love. At least we don't have to worry about your roommate walking in on us now."

"Don't be so sure of that. I wouldn't put it past Iris to barge in here," Zoe said with a smirk.

"You're rooming with Iris? I imagine that's a little intense."

"She grows on you. Besides, she rarely sleeps in here since Dillion showed up."

"Who's Dillion?" It was clear he had a lot of catching up to do.

"He's a friend of Ian's. They went to medical school together, I think, before Ian had to drop out."

"I didn't realize Ian went to medical school."

Zoe nodded and ran her fingers over Cole's chest. He caught her hand and kissed it. "Dillion is actually the one who patched me up after your mom shot me."

"I assume, since you're up and walking, everything healed okay." He should have checked, but it had completely slipped his mind. It didn't seem to slow her down any last night.

"For the most part. It still gets sore when I try to do too much."

"Where did you go after everything happened at Wilborn Headquarters? Jackson told me he saw you in Kentucky. Did you go there first?"

"No, we were at some cheap motel, but your mom's people found us there after a few days. They came pretty close to killing Ian and taking me prisoner, but I was able to fight one of the guys off. Blake killed the other." Zoe's hand went to her throat, and Cole's heart broke as he imagined what she had been through. "From there, we went to Kentucky . . . until your dad showed up and had Hamid killed."

"Jackson told me." Cole ran his fingers over her cheek.

"Hamid was trying to keep your dad's soldiers from taking me back with him. I had a hard time walking for a few days after that."

After Cole's own run-in with his parents' army, he didn't need to imagine what that had been like. It made him sick to think that Gordon had allowed the same thing to happen to Zoe. "I'm so sorry."

Zoe shrugged. "From there, we spent about a few days in a hotel somewhere in Indiana and then in a house in Missouri, I think, before coming here."

"You've been through so much. I wish I could have been there to help you through it."

"It wasn't all bad," Zoe said, but she didn't elaborate. "You were the one I was worried about. I had no idea what your parents would do to you."

"It wasn't bad, especially in the beginning. They kept me locked in my room most of the time. The boredom was the worst part."

"Did you ever try to get away?"

"It was all I thought about. Jackson and I got close once, but Mom found out somehow. She had her army attack me and drag me back. After that point, I had a guard with me at all times."

"Adam?"

Cole nodded. "He's the reason we were finally able to get away. The night we escaped, Adam was ordered to execute me."

Zoe gasped. "Your mom wanted you killed?"

"Apparently I had become more trouble than she was willing to deal with. Obviously, he didn't go through with it."

"Thank God. How long ago was that?"

"It took us about two weeks to make it here, I think."

"I'm glad you're here." Zoe kissed him. "I have to get up. I'm sure there's a huge mess to clean up in the common room, and I promised Dottie that we could go over the food inventory today." Zoe extracted herself from the blankets and grabbed her clothes off the floor.

Cole sat up and watched her get dressed. "You really are in charge here, aren't you?"

"So they keep telling me. I'm just trying to make sure everything runs smoothly. There are people here depending on me, and I don't want to let them down."

"People like Ian?" Cole hated that the question slipped out of his mouth. He had sworn to himself that he wouldn't ask her, but he couldn't get the image of Zoe in Ian's arms, their bodies pressed against one another, out of his mind.

Zoe froze for a moment with her back to him before quickly pulling on her shirt. "We should talk about that." She sat down on the edge of the bed without looking at him.

"Are you two together?" Cole pressed his back against the cold cinder block wall as he braced himself for the answer.

"I don't really know what Ian and I are. We've spent every day together taking care of one another. Protecting one another. We got close, became friends. We all did — Blake, Ian, Iris and me—but eventually my feelings for Ian started to move past friendship."

"And he felt the same way," Cole said, even though

it felt like every word was a fist to his gut.

Zoe nodded. "We agreed to let things progress naturally and see what happened."

Cole took a deep breath as his mind tried to come to terms with what she was telling him. Was this the end of them? Had she chosen Ian over him, and last night was goodbye? "Have you slept with him?"

"No. I told you, we're taking things slow." Zoe looked at him, tears forming in the corners of her eyes. "I love you, Cole. That's what makes all of this so complicated. I thought about you every single day. I came here because I thought for sure you'd be waiting for me, but you weren't here. And I know that wasn't your fault. I know your mom was holding you against your will, that she made you say all those awful things about me on TV, but that doesn't change the fact that you weren't here. Ian was, though. He helped me get through the moments when I wanted to give up. He kept me alive."

"I'm glad you had him. I never want you to feel alone or unhappy." Cole swallowed hard. He didn't want to be mad at Zoe. She had been through something extraordinary, and under any other circumstances, she would have stayed faithful to him. Deep down, he was happy that she had managed to find comfort while they were apart, even if he had never found it while being held by the Arrows. "What does this mean for us?" This was what really mattered. He could forgive everything that happened if he knew they had a future together.

"I love you, Cole. I have for so long. I can't imagine going through life without you."

Cole leaned forward and kissed her before she had a chance to say anything else. "Good answer."

Zoe gave him a weak smile that broke his heart. "I

need to get out there. Why don't you get cleaned up and join me in the dining commons for breakfast?"

"Sure," Cole said trying to sound normal. He watched Zoe get off the bed, wipe the tears from her eyes, and head out the door without looking back at him.

«‹‹◇››»

Zoe's head was spinning. The last twenty-four hours had been a complete whirlwind of ups and downs. She wasn't sure how to handle any of it. Slowly, she made her way to the common room, wanting to assess the work needed to clean up after their Christmas celebrations, but the room was spotless. Normally, she would have been thrilled, but the lack of mindless labor meant she had nothing to focus on other than her current romantic situation.

She sat down on a couch in the back corner of the room and sighed. She had Cole's ring on her finger and Ian's necklace around her neck. She didn't want to give either of them up, but she doubted Ian or Cole would be all right with that. She had been with Cole for so long, she truly couldn't imagine her life without him. But there was no denying the connection she had with Ian. He was gentle and playful when he allowed himself to relax, and he supported her no matter what. Ian believed in her more than anyone else did. Maybe even more than Cole. There was no good answer.

"Good morning."

Zoe looked up to see Ian standing over her. He leaned down to kiss her, like he had done every morning for the last few weeks, but this time, Zoe turned her head and offered him her cheek instead.

"So, that's how it's going to be now." Ian clenched

his jaw and straightened. "I'll leave you alone."

Zoe jumped up and grabbed his arm. "Please don't be like this."

Ian turned back to her. "How do you want me to be? I won't be your guy on the side."

"I care about you, Ian," Zoe pleaded. She was losing him, and she feared it would destroy her.

"But you still went with him last night." There was no malice in Ian's voice, but his words sliced through her heart. The last thing she wanted to do was hurt him, and it was clear that she had done just that.

"I was shocked. I honestly didn't expect to see him ever again. What else was I supposed to do? He's still my fiancé."

Ian pursed his lips and nodded. "So, you made your choice."

"I haven't chosen anything. I told you when we started whatever this is that I still loved Cole, but that doesn't change how I feel about you." Zoe put her hand on her forehead. "I haven't had a chance to even process everything, let alone figure out what's best for everyone."

"This isn't about what's best for everyone. I know what I want, and I'm pretty sure Cole does too. The only one who needs to make up their mind is you."

"I don't know what I want. I wish I did."

"I think you do know, you just don't want to say it," Ian said.

"Oh, really." Zoe put her hands on her hips and glared at him. "Then you tell me what I want, because I have a million different things running through my head, and they are all telling me something different."

"Did you sleep with him last night?" Ian asked, his tone even.

"What?" Had he really just asked her that?

"Did you have sex with Cole last night?" Ian said, slower this time.

Zoe crossed her arms. "Do you really want me to answer that?"

"You just did," Ian said with a hint of pain in his voice. "You made a choice. You just haven't admitted it to yourself yet."

"That's not fair."

"Life's not fair, Zoe. We know that better than anyone," Ian said with a shrug.

"What do you want from me?"

Ian took her hands in his. "Choose me," he said with an intensity she hadn't heard from him before.

"Ian," Zoe said in exasperation.

"Don't you get it, Zoe? I love you." He gently squeezed her hands to drive the point home.

Zoe wanted to say it back, but the words wouldn't come. After a moment, Ian let go of her hands, and Zoe didn't know what to do. No matter what she said, someone would get hurt, but no one more than her. She just stood there, silently pleading with him to understand what she couldn't find the words to say.

She opened her mouth to try to articulate how she was feeling when someone's arms wrapped around her stomach from behind. Judging by the look on Ian's face, it was Cole.

He pulled her close to him and kissed her cheek before looking up. "Good morning, Ian."

"Cole."

Zoe squirmed out of Cole's grasp and stepped away. He was putting on a show, and she wouldn't be part of it.

"I have to thank you for keeping Zoe safe until I got

here," Cole said with an overly large smile; he was trying to stake his claim over her, and she hated it. She wasn't a toy they were fighting over.

"Zoe didn't need me to keep her safe. She's more than capable of taking care of herself. In fact, she saved my life a few times." Ian glanced over at her and smirked. She wondered if he was remembering what happened in the motel and how utterly useless he had been.

Zoe couldn't help but smile back. Ian always saw the best in her.

"Zoe! Ian!" Andre came running over to them; Zoe had never been more grateful for an interruption. "Toby is going to teach me how to shoot!"

Zoe looked at Andre in shock before her gaze fixed on Pearson following behind him. "You're going to teach him to shoot a gun?"

"Yes, I am." Pearson put a hand on Andre's head and tousled his hair.

"He's twelve."

"What's your point?" Pearson said. "I was younger than him when I learned how to shoot. It's important for him to learn the safe way to use a gun. You two didn't learn as kids, and you're still unlearning the bad habits you picked up."

"We aren't that terrible with a gun," Ian countered.

"You were a decent shot, but your lack of concern for gun safety was appalling. Zoe, on the other hand, was a mess," Pearson said with a smirk. "How many times did you almost accidently shoot Ian?"

Zoe put her hands on her hips, choosing to ignore Pearson's dig at her lack of skills. "If you think I'm going to let you put him on your security detail, you're insane."

"Of course not, at least not for a few more years." Pearson winked at Andre.

"Can I, Zoe? Please."

Pearson raised his eyebrow at her. Zoe really didn't like the idea of training kids to be soldiers — Andre had been through enough already without having to deal with that burden — but she could tell this was something he really wanted to do. She let out a breath. "You do everything Toby says."

"I will." Andre gave Zoe a hug.

"If he gets hurt, I'm coming for you, Pearson," Zoe said in what she hoped was an intimidating voice. Pearson waved off her threat and led Andre out of the common room.

"I'll keep an eye on him." Ian reached out and touched Zoe's arm. Their eyes locked, and Zoe's stomach filled with butterflies.

"Thank you," she said softly as she watched Ian leave. Once he was gone, she turned to Cole. "Did you really have to do that?"

Cole blinked at her. "Do what?"

"Don't act innocent. You were trying to stake your claim over me like I'm a piece of property."

"That wasn't my intention. You know I don't think of you that way."

"Very convincing." Zoe rolled her eyes and walked away.

Cole ran to catch up with her. "I'm sorry."

"Can you please try to be civil to him? This is complicated enough without you two entering into some kind of pissing contest."

"Yes, I will. For you." Cole took her hand in his, and her annoyance started to melt away. "Who was the kid?" Cole asked, clearly trying to steer the conversation to a safer topic.

"Andre," Zoe said with a smile. "Most people here have someone from before, but not him. He only drank RiverLife at a friend's house. We've all kind of adopted him."

"That's great," Cole said as he held the door to the dining commons open for her.

"I guess, except for the part where he had to watch his whole family die thanks to the toxin your mom released."

"That's not fair. I'm trying here."

Zoe sighed. Why was being with Cole so difficult now? Had too much happened for them to go back to normal? "I know. I'm sorry. Look, you can go help yourself to some breakfast. There's a ton of that sugary garbage cereal you used to eat." Zoe tried to lighten the mood, but she didn't think it worked. She caught Blake's eye across the room and waved him over. "When you're done, Blake can show you to your room."

"My room?" Cole frowned as Blake arrived. "I assumed I'd be staying with you."

Zoe looked away. She knew what she was about to say was going to hurt Cole's feelings, and she didn't want to see the pain in his eyes. It might be the thing that broke her completely. "For now, I think it would be better if you had your own room. If you need anything, Blake can help." Zoe smiled at Blake, who gave her a knowing nod, then she retreated to the kitchen.

It had never been this hard to be around Cole. Not even when she thought he might be part of the Arrows.

She walked through the kitchen, looking for Dottie while absentmindedly playing with the necklace Ian had given her.

"I wasn't expecting you 'til later this afternoon."

Dottie was standing at one of the large metal prep tables with a mound of dough in front of her.

"What are you making?" Zoe asked, ignoring Dottie's implied question.

"Chicken pot pie. Trying to make the most of the frozen vegetables and canned meat."

"I'm sure it will be delicious." Zoe ran her finger along the edge of the table as she looked aimlessly around the kitchen.

Dottie grabbed a cloth and wiped the flour from her hands. "You're not here to talk about our food supply, are you?"

Zoe shook her head. "I needed to get away from everything for a bit. I was hoping I could hide out in here."

Dottie gave Zoe a knowing smile. "Or course." She ushered Zoe over to a metal stool next to the prep table, then retreated to the freezer and returned with a pint of ice cream and a spoon. "Don't tell any of the kids about this."

Zoe opened the ice cream and took a small bite. The creamy vanilla coated her mouth as it melted, leaving only a swirl of frozen fudge on her tongue. "Where did you get this?" She scooped another spoonful into her mouth.

"Blake finally got that door in the back of the dining commons open. It turned out to be a little snack shop, complete with a freezer full of ice cream. I was saving it for a special occasion, but I think you need it right now."

"Thank you," Zoe said around a mouthful of ice cream. It was amazing how much the simple treat was lifting her spirits—though that might have more to do with the fact that for the moment, neither Cole nor Ian was fighting for her attention.

"Can I offer you a piece of advice to go with it?"

"Sure."

"Don't let guilt or a sense of obligation make this decision for you. Listen to your heart, and do what's best for you."

Zoe set down her spoon. "I don't want to hurt either of them."

"I know," Dottie said, "but trust me, they're already hurting, and so are you. Give yourself some time to figure out what you want. You can't let anyone force you to make this decision before you're ready."

Zoe nodded as the tears started to roll down her cheeks. How would she ever decide who was the right person for her? It seemed impossible — but then again, she was alive, which had also seemed pretty impossible not that long ago.

«‹«›»›

Cole walked through the lower level of Beddow Hall with Blake. He had tried to drag out breakfast as long as possible, hoping Zoe would emerge from the kitchen, but after an hour, she still hadn't returned. He tried to tell himself that she was just busy, but he feared she was avoiding him. This was not how he had expected their reunion to go.

"This is our little shopping mall," Blake said, handing him a canvas bag. "We should have everything you need. There's soap, shampoo, toothpaste, that sort of thing in these rooms." He pointed to a few open doors ahead as they walked. "You can get clothing up there if you need it. Towels and other linens are around the corner."

"This is quite the operation you have set up here,"

Cole said as he grabbed a bar of soap and a toothbrush.

Blake shrugged. "It was all Zoe. It was a bitch getting it all organized, though. We have a few people assigned to maintain it now, so that helps."

"So Zoe really is in charge here?"

"Why do you find that so surprising? She's an intelligent, capable woman."

"I'm aware of that," Cole snapped. "She never liked being in charge, that's all."

"I'm not sure she likes it now," Blake said with a laugh. "But she's good at it. She cares about everyone here and goes out of her way to make sure we're all taken care of. I don't know what more you could ask for from a leader."

"Well, if the choices are Zoe or my mother, Zoe wins, hands down," Cole said as he gathered the rest of the items he'd need.

"Right," Blake said as he scrutinized Cole. He had meant it as a joke, but clearly Blake didn't find it funny. "You're on the second floor with your brother."

Blake opened the door to the stairwell; they walked up to the second floor in silence, though Blake was overly friendly to everyone they passed. They stopped outside of one of the rooms. "This is you."

"Thanks." Cole went to open the door, but Blake stopped him.

"Look, I know things are messy right now. You've been through a lot, and that's changed you; the same is true for Zoe. Have a little faith in her. All she wanted while we were on the run was to find you. That's why she convinced us to come here. She needs time to figure things out."

"She's my fiancée. It really shouldn't be that hard for her to figure out."

"The world's a different place now." Blake shrugged. "Nothing's that simple anymore. You might have to find another way to move forward. Make compromises."

"You think I shouldn't care that she has feelings for Ian?"

"There are worse things in the world to deal with."

"That's insane." Cole's anger bubbled beneath the surface. It was bad enough that Ian had somehow worked his way into his relationship with Zoe, but he didn't need or want Blake's unsolicited advice.

"All I know is that the four of us got close while we were on the run from your parents. We're a family now — Ian, Iris, Zoe, and me. You can either become part of that family or not, that's up to you. But you won't be able to break it apart, and if you hurt her trying, you'll have to deal with me." Blake patted him on the shoulder and left.

Cole opened the door and slammed it shut behind him. Jackson peeked out of the bedroom. "How was your reunion with Zoe?"

"Last night was great, but this morning . . ." Cole's voice trailed off. He didn't know what to say.

"It's that Sutton guy, isn't it?" Jackson sat down on one of the desks in the center room. "I told you they looked cozy last night."

"Apparently she developed feelings for him, and from what I saw this morning, those feelings are reciprocated." Cole paced in front of the door.

"Maybe you two should leave. You can try to start over somewhere else. I'm sure if Sutton isn't around, she'll forget all about him."

Cole stopped to look at Jackson. Was he serious? Where else could they go that would have electricity and clean water? Besides, there were all these people here, and Zoe was making it her job to take care of them. "She'd never go for it."

Jackson cocked an eyebrow at him. "Not even if it means losing you? I bet if you tell her you can't stay here, she'll go with you. She might have the hots for Sutton, but she loves you."

"I can't risk it. Besides, this is probably the safest place for either of us. What do you think Mom will do to me if she realizes Adam didn't follow through with the execution order? What do you think she'll do to Zoe?" Cole shook his head as he tried to erase the thought of Alana killing Zoe from his mind. "We have to stay."

"Even if that means you end up in some weird relationship where you have to share Zoe with the criminal who kidnapped her?"

"It won't come to that," Cole said with a confidence he didn't really feel. "She needs time to process everything she's been through, then I'm sure she'll realize she doesn't really have feelings for Ian. She was just searching for comfort wherever she could find it. Now that I'm here, she can put that all behind her. What we feel for each other is real. We can get past this, I'm sure of it."

"And if you can't, remember I'm here for you. I can fix everything if you need me to. I'm your big brother, it's kind of my job to make sure you're happy."

Cole stared at Jackson. He had no idea what he meant by *fix everything*, but it made him uneasy. He didn't want anything bad to happen to Ian—in fact, he kind of liked the guy. He just didn't want him to be with Zoe.

«<Chapter 22»»

"I think this would be a great space to set up a
school." Zoe stood in the middle of the large, open room
on the lower level of the dorms. While technically
another common room, it was rarely used when she
went to school here. Now they used the space to sort the
items that were brought back from the supply runs, but
maybe they could put it to better use.

She turned to look at Charlotte and Elijah, two
former schoolteachers who had been hounding her for
days to set up a school. Hovering behind them was Cole,
her ever-present shadow. She was trying to be patient
with him as he adjusted to life here, but he hadn't given
her more than a few minutes by herself in the week he'd
been there.

"I don't know," Elijah said as he surveyed the space.
"The kids might get distracted with people trying to get
to the stores."

"We can limit the times people can access the stores,

or close that door. That way people can still get to the stores from the other stairwell without even coming through here. I really think this is the best option," Zoe said.

"What if we set it up in one of the other buildings in the quad?" Charlotte asked.

"We have teams starting to clean out the rooms in the other buildings, so you'll have the same distractions there. Plus, I don't like the kids being that isolated from the rest of the community right now in case something happens. Here you have Pearson's full security team keeping an eye on things. Trust me, we can make this work."

Charlotte took a deep breath and nodded. "All right, we'll give it a shot. We're going to need desks and maybe some whiteboards. Not to mention textbooks and supplies."

"We should be able to get desks and whiteboards from the classrooms on campus without any problems. Put together a wish list, and give it to Ian. I'll work with him to set up a supply run specifically for this."

"Thanks, Zoe," Elijah said.

"No, thank you two for taking this on. I know it's going to be a ton of work."

"The kids here need it. Besides, I'm looking forward to setting up a curriculum that isn't centered around testing. We get the chance to teach these kids things that really matter."

"I'll leave it in your capable hands." Zoe smiled at both of them and went to join Cole.

"You were incredible," Cole said as he leaned over and kissed her cheek.

"Thanks," Zoe said, though her heart wasn't in it. "Maybe you could help them. It'll be a lot of work cleaning this room out and converting it to usable classroom space."

"I'll do whatever you need me to." Cole took her hand in his.

Zoe sighed. He clearly wasn't picking up on the hint that she needed some space. Cole had never been this clingy before, and part of her wondered if it was his way of keeping Ian away from her. Which seemed to be working, as Ian was avoiding her, and she desperately missed his company.

"Hey." Blake met them on the stairs. "Pearson needs to see you."

"Really? What's going on?" Zoe asked as she pried her hand free from Cole's.

"I don't know exactly. He just asked me to find you. He's waiting for us in the dining commons."

Zoe turned to Cole. "I should go."

"I can come with you," Cole offered.

"Sorry, man, he just wants Zoe." Blake put a hand on Cole's shoulder.

"Sorry," she said with a weak smile. "I'm sure whatever it is won't take long. Why don't you go hang out in the common room, get to know some people? I'll come find you when we're done."

"Yeah, sure," Cole said, not even trying to keep the hurt from his voice. Guilt churned in Zoe's stomach, and for a second, she wondered if she should let him come with her, but she really could use a break from him. Besides, Pearson probably had a good reason for not wanting Cole there.

She watched Cole make his way up the steps. "Thanks for the save," she said once Cole was out of sight.

"Trouble in paradise?" Blake asked with a smirk. Zoe

remembered him saying the same thing the first time she had asked him to meet her at her apartment. That felt like a lifetime ago.

"I wouldn't call this paradise." She made her way up the stairs and to the dining commons with Blake in tow. The room was empty when they arrived except for one large table where Pearson, Shane, Mark, Allissa, Dottie, Floyd, Iris, and Ian were waiting for them. Zoe's anxiety melted away the moment her eyes locked on Ian's.

She took the empty seat at the head of the table next to him. "Hi," she said softly.

"Hey." Ian didn't meet her eyes, and it broke her heart.

At the other end of the table, Pearson rose to his feet. "As the original members of this community, there's something we need to discuss."

"Which is—?" Ian turned away from Zoe to give Pearson his full attention.

"The very real possibility that the Arrows will come for our newest arrivals."

"Do you think that could really happen?" Mark asked.

Everyone turned to look at Zoe. "There is a very good chance Alana thinks Cole is dead, in which case I doubt she'd be out looking for him." Zoe hadn't shared what Cole told her about his escape, and she hoped he would forgive her for sharing it now. She wouldn't do it if the safety of her people wasn't at risk.

"Why would she think that?" Iris asked.

"The night Cole was finally able to escape, he was supposed to be executed." Zoe looked at Mark. "Adam was ordered to do it, but he couldn't go through with it."

"Alana ordered her own son to be executed? Why?" Shane asked.

Zoe shrugged. "I guess he was causing too many problems. She needs to maintain power, and the only way she can do that is to keep people from opposing her, even if it's her own children."

"What do you think she's going to do when she realizes they aren't dead? They must have suspected something when Adam didn't return to his post," Pearson said.

"I have no idea. I used to think I knew them, but not anymore. They're insane. There's no telling what they will do."

"It's a good thing you let them stay, then," Ian said. "Their presence is putting everyone at risk."

"Ian, that's not fair," Iris said.

"Maybe not, but it's the truth."

"Are you asking me to tell Cole and Jackson to leave? Because if that's the case, you know I'll have to go with them." Zoe wanted to be mad at Ian, but part of her knew it was true.

"Why would you have to leave?" Ian said.

"Because I'm as much of a risk to this community as they are. Maybe more so. It's no secret Alana wants me dead."

"Zoe, you know that's the last thing I want," Ian said softly.

"I don't think we need to jump to that extreme yet," Pearson said. "But we need to put together a plan for how we're going to handle it if the Arrows show up. Alana Wilborn has the force of the US military on her side. We can't match that kind of firepower."

"What do you suggest we do?" Blake asked.

"You need to talk to Cole and Jackson," Pearson said to Zoe. "Find out what they know about the Arrows' plans and if they would be willing to give themselves up to save the rest of the community. It might be the only chance we have."

"I can't do that. Alana will kill them."

"Even if it means people here will die?" Ian asked.

Zoe looked away. She couldn't give Cole up now that she had him back, even if his hovering was driving her crazy. "There has to be another way."

"Talk to them, see what information they have, then we can work on putting together a plan," Pearson said. "Until then, I want to set up a watch at the town's entrances and start getting as many people ready to fight as we can."

"Fine," Zoe said as everyone at the table nodded and got up. Ian was halfway to the door before Zoe realized their meeting had ended. She jumped up and ran after him. "Ian, wait."

He stopped in the hallway. "What is it?" he said with his back still toward her.

"Will you just look at me?"

Ian sighed, then turned around. "There. Now what do you need?"

"You haven't spoken to me in days. I miss you."

"You have a funny way of showing it. Every time I see you, he's right by your side."

"Cole's still adjusting to life here. He doesn't know anyone else."

Ian crossed his arms. "He knows there was something going on between us, doesn't he?"

"Yes. I told him his first morning here. I didn't think it was fair to keep it from him."

"That's why he won't leave you alone. He's making sure I know that I can't have you."

"He doesn't get to decide who I spend my time with," Zoe snapped. She thought Ian knew her better than that.

"That makes it worse because it means you chose him over me."

"I didn't choose anything. I have no idea how I feel, and it's been difficult to figure out when Cole won't give me a second alone to think and you won't talk to me."

Ian ran a hand through his hair. "I thought staying away would make it easier on everyone. I wanted to give you space to figure out what you wanted without pressuring you. Then again, I hoped Cole would do the same thing, but clearly he took a different approach."

"No kidding," Zoe said with a small smile. "I wish there was a simple answer. One where no one got hurt."

Ian gently pulled her into a hug. "I know."

Zoe relaxed as Ian rubbed her back, resting her head against his chest and breathing in his scent. She had missed him so much. She wasn't ready to give him up.

Out of the corner of her eye, she saw Jackson watching them from down the hall. Gently, she pulled away from Ian as a wave of guilt washed over her. Why did it always feel like she was cheating on one of them?

Jackson shook his head and slipped away. She wondered if she should go after him and try to explain, but she wasn't sure she had it in her. Besides, this didn't involve Jackson. This was something she needed to figure out for herself before someone got hurt to the point that it couldn't be repaired.

«‹›»

It had been two days since their meeting, and Zoe still hadn't found the right way to broach the subject with Cole. The only good thing to come from the meeting was that Ian was talking to her again, though it wasn't like it was before. He was distant and tended to treat her like she was a coworker, but at this point, she would take whatever she could get.

She had spent the day with Allissa's team in the greenhouse, repotting seedlings. It was a nice break from Cole's hovering and gave her some space to think. Not that it did any good. She still had no idea what to do about Ian and Cole. When she finally made it back to the dorms that evening, she had more questions than answers.

She got cleaned up and headed to the dining commons, which was full by that point. She grabbed a bowl of venison stew Floyd had made from the deer that Mark's hunting party had brought back and went to find a place to sit. There was an open seat next to Ian. She started to head in that direction when she saw Cole and Jackson sitting alone in the back corner of the room.

It had never been clearer that they were having a hard time adjusting to life here, and Zoe felt like she was partly to blame for that. People had gotten used to seeing her and Ian together, and they were loyal to him. It didn't help that everyone knew they were Wilborns, and there was a level of apprehension that came with that. On some level, people were afraid of them, even though they had done nothing to warrant it.

Zoe walked over to them and sat down next Cole. She glanced across the room to make sure Ian wasn't looking, then kissed Cole on the cheek. "How was your day?"

"It wasn't bad. We spent most of the day getting the room organized," Cole said.

"I'm sure it's a lot different from what you're used to. Did you ever live in the dorms when we went here?" Zoe and Cole had started dating during his junior year, and at the time, he had been living with a few friends in a house off campus.

"No," Cole said between bites of stew. "My parents bought that house when I decided to go here."

"Of course they did," Zoe said with a small laugh. They used to joke all the time about his disconnect from the real world thanks to his family's wealth, but it didn't feel natural anymore. "Anyway, I've been meaning to talk to you both about your parents."

"What about them?" Jackson didn't look at her as he spoke. He played with the food in his bowl, his entire posture absolutely miserable. Zoe had no idea how to help him, and what she was about to say wasn't going to improve his mood.

She had to choose her words carefully.

"There's some concern that once they realize Adam didn't follow through on your execution, they'll come looking for you . . . and I'm worried about what kind of force they'll use once they find you here."

Cole set down his spoon and looked at Zoe. "You think they might try to kill the people here to get to us?"

"I do," Zoe said, not meeting his eye.

"Don't you pose a bigger risk to the people here than we do?" Jackson asked. "Mom thinks we're dead, but she still has people searching for you."

Zoe didn't have an answer. She glanced across the room, and her eyes instantly locked on Ian's. He was watching her intently, probably waiting to see if she needed any backup. "I guess."

"Then maybe the three of us should leave together. That way, you can protect the people here. Unless you're not willing to leave your new boyfriend behind," Jackson said.

"Jackson, don't," Cole scolded.

"Oh, come on. Why do we have to pretend that she's not cheating on you with that criminal? I saw the two of you hugging the other day, out in the open for anyone to see. You don't even have the decency to hide it."

"It's not like that," Zoe said, but her voice lacked conviction.

"This doesn't concern you, Jackson," Cole said through gritted teeth. "Let it go."

"Hey, you don't want my help, that's fine." Jackson jumped to his feet, knocking his chair over as he did, and stormed out of the dining hall. Across the room, Ian started to rise to his feet; Zoe gave him a weak smile and nodded. Slowly, he sank back into his chair.

"I'm sorry about him," Cole said. "He hasn't been the same since our first escape attempt. Being locked up in that basement messed him up."

"He's not wrong, though. I know my being here is a risk to everyone else. I know I should leave, but I can't . . . and I can't ask you to leave either."

Cole gently grabbed her chin and tilted her face up to his. "I love you, Zoe. That's the only thing that matters to me. We'll figure out the rest of it."

"I love you too." She kissed him. She had to make him understand how hard all of this was for her. She wanted to believe they could find a way forward where she wouldn't lose anyone, but deep down she knew that wasn't possible.

"And you know that if it comes down to it, I'll do whatever I can to help you protect the people here. Even if that means handing myself over to the Arrows."

"I don't want to lose you, Cole." Tears rolled down her cheeks, and she didn't try to stop them.

Cole gently brushed the tears away. "Then let's pray it doesn't come to that."

Zoe nodded, pressing his hand to her cheek. One way or another, she would find a way to keep him safe without sacrificing the people here.

«Chapter 23»»

After a tense dinner with Zoe, Cole went to find Jackson. He appreciated his loyalty, but that didn't mean Cole was fine with Jackson disrespecting Zoe.

Cole wasn't surprised to find Jackson sulking in their shared room. "Why did you go after Zoe like that?"

Jackson glared at Cole. "Are you serious? You went through hell to get here, to be with her, only to find out that she replaced you with the man who kidnapped her. I think the real question is why aren't *you* pissed at her too?"

"Zoe didn't replace me," Cole said with a lot less conviction than he had when he walked in.

"Oh, really?" Jackson rolled his eyes.

"It's more complicated than that." Cole ran his hand through his hair. "Zoe and I are trying to work through it, and you're not helping."

"I don't know why I came here," Jackson said, throwing up his hands.

"Because Mom was going to have us executed if we stayed."

Jackson shook his head. "No, she was going to have *you* executed, not me. I would have been perfectly safe staying there and minding my own business."

"You were a prisoner. Do you really think that's better than being here?"

"Maybe. At least there we had real beds and decent food."

"You can't be serious," Cole said. "You'd rather go back to living under Mom's thumb while she takes over the world if it means you get a bigger bed?"

"I don't know how this conversation became about me. It's Zoe you should be mad at. I've had your back this whole time. She couldn't even wait a few months for you to get away. I'm trying to protect you."

"Well, stop. I'm an adult, Jackson. Zoe and I can work through this without you."

Jackson threw his hands up again. "Fine, but don't come crying to me when this blows up in your face."

Cole sighed. "I know coming here has been harder than either of us expected, but we need to make this our home. Have you even tried to get to know anyone else here?"

Jackson turned away from Cole.

"That's what I thought. Let's go down to the common room, have a drink, and try to get to know some of the people. Maybe you'll start to feel better once you do."

"Fine," Jackson said.

They went back downstairs to the common room, where Zoe was sitting with Iris, Dillion, Blake, and right next to her on the couch was Ian. They were laughing like they didn't have a care in the world.

Cole faltered. He had just told Jackson to let it go, but he had no idea if he could follow his own advice.

He took a deep breath and headed over to them. In his old life, he used to lead meetings with the heads of several manufacturing plants. He had earned their respect. How hard could it be to do the same thing with this group of people?

"Is it all right if we join you?" Cole's eyes flicked from Zoe to Ian.

"Of course." Zoe moved closer to Ian to make room for Cole on her other side.

Ian got to his feet. "I think I'll go get a drink. Anyone want anything?"

"Sit back down, I can get them," Jackson offered with an overly large smile. Awkwardly, Ian sat back down, though he didn't retake his seat next to Zoe; instead, he perched on the arm of the couch. It did nothing to ease the palpable tension.

"How are you settling in?" Dillon asked as he gently stroked Iris's back.

"It's been an adjustment." Cole's eyes shifted to Ian for a moment. "But we're figuring things out. It might help if we had something to do."

"I can add you to the work rotation," Zoe offered.

"Here you go, man." Jackson was back with two drinks. He handed one to Ian, then raised the other to toast him. Ian mirrored his movement, but instead of taking a sip, he set the glass down on the table next to him.

"I've been thinking about our attempts to increase security, and I remembered they used to fire off a cannon at the football games every time Central scored," Zoe said. Cole wondered if she was trying to break the tension in the air.

"They were firing blanks, you know," Cole teased.

"I am aware." The annoyance in her tone shocked him. He had meant it as a joke; she had never minded when he poked fun at her before. "I thought we could use it as a way for our lookouts to warn us that someone was coming."

"It's a good idea," Ian said. "Any idea where they kept it?"

"The ROTC operated out of Finch Fieldhouse on the other side of campus," Cole said as a peace offering.

"I can take a group over there tomorrow and see what we can find," Blake said. He reached over and picked up Ian's drink, taking a long sip.

Out of the corner of his eye, Cole saw Jackson stiffen. He was about to ask him what was wrong when Blake started to convulse in his chair. The glass fell from his hand and spilled on the floor.

"Blake," Zoe whispered next to him.

Dillion was by Blake's side in an instant, his fingers searching his neck for a pulse. "Come on Blake, hang in there, bud. Ian, help me get him flat."

Carefully, Ian and Dillion lifted Blake's limp body out of the chair and onto the floor.

"It doesn't look like he's breathing," Iris said with tears in her eyes. Zoe pulled Iris close, looking at Cole in desperation. He wished there was something he could to do ease the pain that was etched on her face.

"I can't find a pulse," Dillion said. "I'm starting CPR." He pinched Blake's nose and breathed into his mouth.

Ian started on chest compressions. "Come on, Blake."

Dillion breathed into Blake's mouth again. Cole sat frozen as he watched them go back and forth until he lost count.

"Damn it, Blake, wake up," Ian muttered as he compressed Blake's chest.

Dillion breathed into Blake's mouth again, then took his pulse. "He's gone." Dillion touched Ian's arm as he was giving another round of chest compressions. "We can't bring him back."

"No!" Ian shook Dillion's hand off him. "We have to! He can't die."

Zoe released Iris and knelt down next to Ian, pulling him into her arms and holding him as he cried against her. Cole took a step back to give them some space. Blake had told him the four of them had become a family, and watching them now, he could see how true that was.

Pearson and Shane were at their side. Shane covered Blake's body with a blanket while Pearson carefully picked up the glass Blake had dropped. "That didn't look like a heart attack to me," Pearson said as he held the glass up to the light.

"No, it wasn't a heart attack," Dillion said.

"Then what was it?" Zoe asked.

"The toxin."

"Are you sure?" Iris demanded.

Dillion nodded. "I've seen it kill enough people by now to know what it looks like."

"But Blake was immune." Zoe said. "Does this mean the immunity is wearing off?"

"I don't think so." Pearson stood up. "Who gave Blake this drink?"

"It was mine." Ian helped Zoe to her feet and put his arm around her. "Jackson got it for me."

Jackson held up his hands and slowly started to back away from them. "What are you implying?"

"I think you know exactly what I'm implying. You

put something in that drink to kill me."

"Do you know how crazy that sounds?" Jackson said.

Cole turned to Jackson. "Tell me that isn't true."

"Of course it's not true!"

"Grab them both," Pearson said. The next thing Cole knew, someone had snagged his arms and twisted them behind his back.

"You can't honestly think I had something to do with this," Cole said as he tried to pull his arms free. "Zoe, tell them I didn't have anything to do with this!"

Zoe looked at Cole for a moment, then turned away, and Cole stopped fighting.

Zoe didn't believe him, and that hurt more than anything he had experienced so far.

"We need somewhere secure to hold them while we figure out what we're going to do," said Pearson.

"I know what we should do with them." Ian let go of Zoe and advanced toward Jackson with his hands balled into fists.

Pearson stepped in front of him. "You're too emotional to deal with this right now. We all are. Go cool off."

Ian glared at Jackson, then stormed off.

"We can use that room over there." Zoe pointed to the door just past the front desk. "It used to be a computer lab, there are no windows in there."

Pearson nodded. "Put Jackson in there and stage two guards outside. Bring Cole to the security office. I want to question him first."

Pearson's guard pulled them from the common room. Cole saw Zoe drop to her knees next to Blake's body as he was being led away.

«‹«›»

Zoe waited by Blake's body until Dillion had him removed from the common room. She tried to go with them—she didn't think it was right to leave Blake alone—but Dillion stopped her. She only let them leave after he assured her that nothing would happen to Blake's body. When she finally looked around, the common room was empty. Everyone must have retreated to their rooms. The last time she was alone in here was when Blake was helping her set up their Christmas wonderland.

She pushed back the memory as her emotions threatened to overtake her. She couldn't break down yet.

There were two armed men standing outside the old computer lab, and another standing with Pearson outside the small office off the lobby that he had claimed for his security team. Zoe slowly made her way over to them. As their so-called leader, she should do *something*—though she had no idea what.

Pearson met her halfway. "I'm giving Cole some time to calm down before I start questioning him. Do you want to be there when I do?"

Zoe wanted to curl up in a ball and cry, but that wasn't what was needed of her righthint now. "Yeah, I guess, but I need a little time first." She glanced back to the common room where, an hour ago, she had been sitting next to Ian, laughing at Blake's story of his last supply run where he had slipped on a patch of ice and sent several bags of potatoes sliding across the parking lot.

Pearson put a hand on her shoulder. "I saw Ian go out back. Come find me when you're ready, and we'll start the questioning."

Zoe pursed her lips, trying to fight back the tears that would overwhelm her the moment she let them start to fall. "Thanks." She headed back to the dorms, pausing outside of Ian and Blake's room. She leaned against it, wishing at any moment Blake would open it and drag her into some crazy plan that would sound insane but would bring joy and comfort to everyone around him.

But the door didn't open because Blake wasn't in there. He was cold and stiff, lying under a sheet somewhere there was no joy or comfort left.

Zoe kept walking to the end of the hall and out the back door. The cold air cut her skin. For a second, she thought about turning around and heading back inside, but then she saw him. Ian was sitting on the curb a hundred feet in front of her with his back to the building. He was hunched over, and from the movement of his shoulders, Zoe could tell he was crying.

Slowly, she made her way over to him. She sat down next to him and laid her head on his shoulder. His body tensed the moment she touched him.

"Don't." His voice was barely a whisper as he moved away from her.

"I'm sorry. I thought . . ." her voice trailed off. She didn't know what she thought. In fact, she was pretty sure she wasn't capable of any kind of thought at the moment.

"I know," Ian said without looking at her. "Just go back inside before you get anyone else hurt."

Zoe was sure she hadn't heard him right. "What do you mean?"

Ian turned to look at her. "I blame you," he said softly.

"For what?" She started to breathe heavier as the tears welled in her eyes. There would be no keeping them at bay now. In her gut, she knew what Ian meant, but she didn't want to believe it was true.

"I blame you for Blake's death. You brought us here. You convinced everyone that we should let Cole and Jackson stay. You said we could trust them. And now Blake's dead because of those decisions." His voice was calm, which scared Zoe more than if he had yelled at her.

Zoe swallowed hard. "I never wanted anything to happen to Blake. I loved him too, you know that. He was my friend. I never wanted anything bad to happen to him. You have to believe me."

Ian nodded without looking at her. "I do believe you, but it doesn't change anything. I've known Blake most of my life. He was more than my best friend, he was my brother. And now he's gone, and I know you didn't want it to happen, and I know logically I shouldn't blame you for what Jackson did, but I do. I don't want to, but I do."

"Well, if that's how you feel . . ." Zoe said slowly, trying to keep herself from sobbing.

Ian turned to look at her again. The pain in his eyes tore her apart. "It is."

"All right." Zoe slowly got to her feet, turned toward the building, and started to put one foot in front of the other. It took every ounce of concentration she had to keep herself from breaking down right there.

"Zoe," Ian said softly. She turned to look at him. "I'm sorry. I didn't want it to be like this."

"I'm sorry too." She forced herself to keep her head up until she made it back into the building and to her room. A strangled sob escaped her throat as she collapsed on her bed.

«‹‹Chapter 24»»

Zoe allowed herself to fall apart for an hour. Pearson was waiting for her before he started questioning Cole and Jackson; she didn't know if she had the strength to face any of it, but she would find a way to do it. Maybe it would give her something to focus on besides the grief that was threating to never let her go.

She sat up, tossing her tear-soaked pillow to the end of the bed. Slowly, she made her way to the bathroom. The muscles in her face were sore. A chunk of her hair was stuck to her cheek, which was completely drained of color. She splashed some cold water on her face, hoping it would reduce some of the puffiness around her eyes, and quickly ran a brush through her hair. It would have to be good enough. She tried to summon the last shards of strength she had left before heading to the lobby to find Pearson.

He got up from behind the front desk and met her. "Are you ready for this?"

"No." Zoe shook her head. "But I don't want to put it off any longer. We need to know what happened." She glanced back to the common room, her eyes lingering on the chair Blake had been lounging in a few hours ago.

"I'll handle the questioning and you can just listen, if that's easier. If you think of anything I should ask, we can always step out if you don't want to bring it up in front of Cole."

Zoe nodded. She thought telling Cole about the Arrows for the first time would be the most difficult conversation she would ever have, but right now, that seemed far easier than asking Cole about his involvement in Blake's death.

The guard standing outside what was now their security office opened the door as they approached. Cole was sitting in one of the chairs in front of the desk with his head in his hands. He looked up when they entered, but didn't say anything. Zoe fought the urge to go to him. Pearson motioned for her to take the seat behind the desk across from Cole, but she shook her head. She needed some distance if she was going to be able to do this. She leaned on the wall in the opposite corner of the small room while Pearson sat down.

"Sorry to keep you waiting," Pearson said as he took his time getting situated.

Cole looked at Zoe. "You don't really believe that I had anything to do with Blake's death, do you? Zoe, you know me better than that."

"Hey," Pearson said. "You don't get to talk to her. As this community's leader, Zoe is here to oversee the interrogation, nothing more. Leave her out of it, or things could get a lot more difficult for you."

"Okay, okay, I get it." Cole turned back to Pearson. "I'll tell you whatever you want to know. I have nothing to hide."

"Okay, good. Then let's get started. Do you know what was in the drink that killed Blake?"

"No."

"According to Ian, Jackson got the drink for him. Are you aware of any reason why Jackson might want to cause Ian harm?"

Cole shifted in his seat. He shot a quick look at Zoe before answering Pearson. "He had made a few comments about Ian and Zoe being together and that he would take care of it for me if I wanted him to. But I told him to let it go. I never asked him to go after Ian."

Zoe sucked in a breath. Ian was right — this was all her fault. Jackson had wanted to kill Ian because Zoe had feelings for him.

"Hey! Back off!"

Zoe shot Pearson a look at the shout that echoed down the hall. Someone was in trouble, and from the muffled sound of their voice, they were behind a closed door somewhere. Pearson shot to his feet and followed Zoe out of the door.

"I mean it! Stay away from me!"

That was Jackson's voice. He was supposed to be locked up alone. Zoe ran over to the guards standing outside of the room they were holding Jackson in. "Who's in there with him?"

They looked at her, confused. "Ian went in a few minutes ago. He said you all had agreed on how to handle him."

"What? No, we haven't agreed on anything," Zoe said.

"Open the door. Now!" Pearson yelled.

The guard opened the door, and Pearson rushed into the room with Zoe at his heels. Inside, Ian had Jackson pushed up against a wall with one hand, and a syringe was in his other. Zoe recognized it from the motel; she would bet that it contained the same thing Jackson had used to poison Blake.

"This guy's insane! You have to get him away from me!" Jackson said as he tried to fight his way free of Ian's grasp.

"Nobody's coming to help you," Ian said, as if he didn't even realize they were in the room with him. He held the syringe up inches from Jackson's face. "Do you see this? Your mom tried to have her assassins use this on me. I've been holding on to it since then, just in case we found a use for it. We don't know for sure what's in it, but I'm sure it's not good. How about we find out?"

"Ian, put the syringe down," Pearson said calmly.

Ian ignored him. "The problem I'm having is figuring out where to inject you. I'm afraid if I plunge it into your heart, it will kill you too quickly, and I want you to suffer. On the other hand, if I inject it in your arm, there's a chance it will take too long to have any effect, and I want to get rid of you."

"That's enough, Ian. This isn't the way," Zoe said.

"There are so many options, it's hard to decide which is best." Ian still hadn't acknowledged them. Zoe wondered if he could even hear them through his grief and the constant whimpering coming from Jackson.

She would need to do something drastic to get through to him.

With a confidence she didn't feel, Zoe grabbed Pearson's sidearm from the holster on his hip and pointed it at the side of Ian's head. "Let him go," she said through gritted teeth.

Ian turned his head a fraction of an inch, finally looking in her direction. "Zoe, what are you doing?"

"What does it look like I'm doing?"

"Be careful, it's loaded," Pearson said, but he made no move to take the gun from her.

"I'm aware of that," Zoe said as she concentrated on keeping her hand from shaking.

"Why are you trying to save him? He killed Blake."

"I don't give a shit about him," Zoe said. "I'm trying to stop you from doing something you'll regret for the rest of your life."

Ian shook his head and brought the needle up to Jackson's neck. "He deserves to die."

"I'm not disagreeing with you, but not like this. This is revenge, not justice."

"Does it really matter? The end result is the same."

"Killing Jackson won't bring Blake back," Pearson said.

"No, but it might make me feel better." He pressed the needle into Jackson's skin.

"Don't make me shoot you," Zoe said as she held the gun steady with her other hand. "Please, Ian. You're not a murderer."

Tears ran down her cheeks. This was too much to deal with so soon after Blake's death.

Ian sighed and pulled the syringe from Jackson's neck. Without saying a word, he handed it to Pearson and left.

Zoe lowered the gun and let out a breath she wasn't aware she had been holding.

"Thanks for saving my life," Jackson said as he pressed his finger to the spot the needle had just been.

Zoe pointed the gun at Jackson. "Understand, I don't care about your life. I did this because Blake wouldn't want Ian to become a murderer because of him. Your life means nothing to me. In fact, maybe I should finish what

Ian started." Her finger hovered over the trigger.

"Zoe." Pearson put his hand on her shoulder.

She lowered the gun. He wasn't worth it.

She turned to Pearson and handed him back his gun. "Lock Cole up in here tonight. I can't handle anything else right now. We can pick it up in the morning."

Pearson returned his gun to his holster. "I'll handle it. Go get some rest."

«‹‹›»

Cole was given no explanation as to what was going on as they took him from the security office and locked him in the same room as Jackson. His brother was sitting on a table with his eyes closed, pressing a tissue to his neck. Cole paced on the other side of the room, a stark contrast to the last time he was locked up with Jackson.

"Enough with the pacing, I'm trying to get some shut-eye over here," Jackson said without opening his eyes.

Cole whipped around. "Tell me why I should do anything for you after what you did."

Jackson opened his eyes and sat up straighter. "I did what I had to do."

"You killed Blake!" Cole yelled, waving his arms at Jackson in disbelief.

Jackson pointed at Cole. "To be fair, my intention was to kill Sutton."

"You say that like it makes everything better. Killing Ian would have been just as bad as killing Blake."

"Would it, though? Or would it have solved all of your problems?" Jackson raised an eyebrow at him.

Cole put his hands on his head. He couldn't believe what Jackson was saying. This wasn't the same person he had grown up with. "I'm not thrilled about the Ian and Zoe situation, but I never wanted him dead. When did you become so cavalier about murder? I remember you freaking out when you hit a bird while driving, and now you're going around poisoning peoples' drinks?"

"The world is a different place now. We have to look out for ourselves."

Cole shook his head and turned away. Those weren't Jackson's words coming out of his mouth. Someone had put them there, and Cole had a sinking suspicion who. The question was, did he really want to know?

"What did you put in that drink?" he finally asked.

Jackson smirked. "A super concentrated dose of the Arrows' toxin. Strong enough that no amount of built-up immunity could stop it."

Cole froze. His blood turned to ice as Jackson confirmed his worst fears. This was bigger than his older brother taking extreme measures to protect him from heartbreak. In fact, Cole doubted this actually had anything to do with him at all.

"Where did you get a concentrated does of the Arrows' toxin?" Cole's words were evenly measured as he tried to keep his rising panic under control.

"Mom gave it to me before we left." Jackson got off the table and walked over to Cole. "I'm sorry to break it to you, but this whole thing — the escape, coming here — it was all a setup to lead the Arrows to Zoe."

Cole stumbled backward until he bumped against a table. "No," he said, shaking his head. "That can't be true. What about the execution order? Adam said that was real."

"It was and it wasn't."

"What does that mean?"

"The order was real, but we were pretty sure Adam

wouldn't go through with it. Especially after all the time you spent helping him. Mom needed you to think that you had escaped without her knowing. We couldn't risk you thinking the Arrows were following you, or else you might not have led us to Zoe."

Cole's head spun. How had he not seen that he was getting played? He had put everyone here in danger. He had put Zoe in danger. "But there wasn't an execution order for you. How did you get Adam to bring you with us? Was he in on it?"

"No, he wasn't, so I had to make sure he knew that I wanted to get away too. It was a risk, but it all worked out."

"What about the first escape attempt? Mom knew exactly where to wait for me. That was a setup too, wasn't it?"

Jackson nodded. "Mom thought if you saw how pointless trying to get away was, you would give up and start supporting the family again. She underestimated your sense of self-preservation, or lack thereof."

"This can't be happening," Cole muttered to himself. He turned back to Jackson. "How long have you been an Arrow?"

"I wouldn't say I'm officially an Arrow. It's not like I took some kind of blood oath or anything, but I've been helping Mom and Dad with their plans since I got back from Kentucky."

"But I thought you let Zoe go."

"I did, but Dad and I had a long talk on the drive back. He made me see how Zoe and her friends are a threat to everything Mom and Dad are trying to create. That she's a threat to the safety of our family."

"You're insane." Cole started to pace again. How had he missed the fact that his brother had betrayed him?

"I'm not the one whose fiancée locked him up for no reason," Jackson countered.

"No reason? You killed Blake!"

Jackson closed the gap between them. "And they all think you had something to do with it. That's why you're in here with me. But don't worry; as usual, I have your back. We just have to hold out a few days."

All the color drained from Cole's face. "What are you going to do?"

Jackson took a step back and held up his hands. "I'm not going to do anything. But when I miss my check-in with Mom tomorrow morning, she'll know I've been discovered. You know how protective Mom and Dad are. They'll come get us. Mom's army has been on standby since we got here."

Cole rushed at the door, banging against it with his fist. "I need to talk to Zoe!" He had spent enough time as a prisoner lately that he knew there would be a guard of some kind on the other side who would be able to hear him. "Please, it's important. I need to talk to Zoe. Now!"

Cole tried to open the door, but it was locked. He kept banging on it instead, praying that the guard on the other side would eventually get annoyed and give in to his demands.

When the door finally opened, it wasn't Zoe on the other side. Pearson filled the doorway, looking more pissed than Cole had ever seen him. "You're not going to see Zoe, so whatever you have to say, you can say it to me."

Cole weighed his options. He had no idea if Pearson would believe him or not, but if he didn't tell someone, they'd all be killed.

He took a deep breath. "The Arrows are coming."

«‹«‹›»›»

Zoe sat on her bed, her body wrapped around her legs as she cried into her knees. It had been dark outside when she sat down, but now a soft light shone through the cracks in the curtain. Her eyes were sore and heavy. She hadn't slept. How could she, when everything was such a mess? People would be looking to her for guidance on what to do now, but she had no idea what to tell them.

Someone knocked gently on the door, but she didn't have the strength to get up. She wasn't surprised when the door opened a few seconds later; she looked up, hoping to see Ian, but it was Shane standing in the doorway.

"Mind if I come in?" He didn't wait for an answer before walking over and sitting down on the bed next to her. "How are you holding up?"

"I'm not," she confessed as she slowly unfolded her body and stretched her stiff muscles.

"That's understandable."

"Especially since this is all my fault." She didn't meet his eyes as the words left her mouth.

"Who said that?" Shane asked. Zoe cocked an eyebrow at him in response. "I see. Then let me tell you that Ian is wrong. None of this is your fault. You didn't do anything differently welcoming Cole and Jackson into this community than you did for everyone else here."

Zoe laughed weakly. "That's not true. I never should have let them in. If I had told them to leave, Blake would still be alive."

"It's not that simple, and we both know it," Shane said as he gently rubbed her back. "Toby questioned them and didn't think there was anything to be concerned about. Sometimes people betray you, it's part of life. The only person to blame for Blake's death is Jackson."

"I really want to believe that," Zoe said as she brushed away the tears on her cheeks.

"Then believe it. Now, I hate to ask, but Toby needs to talk to you. He says it's important. Do you think you can handle it?"

Zoe took a deep breath. "Doesn't sound like I have a choice." She stretched her legs again as she got off the bed. "Thank you."

Shane wrapped Zoe in a hug. "Any time. We all care about you. You know that, right? This is a family now, and you're the heart of that."

Zoe nodded against his chest as she gathered her courage. When she felt ready, she released him and followed him over to Thorpe Hall.

"Why are we meeting over here?" Bile filled her gut as she walked into the room. Meeting away from the rest of the community had to be a bad sign.

"I didn't want anyone to accidently overhear us," Pearson said from the common room. Ian and Iris were sitting on a couch near him, looking as bad as she felt. Cole stood off to the side.

Zoe looked from Ian to Cole before taking a seat in an armchair. She wanted them both, and since she couldn't have that, she would choose neither.

"I know this is the last thing any of you want to be dealing with right now," Pearson started, "but I don't think it can wait." He turned to Cole. "Tell them what you told me."

"After you locked me up with Jackson," Cole started, annoyance heavy in his voice, "he confessed that he's been working with my parents since they found you in

Kentucky. He's been in contact with them the whole time we've been here. I swear, I had no idea. I thought he wanted to escape just like I did, but it was all a ploy to get me to lead the Arrows to you." Cole looked at Zoe with pain in his eyes.

"Wait." Ian shifted in his seat. "Are you saying the Arrows are coming here?"

"Yes. According to Jackson, he's supposed to check in with them sometime this morning. When that doesn't happen, the Arrows will start making their way here."

"Fuck," Ian said, running his hands through his hair and looking at Zoe. "You fucking led the Arrows right to us!"

"How dare you blame her?" Cole snapped.

Zoe jumped to her feet and held her hands up between them. "Don't. Fighting right now wouldn't do any good."

Ian rose his feet as well, taking a few steps closer to Cole. "You don't get a say in this. It might have been Zoe's emotions that got in the way of her better judgment, but as much as I blame her for Blake's death, I blame you more."

"Ian," Iris scolded.

"Enough." Zoe took a step closer to Ian. "You can blame me all you want later, but right now we need to figure out what we're going to do."

"There's only one thing we *can* do," Iris said, looking around the group. "We need to leave. All of us."

"Where are we going to go?" Shane asked. "It's freezing out there, and there's no way to know where else we can get power. I can't imagine walking away from everything we've built here."

"If we don't, the Arrows will kill us. It's the only choice we have," Iris said. "If we go now, we'll have a decent head start. They won't know where to look for us next."

"I'm not leaving," Zoe said, her voice even.

"What do you mean you're not leaving?" It was the nicest thing Ian had said to her since Blake died.

"We all knew the Arrows were likely to show up eventually. Isn't that why you asked me to talk to Cole and Jackson about turning themselves over to Alana to save the people here?" Zoe said to Pearson.

"Yes, but—"

"There are no buts. We can all pretend that the Arrows will leave us alone, but the truth no one wants to admit is that Alana Wilborn wants me dead, and she won't stop until it's done. If I leave, it might buy me some time, but rest assured we'll end up right back where we are now. So, I'm staying, and I'll have it out with her once and for all."

"Zoe, you can't," Cole said.

"Yes, I can."

"We need to talk about this," Ian said, desperation bright in his eyes. He might have spent the last several hours blaming her, pushing her away, but she knew that no matter what, he still loved her.

"This isn't up for discussion. Staying is my decision. Everyone else needs to decide what's best for them."

"When should we tell the rest of the community?" Pearson asked.

Zoe glanced at the sun rising through the windows. "We'll gather everyone in the dining commons for breakfast in a few hours. I'll tell them everything then."

Zoe got up and walked back to her room. The only thing left to do was to find the right words to convince everyone to save themselves while she stayed behind to face the Arrows on her own.

«Chapter 25»

Zoe knew she should try to get some sleep before she had to address the whole community, but every time she closed her eyes, a fresh wave of guilt threatened to consume her. So instead, she sat at her desk and attempted to write a speech that would convince everyone to leave behind everything they had built here.

Two hours later, all she had was a pile of crumpled paper and a new sense of guilt for wasting the community's resources.

Frustrated, she headed to the dining commons. People would start trickling in for breakfast soon, and she would need coffee if she hoped to put a coherent thought together. She made her way back to the kitchen where Dottie and Floyd were busy getting breakfast ready.

"How are you, sweetheart?" Dottie wrapped Zoe in a hug that almost made her break down on the spot.

"I've been better," she said with a weak smile.

Floyd handed her a cup of coffee. "It'll get better, just give it time."

"Thanks. Could you do me a favor?"

"Anything," Dottie said.

"Can you go through the food stock and put together some care packages for everyone? Things that would be easy to eat on the go. Enough to last for, like, a week."

"Why? What's changed?" Floyd asked.

Zoe had assumed Pearson would have filled his parents in after their meeting last night. "I'll tell you once everyone gets here." She didn't have the strength to say it more than once.

She wandered out to the dining room and sat down at a small corner table to wait for everyone to arrive. Slowly, the room started to fill. Iris came over and sat down across from her. "Are you sure you want to go through with this?"

Zoe nodded. "I am."

"I hope this isn't because Ian is being a colossal ass right now because that's just what he does when he's hurting. He pushes people away thinking that will make it hurt less, which of course, it doesn't. He misses Blake, and he's taking it out on you."

"We all miss Blake," Zoe said.

"I know, and I promise I'm not trying to make excuses for Ian. I just don't want you thinking that you have to face the Arrows alone as some way to atone because none of this is your fault, no matter what my asshole brother says."

"This doesn't have anything to do with Ian. As long as the Arrows want me dead, I'm putting everyone at risk. The only chance they have is if I stay while the rest of you go."

"You're not the only one the Arrows want dead," Iris

said.

"I know, but I'm sure I'm at the top of Alana's list."

Pearson made his way over to them. "Everyone's here."

Zoe nodded and got to her feet. "Excuse me, can I have everyone's attention?" she said, even though no one was really talking. "There's something you need to know. We have reason to believe that the Arrows are on their way here. Jackson Wilborn, whom I believed we could trust, has betrayed us. He's been in communication with the Arrows since he arrived. He killed Blake for them." Zoe paused as a wave of tears threatened to overtake her. She needed to stay strong. She scanned the crowd, hoping for a sign of reassurance from Ian, something to give her the strength to keep going. Instead, her eyes settled on Cole, who was standing alone in the back of the room. She smiled at him weakly. "We can't know for certain what the Arrows want, but I doubt it's going to be a friendly visit. I will be staying here to face them, but I don't expect anyone else to do the same. You need to do what's best for you and your family. I don't know how long we have before they arrive. I suggest everyone starts getting ready to leave now. I've asked Floyd and Dottie to get some provisions ready."

"Where are we supposed to go?" Mark asked.

"I don't know," Zoe said.

Elijah stood up. "Why should you stay and face them alone? We have numbers here. We can protect you. Whatever we do, we should all stay together." People nodded throughout the room.

"I wish it was that easy, but it's not. The Arrows have been after me since this all started. If I go with you, I'll be putting everyone at risk. I can't do that any longer.

Staying here to face them is the best way I can protect all of you. This community is the greatest thing I have ever been a part of, and I won't let it be destroyed when I can do something to save it. I love you all."

Unable to hold back the tears, Zoe slowly made her way out of the dining commons. People reached out and squeezed her hand as she passed. Andre ran over and hugged her so tight, she was afraid he would crack her rib cage. She couldn't stop the tears as she pried his arms from around her and all but sprinted back to her room. Closing the door, she slid down it to the floor and allowed the tears to overtake her.

«‹›»

Cole had no idea if Zoe wanted to see him or not, but he couldn't leave her alone. He had seen a side of her today that he had never seen before, and it made him love her even more than he already did. He wondered if she had any idea the effect she had on people. The people here would follow her to the ends of the earth if she asked them to.

Iris let him into their room, and he gently knocked on the door to Zoe's bedroom. "It's me. Can I come in?" he asked softly.

From behind the door came a sound like someone getting up off the floor. A moment later, the door opened. "Hi," Zoe said meekly as she stepped aside to let him in.

Cole pulled her into his arms and held her. "Are you all right?"

"Why does everyone keep asking me that when it's very clear that I'm not?" Zoe said against his chest.

"I guess even in the apocalypse, we can't let go of

some social norms." Cole stroked her hair.

Zoe pulled away and looked him in the eyes. "I'm sorry I let them lock you up. I should have known that you had nothing to do with Blake's death. I wasn't thinking clearly."

"It's okay." Cole leaned down and kissed her. "You did what you thought was right at the time. I'm not mad. If I were in your shoes, I probably would have done the same thing. You have to do what's best for the people here, regardless of your own feelings. That's what being a leader is, and you are an amazing leader, Zoe. The people here are lucky to have you."

"You don't have to say that just to make me feel better."

"I'm not. I mean every word. Besides, if you hadn't locked me up with Jackson, we might not have found out about the Arrows until it was too late."

Zoe walked over to her desk and grabbed a few tissues. "Have people started to leave yet?" She rubbed the tissues over her eyes in a vain attempt to erase the evidence of her tears.

"Zoe, no one is leaving," Cole said. "After you left, everyone started talking. They don't think they can find somewhere to resettle that's better than this. They're as invested in this community as you are, and they aren't willing to give it up. They want to stand with you when you face the Arrows."

"They can't!" Zoe said desperately. "Alana will kill everyone here, we both know that. You have to help me convince everyone to leave. I can't be responsible for any more deaths."

Cole's heart broke at the panic in her eyes. He gently took her face in his hands and looked her in the eye. "You are not responsible for any deaths. The people here love you, and they want to help you. You need to let them. They know the risks, and they've decided to stay anyway. They know what you've built here is worth fighting for. Come and see."

Cole took her hand and led her out to the common room. People rushed past them carrying mattresses to block the floor-to-ceiling windows. Piles of furniture were positioned near the doors to barricade them if needed. Pearson was at the front desk, organizing and distributing their weapons. Adam was with him, discussing defensive strategy.

Zoe stopped and looked at Cole. "It's not going to be enough."

"You don't know that. I have to believe that there's a way to get through to my mother. If anyone can make her see reason, it's you, and if it comes down to it, use Jackson and me as leverage."

"I won't hand you over to Alana just so she can follow through on her execution order."

"I'm not sure how real that actually was. Jackson confessed that it was all part of their plan to get me to lead the Arrows here. I don't think she wanted me killed. It was just her twisted way of manipulating me."

"I don't think you're making the case you think you are," Zoe said with a smirk. Cole watched as she scanned the room. He could almost see the gears turning in her mind as she assessed the situation. "I hope this works."

Cole squeezed her hand. "Me too."

Zoe wrapped her arms around him and pulled him close. "I would be so lost without you right now. Thank you for still being here for me after everything I've put you through. I really don't deserve you."

Cole tilted her head up to his and kissed her. "There's nothing I wouldn't I do for you, Zoe Antos."

«Chapter 26»»

It was nearly dusk as Zoe made her way out and into the cold. They had spent most of the day trying to prepare for the Arrows' arrival, but this was far more important.

She followed the line of people out the front door to a patch of grass surrounded by a few pine trees. The ground was freshly turned, and a body wrapped in a sheet was gently being lowered down into the hole.

Blake deserved better. He deserved a real funeral with flowers and a room packed with mourners. He deserved to be buried in a casket with an elaborate headstone to mark his final resting place. But they couldn't give him any of that. At least the trees blocked some of the wind as the snow and sleet began to fall from the sky.

Ian and Iris stood off to one side, while Zoe and Cole stood on the other. They watched in silence as their friends covered Blake's body with dirt. Zoe wanted to go to Ian, to take his hand and try to comfort him, but he wouldn't want that; so instead she stayed where she was, clutching Cole's arm for support as her tears froze to her cheeks.

Once the hole was filled, Nina and Gemma stepped forward with a bouquet of paper flowers that they placed on the grave. "Goodbye, Blake, we'll miss you. You looked like an adult, but you always acted like a kid. I wish more adults were like that," Nina said, and Zoe cried even harder.

Blake had touched the lives of everyone here. How were they ever going to get through this without him?

One by one, people stepped forward to say their final goodbyes until Zoe, Cole, Ian, and Iris were the only ones left. Zoe let go of Cole's hand and forced herself to step forward. She looked up at the sky and took a deep breath, letting the snow fall on her face. "I'm so sorry, Blake," she said through her tears. "I never wanted anyone to get hurt, and I wish every second that it had been me instead of you. But since I can't change what happened, I promise I'll live every day of my life trying to make the world a more joyful place. Like you did. We didn't know each other for very long, but it always felt like we had been friends our whole lives. You were the first one to accept me and make me feel welcome. Well, except for that one time you threatened to kill me." Zoe let out a small laugh. "But even then, you were only trying to keep the people you loved safe. I will miss you every moment of every day."

She let out a sob and turned away from the grave; she needed to give Ian and Iris space to say their goodbyes in private. She reached out for Cole's hand, and they started the slow walk back to the building.

They were halfway there when a boom resonated

through the air.

"Was that a cannon blast?" Zoe turned toward the football stadium.

"Yeah," Cole said. "Shane took some people to get it after breakfast."

She looked toward Blake's grave, where Ian and Iris were running toward her. "The Arrows are here," Ian said.

"No. It can't be. It's too soon." Panic lanced through Zoe's body.

"Alana must have been waiting nearby," Cole said, looking down the empty street.

"We were supposed to have more time." Zoe whispered in disbelief.

"We need to get inside." Ian gently grabbed her arm and turned her back toward the entrance of the building.

"How long do you think we have?" Zoe struggled to keep up with Ian and Cole, who both seemed intent on dragging her into the building.

"Not long," Iris said. Zoe glanced down the road, where she could make out a line of headlights coming toward them.

Pearson was holding the door open for them and locked it the moment they were inside. "Here," he handed guns to Ian, Zoe, and Iris.

"What do we do now?" Zoe asked as she adjusted her grip on the gun. She hadn't had to carry it for a while now, and it took her a moment to remember what Pearson had taught her.

"We wait and see what they want." Ian stationed himself by the door.

Zoe turned to Cole. "You need to stay out of sight. I don't want anyone to see you yet."

Cole nodded and retreated to the common room,

where most of the community had gathered. If the Arrows decided to attack, everyone could be lost in minutes.

"Allissa," Zoe called. "Take the kids through the dining commons and hide in Sweeney Hall. It's the farthest away from here. If something happens, get them out. Take Mark and Adam with you."

They all nodded and quickly gathered all the kids and ran through the building. At least they had a shot at staying safe.

"Here we go," Iris said from the door.

Two black SUVs had pulled up in front of the building. At least it didn't appear they had brought any heavy artillery with them. Soldiers got out of the cars, followed by Alana and Gordon. One of the soldiers handed Alana a bullhorn.

"Zoe, I know you're in there. Come out. I want to talk to you." Alana's amplified voice shook the glass in the windows.

Zoe moved toward the door, but Pearson stopped her. "If you go out there, she could kill you before you even have a chance to say anything."

"What else do you suggest we do? Are you really ready to open fire and start a war with the Arrows? How much do you want to bet that they have the full force of the military waiting just out of sight in case we don't play along? I have to do this."

Pearson sighed. "Then I'm coming with you."

"Me too," Ian said.

Zoe nodded. She really didn't want either of them to risk their lives for her, but she didn't know if she had the strength to do this alone. She turned to Iris. "No matter what happens out there, don't let Cole get out. I want them to think that we're holding Cole and Jackson prisoner. It might be the best chance we have."

Iris nodded. "You got it. Be safe, Zoe." She pulled Zoe in for a quick hug, then did the same to Pearson and Ian, surprising them all.

"I'm waiting, Zoe," Alana said. "And the longer I have to wait, the worse this will be for everyone."

Zoe took a deep breath and nodded to the two men guarding the doors to open them.

She walked out with her head held high. She didn't want Alana to know how terrified she was. Ian and Pearson walked on either side of her, each with a rifle in their hands. "Alana," Zoe said coolly once she reached her.

"Zoe, I'd say it was nice to see you, but we'd both know I was lying. I wanted to try to move past that day in the control room, but you keep causing problems. I can't let it go on any longer." Alana looked the same as Zoe remembered: perfectly tailored power suit with hair pulled back into a tight bun. Even her makeup was immaculate. The only change Zoe noticed was the vindictive smirk on Alana's lips, and it terrified her.

Ian stepped forward. "Tell me why I shouldn't put a bullet in your head right now and end this once and for all." He raised his gun. Alana didn't even flinch.

"You could, but my snipers would kill Zoe before I even hit the ground, and then my army would kill everyone here. I don't think you want that much blood on your hands, Mr. Sutton, so why don't you lower your weapon?"

Zoe touched Ian's arm, and reluctantly, he lowered the barrel of the rifle.

"What do you want, Alana?" They needed to get to the point before the reserve of courage Zoe had somehow tapped into was depleted.

"I want you to hand yourself over to me to be tried for your crimes and promptly executed. As for your little community here, they will be given the choice to relocate to one of our resettlement colonies or be charged as traitors."

"Why would I agree to any of that?"

"Because you know you can't win. You can try to fight back, but that would only result in more death." Alana glanced over at Blake's grave. "How many more of your friends do you want to die because of you?"

Ian launched forward, but Pearson grabbed the back of his shirt, preventing him from reaching Alana. For a second, Zoe wondered what would happen if they really did try to kill Alana right now. Would her soldiers really follow through and kill everyone? Zoe wished she had some way of knowing if Alana was bluffing.

"You have the rest of the world," Zoe said. "Why can't you let us have this little piece of it? Is what we're doing here really that much of a threat? No one even knows we're here."

"Believe me, I'd love to move forward pretending you don't exist but unfortunately, I can't. Until you pay for what you've done, the other Arrows won't see me as a competent leader. This is the only way for me to maintain control to rebuild the world how I see fit. If people knew there was no punishment for going against us, we would have chaos. The billions of people who have given their lives to reset balance on the planet would have died for nothing."

Zoe let out a laugh. "'*Given their lives.*' You murdered them. They didn't have a choice in the matter. You're the one who should be concerned with the amount of blood on your hands."

Alana made a show of checking her hands. "They

seem fine to me. Now how about it, Zoe? It's your life or theirs." Alana nodded toward the building.

Zoe didn't know what to say. She would turn herself over right now if she could guarantee that Alana wouldn't hurt the people here, but she hated that they were forced to play by Alana's rules again. She wanted to fight back, but doing so would put everyone at risk. She couldn't risk their lives just to satisfy her ego. She really only had one choice. "I have your word that the people here won't be harmed?"

Ian grabbed her arm and turned her toward him. "What are you doing?" he said through gritted teeth.

"The only thing I can do," Zoe whispered back.

"No." Ian turned back to Alana. "Lay one hand on her, and I'll kill your sons."

Gordon stepped forward; Zoe had almost forgotten he was there. She wasn't used to seeing him in a supporting role. "Zoe, I know you don't want Cole or Jackson to get hurt. Let them come back home."

"I'm not sure it's up to me." Zoe stole a glance at Ian. She had no doubt that his threat was real.

Alana closed the gap between her and Ian. "Let me make one thing perfectly clear. If you hurt my sons, I will personally see to it that every single person here suffers before they're killed, and I'll make you watch as each is tortured before I finally kill you."

Zoe pulled Ian behind her. "That won't be necessary."

Alana nodded. "I'll give you twenty-four hours to say your goodbyes and prepare your people to move to one of the resettlement locations. If you aren't prepared when we return, the offer is off the table." Alana nodded to the soldier next to her. They turned back toward the cars.

Zoe walked back inside with Ian and Pearson in her wake. She heard car doors shutting behind her, and she didn't release the tension in her body until she was sure they had left.

She nearly collapsed in the doorway as a wave of cheers crashed over her. She didn't know how to tell them that they hadn't won. In fact, Zoe was pretty sure she had just signed her own death certificate.

«‹«›»»

Cole cornered Ian as everyone congratulated Zoe on standing up to Alana. There was no way it was that easy. She wouldn't have gone to all the trouble of having Jackson trick him into leading the Arrows here just to walk away because Zoe told her to. "What happened out there?"

Ian set his rifle down on the front desk. "Your mom gave Zoe twenty-four hours to hand herself over to them, or she'll kill everyone here." Ian didn't look at Cole as he spoke. Instead, he was scanning the room behind Cole.

"Hand herself over for what purpose?" Cole asked, but Ian walked past him without saying another word — not that Cole really needed an explanation. He knew exactly what Alana would do to Zoe if she got her hands on her.

It made him sick to think about it. All those times that Alana and Gordon told him that Zoe was family, that they loved her like she was one of their own, Cole wondered if they'd ever meant it. And if they did, how could they now be so determined to kill her just because she'd been brave enough to stand against them?

He needed to find Zoe and come up with a way to

get her out of this.

Cole scanned the common room, but Zoe wasn't there. He headed toward her room; she would want to get away from everyone while she thought through her next move. The door was open when he got there.

"You can't honestly be thinking about doing what she says?" Ian's voice traveled through the opened door. Cole heard his own fear and anxiety reflected in Ian's voice.

"Of course I am," Zoe said. "It's not even a hard decision."

"But she'll kill you!"

Cole walked into the room. "He's right," he said, trying to keep his voice calmer than Ian's. He knew a surefire way to ensure Zoe did something was to tell her not to. If Ian wasn't careful, he'd push Zoe into Alana's waiting clutches before they had a chance to come up with a different plan.

Zoe put her hands on her hips. "I'm well aware of that, but what choice do I have? I can't let her kill everyone here. This is exactly why I wanted everyone to leave before the Arrows arrived! If everyone had listened to me, you all would be safe right now."

"And you would be dead," Ian said.

"I am anyway." Zoe waved her hands.

"We can fix this—"

"No, Ian, we can't. There's only one way for this to end, and we both know it." Zoe stared at him, desperation stark in her eyes. It was like Cole wasn't even there.

"We can still leave," Ian said.

Zoe shook her head. "I can guarantee there are guards watching this place. I'm sure they have orders to kill anyone who tries to leave. We are out of options."

"Then we fight," Cole said, interjecting himself into the conversation. He looked at Ian for support, but he turned away and rolled his eyes. "I know the odds aren't on our side, but it's got to be better than giving up."

"It's not if the end result is the same and everyone ends up dead," Zoe argued. "I'm not willing to risk anyone's life to save mine. The resettlement camps can't be that bad. If we do what she wants, then the people here have a chance."

Ian turned back around and took a few steps closer to Zoe. "We'll figure out another way out of this. You aren't leaving, even if I have to handcuff you to that futon to keep you here."

With that, Ian stormed out of the room.

Zoe ran her hands over her face, then turned to Cole. "You understand why I have to do this, don't you?"

"I understand why you feel that way, even though I don't agree."

Zoe sighed and sat down on the edge of the futon, keeping to the middle, out of reach of the armrests. He sat down next to her and took her hands in his. "The Arrows won't be back for twenty-four hours. We have time. Don't give up yet. It's been a long day. Everyone's on edge. Let's try to get some sleep and start fresh in the morning."

Zoe nodded as she looked at their joined hands. "Will you stay with me tonight?" She looked at him with pleading eyes. He wished there was a way for him to take her pain away.

"Of course." Cole brought her hand to his lips and kissed it. "I just got you back, Zoe, I'm not ready to give you up again."

"I love you, Cole." Zoe stood up and without letting go of his hand led him into her bedroom.

«‹‹›»

It was the second time Zoe had snuck out of bed in the middle of the night while Cole slept next to her. The first time had resulted in her getting shot in the leg and the Arrows' toxin getting released three days early.

She knew this time would end in her death, but she hoped the others would be spared.

The common room was empty except for the guard Pearson had stationed at the front door. It was a smart move, but it complicated what she had to do. She hung back and watched him; his name was Gary, and he had come here with his wife and two teenagers. He didn't have any kind of military or police background but had offered to help on the security team shortly after he arrived. He was a nice guy, and Zoe felt bad she would have to deceive him.

"What are you doing up?" Gary asked as she approached.

"Couldn't sleep," Zoe said with a shrug.

"Wish I had that problem," Gary said with a tired smile. "It's a struggle not to doze off out here."

There was her opening. "Why don't you go to the kitchen and get some coffee or something? I can keep watch for you."

"Are you sure?"

"Of course. I'm awake anyway." Zoe shooed him away.

When she was sure he was gone, she headed behind the desk to grab the jackets and zip ties she had stashed there earlier. She pulled out a piece of paper, scribbled a quick note, then took off the necklace Ian had given her for Christmas and her engagement ring. She left them on the note—her final goodbye to both of them.

For a second, she reconsidered what she was about to do. There was still time to go back to bed and see if the morning brought any better ideas. The moonlight shone on the pictures the kids had taped to the wall, and Zoe knew there was no better solution. Not one that ensured the safety of the community.

She put on her jacket, pulled out her gun, and headed to the computer lab, where they were holding Jackson. She opened the door to see him sleeping soundly on a mattress in the corner. She kicked the corner of the mattress while pointing the gun at him.

"Zoe?" he said sleepily. His eyes widened when he saw the gun in her hand. "What are you doing?"

"Put this on." She tossed the jacket at him. "Then stand up slowly and put your hands behind your back."

"Okay, just be calm," Jackson said as he slipped his arms through the sleeves.

"I am calm." Zoe secured his hands behind his back with the zip ties.

"Does Cole know you're here?"

"This doesn't concern Cole." She pushed him out of the room with the gun pointed at his back. "Try anything, and I won't hesitate to shoot you."

Zoe led Jackson out the front door to the sidewalk. "Can you tell me where we're going?"

"We're going to see your mother."

Zoe marched Jackson down the street. If she was right, someone would try to stop her soon—she hoped they wouldn't shoot first. They made it a few hundred yards before a car pulled up and several soldiers jumped out.

"Release him," one of the soldiers said.

"That's not going to happen, and I'm assuming since

you haven't killed me yet, you're under orders not to." They exchanged a look that confirmed her suspicions; Alana would want to make a show out of her death. Prove to the world that she was in control. "That's what I figured. Go tell Alana to meet me in the Wayside parking lot at the end of the street. Tell her to come alone, or I'll kill her son."

The soldiers exchanged another look, then got back in the car. Zoe pushed Jackson forward, and the SUV trailed a few yards behind them as they made their way down the street. The walk was less than a mile, but every step felt like it took an eternity. It didn't help that Jackson was dragging his feet the whole way. Had he always been this annoying and Zoe had never noticed before?

Alana was waiting when they arrived. The soldiers must have radioed ahead.

"I hear you want to talk to me," Alana said.

"I want to renegotiate the terms of our situation," Zoe said in what she hoped was an authoritative tone. She had no idea if this would work, but she had to try.

"What makes you think you have that kind of power?" Alana challenged.

"Maybe I don't, but I do know you, Alana. I've known you for ten years. I'm banking on the fact that under that evil-dictator facade you have going on, you still care about your son. So, unless you'd rather I shoot him, you'll hear what I have to offer."

"You're forgetting I know you too, Zoe. And I know you don't have what it takes to pull that trigger."

"Oh, really?" Zoe lowered the gun and fired a shot into Jackson's leg, just like Alana had done to her. Jackson screamed and collapsed to the ground, and Zoe grabbed a fistful of his hair with one hand, pressing the barrel of the gun to his temple. "You have no idea what I'm capable of."

Alana held up her hands. "All right, you've proven your point. What's your offer?"

"I hand myself, as well as Jackson, over to you, and in exchange, you leave everyone else here alone. You don't force them to go to one of your resettlement camps. You take your army and leave Mount Pleasant. You never set foot in this town again. You will put out a public announcement that this town and the people in it are off-limits. You agree to that, and I'll come willingly."

"Deal," Alana said without hesitation.

"Just like that?" This was way too easy. She'd expected Alana to counter, or at the very least take few minutes to think it over.

Maybe coming here alone wasn't the best idea, but it was too late to back out.

"Yes. You're the only one I really want. I don't want to waste lives if I don't have to. Your people can have this town. There's not much as far as resources here, I doubt they'll survive more than year or two anyway. And if they set foot outside of the city limits, then they will be labeled traitors to the Arrows and will be dealt with accordingly."

"All right." Zoe's head was spinning. "Once you make your announcement, I'll come to you." She slowly started to step backward.

"Oh, I don't think so. You're coming with me now." Alana nodded to the soldiers, who were on Zoe in seconds. They ripped the gun from her hand and threw her to the ground. Zoe tried to fight back, but all it won her was a black eye. They slammed her face on the concrete and twisted her arms behind her back to cuff her. Then they threw her into the back of an SUV and sped away.

«Chapter 27»»

The door to the dorm flew open, jerking Cole from sleep.

"Zoe!" Someone yelled from the main room before the bedroom door burst open. Ian stood in the doorway, glaring at Cole before he turned and left.

It was only then that Cole realized he was alone after falling asleep with Zoe beside him. He scrambled out of bed, pulling on his T-shirt as he chased after Ian. "What the hell is going on?"

Ian stopped at the front desk and turned to Cole. "She did it again."

"Did what again?"

Ian rubbed his hands over his face. "She went to face the Arrows on her own."

"How do you know?" This couldn't be happening.

"I found these on the front desk." Ian handed him Zoe's engagement ring, a necklace he had seen her wearing, and a note that simply said *I'm sorry, it was the only way.*

"Damn it, Zoe." Cole scanned over the note again as if it would suddenly reveal her location, then he clutched the note in his hand, Zoe's ring biting into the palm of his hand as he joined Ian and Pearson at the desk.

"If we can figure out where the Arrows are holed up, maybe we'll be able to find Zoe and bring her back before it's too late." Pearson turned to Cole. "Do you have any idea where your mom might be?"

"No. They rarely came up here when I was in school. Maybe Jackson would know." Cole ran over to the room they were using as a holding cell, trying the door and finding it unlocked. He opened it anyway, hoping to find his brother on the other side, but the room was empty. "Jackson's gone too."

"He couldn't have gotten out on his own. Zoe must have taken him to use as leverage," Pearson said.

"How did this even happen? I thought you had someone on watch last night!" Ian snapped.

"I did. He said Zoe came out claiming she couldn't sleep and offered to take over for him while he got some coffee. He fell asleep waiting for it to brew, and when he came back out, Zoe was gone."

"You should have better people standing guard," Cole accused.

"It's not like I'm working with trained people, here. Gary worked insurance before your parents started this."

"You were in bed with her and didn't know she left, so don't go placing blame where it doesn't belong," Ian said.

Cole ignored Ian's accusation, mainly because he was right. He should have known that Zoe would try something like this and been ready for it. "She agreed to wait 'til the morning to make any decisions. I didn't think she'd change her mind."

"No, when has she ever gone back on what she said?" Ian rolled his eyes and turned away from Cole. "This is all my fault," he muttered under his breath. "I pushed her away. Made her think I didn't want her anymore."

Cole scoffed. "What makes you think you're that important to her?"

Ian whipped around, took a deep breath, and nodded. Then he calmly closed the gap between them and punched Cole in the jaw. "I've wanted to do that for a very long time."

"What the fuck was that for?" Cole massaged his jaw.

"You know damned well what that was for."

"All I meant was that Zoe wouldn't have given herself over to the Arrows just because you were a jerk. She sacrificed herself because she thought it was the only way to save the rest of us."

"We need to find her," Ian said. "They couldn't have gotten far."

"I don't think that's going to be possible." Pearson nodded to the window.

Cole walked over to see a line of soldiers approaching the front of the building. They stopped about a hundred yards away and drew their guns. "We need to get out of here."

"It's too late," Iris said as she walked over to them with Dottie and Floyd. "We were just in the dining commons. They have soldiers posted at every exit in the whole damned quad. We're trapped."

«‹«›»»

Zoe sat in the corner of a dark, freezing room with her hands still secured behind her back. She had no idea where Alana had taken her; she only knew she was cold and that her life was coming to a swift end. She tried to keep her knees pulled close to her body in a vain attempt to stay warm. They had taken her jacket from her before locking her in. Alana knew how much Zoe hated the cold; this was just another way to make her suffer before the Arrows finally killed her.

The door opened, and Zoe squinted as light flooded the room.

"It's time," the guard said as he walked over to her.

"Good." Zoe struggled to get to her feet. She wanted this to be over. The guard grabbed her under the arm and helped her up. His touch was not unkind, and Zoe gave him a weak smile as he led her out of the door. He was only doing his job.

He led her through the building and outside to a large stage. She was at the casino concert venue; Cole had brought her here once to see a show when they first started dating. She wondered if Alana knew that.

A ten-foot-high platform had been constructed in the middle of the stage. They were going to hang her.

Zoe's feet turned to lead as she slowly mounted the stairs. Alana and Gordon were standing at the top; on the stage below, two cameras were pointed at her. Of course Alana would want to broadcast this. That was the whole point, to prove that she had taken out her biggest threat.

Zoe only hoped Alana would hold up her end of the deal and announce that Zoe's people were to be left to alone.

The guard put the noose over her head and tightened it around her throat. The coarse rope irritated her skin as he adjusted it.

Alana stepped in front of Zoe. "Now, isn't this nice? I had a hard time figuring out the best way to kill you, but this used up the least amount resources." Alana ran her finger over the rope around Zoe's neck. "Besides, it will play nice for the cameras."

Zoe turned her head away. She had nothing left to say to Alana.

"Come now, don't be like that." Alana turned Zoe's head back. "You had to know it was going to come to this. There's no other way for it to end."

"Then stop dragging it out and get it over with," Zoe growled.

"Ma'am." A disembodied voice came from the radio in Alana's hand. "We have the dorm surrounded and are awaiting your orders."

"Good. If anyone takes a step outside, shoot them."

"I did what you want. I came to you willingly. Going back on your deal now shows who you really are, and once they know, they'll come for you." Zoe's eyes darted to the soldier standing next to her.

"Our deal stated that my sons wouldn't be hurt. You broke the deal when you put a bullet in Jackson's leg. Once again, you've failed to save the people you've promised to protect," Alana said with a smile. "So now I'm going to watch you die, and then I'm going to order everyone in that building to be killed."

Zoe should have expected Alana to do something like this, but to hear her say it was still a shock. "You can't do this."

"I can do whatever I want. Did you really think you had any kind of power to bargain with me?"

"But Cole is in that building! If you really wanted to protect your son, you wouldn't do this."

"That is unfortunate, but we all must make sacrifices for the cause."

Gordon stepped forward with a stern scowl; he had been uncharacteristically quiet during the whole ordeal. "Alana," he said in a harsh whisper, "when we started this, we vowed that no matter what happened, we would keep our family safe." He shot Zoe a sideways glance. "I've made allowances for your vendetta against Zoe. I understand the position you're in, but I can't stand by while you kill our son."

"Cole has betrayed this family." Alana pointed to Zoe. "She poisoned his mind and turned him against us. I tried everything I could to get him to see reason, but he continues to refuse us. He doesn't deserve our protection anymore."

"He is still our son," Gordon said through gritted teeth.

"Not anymore. I need to get ready. We'll be on the air soon." Alana walked off the platform.

"Gordon," Zoe said desperately, "you can't let her kill Cole. You have to do something. You can stop this. I don't care what you do to me, but save Cole. He doesn't deserve to die."

Gordon looked at her with a pained expression. "I'm sorry, Zoe. I really wish it hadn't come to this." He followed Alana off the platform.

«‹«›»»

Cole helped Iris lean a mattress against the front window. News of the soldiers' arrival traveled through the building like wildfire, and everyone quickly began to gather in the common room. They were all looking for Zoe to come up with a plan to save them, but Zoe wasn't there.

Cole went to the front desk where Ian and Pearson were debating their next move.

"We could go on the offensive, make the first strike, try to catch them off guard," Ian offered as he picked up a rifle from behind the desk.

"I don't like it. There are too many of them. Even if we catch them by surprise, it won't give us more than a few seconds' advantage before they start to fight back. At best, we're able to take out a few before they overpower us," Pearson said.

"And we're sure there isn't a way out of here that isn't covered?"

"Positive, though I have men stationed around the building to let us know if the soldiers move and there's an opportunity for us to get out."

"There has to be something we haven't thought of," Ian said.

Cole stepped forward. "I could go out there and try to talk to them."

Ian and Pearson both turned and glared at him. "No way," Ian said.

"It's too dangerous," Pearson added.

"I'm still a Wilborn, they might listen to me. Besides, it might be the only chance we have." Cole needed to do this. Zoe had sacrificed herself, and if Cole couldn't save her, then he would try to save the people she cared about.

"I don't like it. Zoe wouldn't want you to sacrifice yourself for nothing," Ian said.

"Look around, Zoe's not here! And it's not like she took our feelings into consideration before she gave herself up. Let me do this," Cole urged.

"Someone, turn on the TV," a voice yelled from the

security office, and a woman bolted out of the room. "The Arrows are broadcasting."

Cole followed Ian and Pearson to the common room. Someone had already turned on the TV, which was currently showing a large stage Cole vaguely recognized. "That's the concert venue at the casino on the other side of town."

"That must be where they have Zoe," Ian said.

"I'd say that's a safe assumption." Pearson nodded toward the screen. The camera was zooming in on the elevated platform in the middle of the stage. Zoe stood in the middle of it with a noose around her neck.

"This can't be happening." Cole stepped closer to the screen. His mom was really going to kill Zoe and make the whole world watch while she did it. The rage building up in Cole was more intense than anything he had experienced before.

"We have to get her," Ian said. "We have to find a way to save her." His eyes were glued to the screen. Alana was walking out to the podium on the stage below the platform.

"I'm going to put a stop to this." Cole pushed his way through the crowd that had formed behind him. He refused to stand by and watch Zoe die.

He could stop this. He had to stop this.

"Cole, wait!" Ian called.

He did not look back. This was his responsibility. This was his family. He pulled the mattress off the front door. His hand hesitated on the handle; he had no idea if this would work.

"Don't do this!" Pearson yelled.

Cole took a deep breath and stepped outside with his hands held over his head.

"This is your only warning to get back inside, or you

will be shot," one of the soldiers yelled.

Cole froze, but he couldn't go back. Not when there was a chance he could save Zoe. "I'm Cole Wil—"

He felt the bullets tear through his skin before he heard the gunshots. He fell to the ground, his head hitting the concrete hard.

"Cole!" Ian sounded far away.

Behind him, he heard glass shattering and distant screams, but they were fading. Everything was fading.

His eyelids grew heavy. He wished he had told Zoe that he loved her one more time before they fell asleep last night. He never dreamed it would have been the last time he said it.

They were supposed to have more time.

«‹›»

Zoe held her head high despite the weight of the rope around her neck. Alana might be moments away from taking her life, but Zoe wouldn't let her take the last shards of her self-respect as well. She refused to let the world see how scared she was.

Below, Alana stepped up to a podium. Floodlights switched on, momentarily blinding Zoe.

This was it. She was going to die.

"Good morning," Alana said. "I come to you this morning to announce that the terrorist responsible for the release of the toxin that decimated our world has been caught. While her death won't bring back all those we lost, I hope it provides some solace that justice is finally being served."

Zoe laughed; this wasn't justice, this was murder. Plain and simple.

Gordon stepped forward, his back to the camera. He

glanced up at Zoe, their eyes locking, then spoke to his wife. "You can't go through with this."

Alana shifted her weight as her hands tightened on the edges of the podium. Zoe would have given anything to see her face in that moment. "Yes, I can. Now get out of the frame."

"I can't let you do this. I'm sorry, my love." Gordon pulled out a gun, brought it to Alana's stomach, and squeezed the trigger.

Shock almost made Zoe miss the sound of the gunshot.

Gordon dropped the gun and caught Alana as she collapsed to the ground. "I'm so sorry," he said through his tears. "This was the only way to keep our family safe."

Alana's last gasps traveled through Zoe like an electric current. She had no idea what it meant for her. She assumed Gordon would still kill her, but hopefully he would call off the attack on the dorms. His goal was to save Cole, and that would be enough.

She tried to stand tall as she waited to find out her fate.

Gordon gently laid Alana's body down on the platform. He picked up the radio from the podium and held it to his mouth. "All troops are to stand down at once. Do not engage. I repeat, *do not engage*."

"Identify yourself," a voice said through the radio.

"This is Gordon Wilborn, leader of the Arrow Equilibrium, and I'm ordering you to stand down and return to base at once! Is that clear?"

"Yes, sir."

Zoe breathed a small sigh of relief. She could die happy knowing that her people were safe.

Gordon stood up and turned to her, and Zoe tensed

again. This was it. She closed her eyes and braced herself for what was to come.

Gordon sighed and spoke to the soldier on the platform with her. "Release her."

Zoe was sure she had heard him wrong, but when her eyes flew open, the soldier was already removing the noose from her neck. The next second, the handcuffs were gone.

Zoe rolled her shoulders and messaged her wrists as she cautiously watched Gordon for some sign of what he was planning. Slowly, she made her way down the steps to the main stage. "What happens now?"

Gordon looked down at Alana one more time and ran his hand through his hair. Then he turned to Zoe. "I'll take you back to the dorms and we'll leave."

"You're letting me go," Zoe said in disbelief.

He nodded. "There has been enough death today. I'll honor your agreement with Alana. We'll let you run this town without interference from the Arrows. I'm even going to reverse the resettlement requirements. I think it will be better for people to come together so we can provide a higher quality of life while working to restore the planet, but we won't make it mandatory. Maybe once I've restored the Arrows to what we had intended them to be, we can find a way to work together."

"Thank you, Gordon."

"I do have one thing to ask in return."

Zoe's stomach dropped. She should have known it was too good to be true. "What is it?"

"I'd like a chance to talk to Cole. To apologize and beg for his forgiveness."

"I can ask him, but the decision will be up to him." She wouldn't force Cole to talk to his father, but she knew deep down how much Cole must miss him. He was always so close to his dad.

"That's all I ask. Now, let's get you back to your people." Gordon held out his arm to usher her off the stage, away from the cameras, the noose, and Alana's body.

«‹‹Chapter 28»››

Zoe was afraid to say anything during the ride back to Beddow Hall for fear that Gordon would change his mind and decide to kill her after all. It was just the two of them in the car — no soldiers, and as far as Zoe could tell, no weapons. Her heart rate quickened as they turned onto West Bloomfield Street and the dorm came into view. He was really taking her back.

They pulled up to the front of the building, and Zoe prepared herself to tell Cole that his father was here and wanted to see him. Part of her felt obligated to convince Cole to see Gordon, yet another part of her hoped Cole would flat out refuse. Even though Gordon had saved her life and hopefully brought an end to the Arrows' reign of terror, it didn't mean she could forget everything he had done. How he had ordered Hamid to be killed, how he had done nothing to stop Alana from torturing Cole, how he would have allowed Alana to kill her if Cole's life hadn't been on the line.

"Let me go in first and explain what's going on," Zoe said.

"All right," Gordon said.

Zoe slowly got out of the car and started to make her way to the front door. Behind her, a car door opened and closed; she looked back to see Gordon standing next to the car. Maybe he thought Cole would have a harder time refusing him if they saw each other.

She turned back to the building to see Ian running toward her, grief and disbelief etched onto his face. He grabbed the base of her face and ran his thumbs over her cheeks, then he pulled her close and kissed her.

Zoe was vaguely aware that Gordon was watching her, but she didn't care.

"I thought I had lost you forever." Ian pressed his forehead to hers, never taking his hands off her. It was like he thought she would disappear if he wasn't touching her.

"I'm sorry. I didn't think there were any other options."

"I thought I would die when I saw you on that platform." Ian ran his thumbs over the rope burn on her throat. "Then the broadcast cut off, and we didn't have any idea what happened."

"Alana was going to order everyone here to be killed after she hung me, but Gordon shot her before she could issue the order. She's dead . . . we're safe. Everything's going to be all right now."

"Oh, Zoe, I wish that was true." Ian's voice was thick with pain.

"What do you mean?" She pulled away slightly so she could see him better. She put her hands on top of his. That was when she noticed his sleeves were stained. "Is that blood?" She took his hands off her face.

"It's Cole's." Ian didn't meet her eye.

"What? What do you mean it's Cole's?" Zoe's voice rose a few octaves higher than normal.

"The army showed up right before the broadcast started. Once Cole saw you on that stage, he wanted to do something to save you. He thought he would be able to talk the soldiers down." Ian's voice was halting. "He didn't even get a chance to tell them his name before they shot him."

"No." Zoe didn't recognize her own voice. She couldn't have heard him right. Ian had to be confused, or maybe this was his way of getting back at her for scaring him. Any moment, Cole would come out and take her into his arms.

"I tried to get to him, see if we could save him, but every time someone stepped near the door, they started shooting. They just left him there to die."

Zoe shook her head, tears streaming down her face. This couldn't be real. This couldn't be happening. She glanced over Ian's shoulder and saw the shattered glass on the doors and a large, dark stain on the cement.

Zoe turned to look at Gordon, who was by her side now. "But you called off the attack. I heard you." Her voice had a faraway quality as if someone else was speaking through her.

"I must have been too late," Gordon said softly.

"We tried everything we could once the soldiers left," Ian added. "But he was already gone."

"No," Zoe said between sobs. "No! He can't be dead." Her body grew heavy, and her legs gave out; Ian caught her and slowly lowered her to the ground.

"I'm so sorry, Zoe. I wanted to save him for you," Ian said as he stroked her hair.

"No, no, no," Zoe repeated over and over until it was

nothing but a chorus of sobs.

This wasn't real. This had to be a dream. This *couldn't* be real. She needed Cole. How could he leave her like this?

"Please, can I see my son?" Gordon begged above her.

"I'll take you," Pearson said. Zoe had no idea when he had come outside.

"You're freezing," Ian said as he held her close. "Let me take you inside."

Zoe didn't say anything. She didn't feel cold. She didn't feel anything. She was numb.

Ian helped her to her feet and brought her into the dorm. He kept his arm around her the entire time; she was pretty sure she wouldn't have been able to move without his help.

She was only vaguely aware of everyone watching them as he steered her over to the common room and lowered her onto the nearest couch. Zoe stared blankly across the room, not seeing anything.

How could Cole be dead? How could any of this be happening? She was the one who was supposed to die, not him.

"Zoe, you're back!" Andre's voice sounded far away.

"Hey, buddy, Zoe's really not up to seeing anyone right now," she heard Iris say, but her voice was muffled, hazy, like everything was at the moment.

"Is she going to be all right?"

"Yeah, she's just sad right now."

"Is it about that guy that died?"

Zoe closed her eyes, hoping things would go back to normal when she opened them. Instead, she saw Ian kneeling in front of her, his hand holding hers. The pained look on his face was all she needed to tell her that this wasn't a dream.

Cole was gone.

She stood up and walked out of the common room. She didn't want to be near anyone. Slowly, she made her way down the hall to the rooms Dillion had taken over for the medical equipment. She needed to see Cole. She needed to see for herself that what they had told her was true.

Pearson was standing outside one of the rooms. He didn't stop her as she walked in. Cole was lying on the bed, a sheet covering everything but his face. Gordon was hunched over the bed crying, his hand clutching Cole's.

It was too much. She couldn't do this. She couldn't say goodbye to Cole.

She backed out of the room and ran down the hall to her room. She threw herself on the bed and buried her face in the pillow Cole had slept on. It smelled like him.

How was she going to do this without him?

«‹›»

"Hey, Zoe," a soft voice said.

For a second, she thought it was Cole, but when she opened her eyes, he wasn't there. Instead, she saw Ian standing next to her bed. At some point, she must have cried herself to sleep.

"They're going to bury Cole soon. I thought you would want a chance to see him before they do."

"I guess I should." Zoe slowly got out of bed. "Let me get changed first."

"I'll be right outside if you need anything."

Zoe methodically stripped out of her clothes. She took her time selecting something clean to wear. If she didn't go see Cole one last time, she would regret it for the rest of her life, but she wasn't sure she could do this.

She ran a brush through her hair as she tried to buy herself time to work up the courage to go to him. When she could put it off no longer, she went out to the main room where Ian was waiting for her.

"Will you come with me? I don't know if I can do this on my own."

"Of course." Ian took her hand and led her down the hall to the medical rooms.

Cole's face was covered this time, but that only made it harder. Her hand shook as she pulled the sheet down. He almost looked like he was sleeping, but his lips were missing the hint of a smile he always seemed to have when he slept next to her.

Zoe kissed his forehead, and the chill in his skin almost made her gasp.

This was really happening. He was really gone.

"I'm so sorry. It should have been me," she whispered as the tears started to flow again. "I love you. I will always love you." She gently placed the sheet back over his face as a strangled sob escaped her lips, and her legs started to tremble.

Ian rushed forward and pulled her into his arms. He didn't say anything as he stroked her hair. Zoe had no idea how long they stood like that, but eventually her sobs slowed to a soft cry, and Ian led her out of the room where Dillion and Pearson were waiting.

"We're ready," he said.

They nodded and headed into the room. Ian took her back to her bedroom, helped her put on a jacket, and led her outside. There was a fresh grave dug next to Blake's, and everyone was gathered around it. They moved aside to let Ian and Zoe through, and Zoe spotted Gordon standing alone on the other side.

She went to him and took his hand in hers. She didn't think she could ever repair her relationship with Gordon, but they were the two people in the world who loved Cole the most, and that was all that mattered right now.

Pearson and Dillion brought Cole's body out and carefully lowered him into the ground. Zoe turned away as they started to cover his body. No one said anything. Most of them barely knew Cole. Slowly, people started to file back inside.

Zoe had no idea how long she had been standing there when Gordon finally guided her back inside. Zoe went directly to her room and sat down on the futon, curling her body around her knees.

"Are you going to be all right?" Gordon asked.

Zoe glanced at him and shrugged before returning her gaze to the white cinder block wall on other side of the room.

"I'll take care of her," Ian said from the doorway. He hadn't left her side all day. Zoe wished she could express how much it meant to her to have him there, but she couldn't put the words together. She couldn't do anything.

"I need to get back to DC," Gordon said. "Most of the Arrows did not approve of the way my wife had been handling things, but she had a handful of loyal followers who might try to take over now that she's gone. I need to make sure that doesn't happen."

"Don't let me stop you." Ian stepped out of the doorway, clearing the path for Gordon to leave.

"I'd like to come back in a few weeks to check on Zoe, if that's all right. I can bring any supplies you might need." Gordon looked from Zoe to Ian. She knew she was the one who was supposed to be making the decisions, but she couldn't. The last decision she'd made had resulted in Cole being killed.

She was done taking the lead. Someone else could take charge and shoulder the responsibility. She didn't want it.

Ian shifted his weight. Zoe felt his eyes on her, but she didn't look at him. "No."

"No?"

"Look, I'm grateful you brought Zoe back, but now that Cole is buried, you are no longer welcome here."

Gordon glanced at Zoe. "Please . . . I just want to make sure she gets through this okay."

"I'll make sure she's all right. You can't act like you have her best interest at heart after everything you've put her through."

"Then what if I send someone else to check on her? I'll draw up a peace agreement between this community and the Arrows, ensuring that no one tries to take this town away from you again, and have them bring it."

"A piece of paper means nothing." Ian crossed his arms as he stood between Zoe and Gordon. Zoe wished they would leave her alone with her grief, but she would get no peace until this ended.

She got up and put her hand on Ian's shoulder. "Who would you send?"

"I could send Victoria. She doesn't have anything to do with the Arrows. I'm sure she'll want to see you." Gordon looked away for a moment. "And have a chance to say goodbye to her brother."

"Fine," Zoe said without any emotion. "Now both of you should go. I'd like to be alone." Zoe headed to the bedroom without waiting for a response.

«‹›»

It had been over a month since Cole died, and every day still felt impossible to get through. Zoe was reminded of him everywhere she went. People kept trying to get her to do something. They told her that keeping busy would help, but Zoe refused every time. She didn't want to move on and leave Cole behind.

"How is she?" Victoria's voice floated through the open door to her room, jerking Zoe out of the haze she spent most of her time in.

She sat alone on her bed. The tray of food she had gotten that morning sat untouched on the desk. She didn't have much of an appetite, but she knew if she didn't at least take something to eat, Ian, Iris, or Dottie would show up with food and watch her while she ate it. It was easier to keep up appearances during the brief moments she had to leave her room.

"Not great," she heard Ian say. She knew he was worried about her; Zoe hated that she was causing him stress, but she didn't have the strength to pretend like everything was fine. Not even for him. "She barely speaks or eats. She's pulled away from everyone, spends most of her time alone in her room."

"Can I see her while you look over the trade agreement? Then I'd like to see where my brother is buried before I leave."

"We're not going to make any kind of decisions until Zoe's had a chance to weigh in. She's still in charge."

"That's fine. There are instructions in there on how to get in touch with Arrows once you've made your decision. Take as much time as you want to review it and make changes. The way my dad is acting right now, he'll give you just about anything you want. I think it's his way of atoning for everything."

"We just want to be left to live in peace."

"I get that, but eventually you'll run out of resources. Just think about it," Victoria said. "You might not agree with the Arrows—I don't either, if I'm honest—but if you can make life better for your people, you should consider it."

"Even if—and that's a big *if*—we sign this agreement, Gordon Wilborn will never be welcomed back here."

"I understand. I'll go talk to Zoe, then get out of your hair." There was a knock on her door, and Zoe looked up to see Victoria standing at the edge of the bed.

"Hey, Zoe. It's really good to see you," she said as if she were talking to a child. "How are you?"

Zoe shrugged. "I'm here."

Victoria sat down next to Zoe on the bed and wrapped her arms around her. "I can't imagine the pain you're feeling right now. You've lost so much. Being here is enough."

Zoe gave her a weak smile.

"But eventually you're going to have to find a way forward. I know Cole wouldn't want you to live like this. He'd want you to be happy."

Zoe shook her head. "It's not that simple."

"It can be."

"No, it can't." Zoe nodded to the desk.

Victoria got up and went over to it; Zoe knew it wouldn't take her long to find what she was referring to.

A moment later, Victoria spun around with a pregnancy test in her hand. "This is yours?"

She nodded and put her hand over her stomach. "It's Cole's."

Victoria put the test down and went back to Zoe. "I know it might not feel like it right now, but this is incredible news. Cole gets to live on in his child. You're going to make an amazing mother."

"Except I'm not. I have no idea how to raise this child on my own. Cole was the one who was good with kids. I can't do this without him. I shouldn't have to, but he had to try to be the hero."

"From what I hear, you were also off trying to be the hero," Victoria said with a gentle laugh. "You and Cole had so much in common. I was always jealous of the relationship you two had."

"And now it's just me, and I have to figure out how to do this on my own."

"Oh, Zoe, you aren't alone. You have a whole community of people here who care about you. I've seen the way the people here take care of one another. I know they'll do that for you and this baby. Besides, there's a super-hot guy hovering outside the door who is clearly in love with you."

Zoe's gaze shifted to the door where, sure enough, Ian was waiting, pretending not to be listening to everything they were saying.

Would he still want to be with her now? Would he really be fine helping her raise Cole's child? "I don't know if that's enough."

Victoria took her hands in hers. "It's more than enough. Cole would want you both to have full and happy lives. The best way for you to honor him is to do that. You need to find a way to move on."

"I don't want to forget him."

"You never will," Victoria assured her.

Zoe nodded. She would find a way forward. She had to. For Cole.

««Epilogue»»

Zoe changed positions in bed for the hundredth time. At this stage in her pregnancy, it was nearly impossible to find a comfortable position, especially in the twin-size dorm beds they had pushed together to give the illusion of a queen-size bed. They had managed to find better furniture for most of the people here but somehow had never upgraded what was in their own room.

Ian didn't seem to have any issues with it as he slept soundly next to her.

The door to their room flew open, banging off the wall as Ava ran in. "Mommy, Daddy, wake up! They're coming today!"

Zoe closed her eyes and pretended to be asleep. She wasn't ready to deal with the bundle of energy that was her three-year-old daughter.

The bed moved as Ian sat up. "Come here, peanut. Let Mommy sleep."

She opened her eyes a crack to see Ian scoop Ava up

in his arms. Zoe loved watching the two of them together. There was no doubt that Ian loved Ava as if she was his own. All the anxiety Zoe had felt around telling him that she was pregnant with Cole's child had been unwarranted. She had even overheard the two of them talking a few times about her Daddy in heaven.

Ian and Ava snuck out of the room, and Zoe allowed herself to relax into the mattress.

When she opened her eyes again, the room was filled with light. She must have fallen back asleep. It was probably for the best. She would need all the energy she could muster for when the trade delegation arrived.

Zoe awkwardly rolled out of bed and put on the few items of clothing that currently fit her before heading out to the common room. Iris was behind the front desk, directing the prep teams.

"I saw Ian and Ava running around at some ungodly early hour this morning," Iris said as Zoe approached.

"Were you up with Patrick?" Iris's son was only a few weeks old and needed to be fed every few hours. Zoe was not looking forward to going through that again.

"No, Dillion took the night shift."

"Down with the patriarchy, right?" Zoe said with a laugh.

Iris returned her laugh. "Ava was certainly putting Ian through his paces."

"She's excited. I'm surprised she slept at all last night."

"How are you doing?"

Zoe shrugged. "It gets a little easier every time they come." Her eyes drifted to the front door. They had replaced it with one from another building on campus. The blood stain on the concrete had faded a long time ago, but Zoe knew the exact spot where it had been. The spot where Cole had lost his life. "Is the welcoming committee ready?" She asked to keep her mind from traveling down that dark path.

"Just about. We have fifteen rooms we're prepping with fresh supplies in Sweeney. We'll be doing orientation in the dining commons during lunch if you're available to swing by and meet everyone."

"I'll try. Have you seen Pearson yet?"

"He was up early doing his rounds the last I saw him."

"I'll try to catch him on the radio. I want to make sure the security team is ready."

"It's been almost four years of these trade delegations, and you still don't trust them, do you?"

Zoe cocked an eyebrow. "No, I don't."

"Good," Iris said with a smirk.

"Mommy!"

Zoe turned around to see Ava running toward her at top speed. Ian darted forward and swooped her up before she plowed into Zoe. He held Ava out like an airplane and brought her to Zoe's face for a kiss. "Good morning, baby girl."

"When's Aunt V getting here?"

"Should be anytime now." Zoe gave Ian a quick kiss. "Are we ready for them?"

"We should be." Ian tensed slightly, though Zoe was sure she was the only one who noticed; he wasn't comfortable with these visits and only put up with them for her. If it wasn't for the supplies they brought, Zoe would have called them off a long time ago, but the benefits to the community far outweighed her own feelings.

Andre came in the front door. He was at least a foot

taller than Zoe now. Ava jumped out of Ian's arms. "They're here," Andre said as he struggled to catch Ava.

Zoe took a deep breath and nodded. She laced her fingers through Ian's and slowly made her way outside as the convoy of vehicles pulled up.

Ava came running out, nearly knocking Zoe over as she went. The girl's arms were wide as she flung herself at Victoria. Ian's hand tightened around Zoe's as they watched Ava release her aunt to greet Victoria's sons, who were getting out of the back of the lead vehicle.

"Welcome back," Zoe said. "Hi, boys."

"Hi, Aunt Zoe!" They yelled in unison as they chased Ava around the patch of grass next to the entrance. It was one of the few patches of grass they hadn't turned into a garden.

"You're both looking good." Victoria gave Zoe a hug and nodded to Ian, who hadn't been won over by her charm and energy. The smile on Victoria's face reminded her of Cole.

"You too," Zoe said.

"When's the baby coming?"

"Soon," Ian said.

"Not soon enough." Zoe grunted as the baby kicked her kidney.

"It doesn't seem as busy as the last time we were here." Victoria looked over the building.

"We've been able to start moving people into a nearby apartment complex now that we got the town's water treatment plant back up," Zoe said.

"How large is your population now?"

"A few hundred people," Ian said. Zoe knew he wasn't comfortable giving the exact number; he worried what the Arrows would do if they got too big.

"Let's go inside and talk," Zoe said as the baby

kicked again.

"Come on, boys," Victoria called and waved them all over. "So, how are things going here?"

"The electric trucks you brought last time have been a huge help to our farming operations. We've been able to plant five additional fields this year," Zoe said as she waddled toward the dining commons. Victoria and Ian matched her speed, though she was sure it was a struggle for them not to outpace her.

"I've brought another one in exchange for the crops we agreed on last time," Victoria said as she herded the children into the dining commons. There was a tray of cookies on the end of one of the tables, along with Ava's favorite board game.

Ava grabbed the cookies and brought them over. "Grandma Dottie helped me make these just for you, Aunt V."

"Thank you, sweetheart." Victoria made a show of eating one of the cookies. "That was the best cookie I've ever had! Now, why don't you go teach your cousins how to play that game you have set up over there?"

They all watched as Ava ran to the other end of the table with the tray of cookies. Zoe was impressed that only two hit the floor during the process.

"She reminds me so much of Cole," Victoria said softly.

"I know," Zoe said.

"We should have some livestock to trade on your next visit." Ian steered them back to a safer topic.

"That would be great. We're having a hard time maintaining herd populations in some areas." Victoria pulled out a tablet and started to take notes. "What do you need in exchange?"

"Medical supplies. We're running low on antibiotics,

bandages, that sort of thing. I'll get you a list."

"I'll see what we can do." Victoria hesitated. "I promised Dad I'd ask again . . ."

"No," Ian said before she could get the rest of the question out. Every time they came, Victoria asked if Gordon could meet Ava. Maybe once Ava was older and could understand everything Gordon had done, they'd let her decide for herself if she wanted to meet him; but for now, it was better that she didn't know anything about him.

"I should tell you," Victoria started, giving Ian a cautious glance. "The Arrows are planning on decommissioning the chemical factory in Midland soon. Dad will be leading the project and staying there until it's done."

Zoe saw her own concern mirrored on Ian's face. Midland was less than thirty miles away. She did not want a town full of Arrow loyalists that close to them. And there was only one reason why Gordon would stay through the decommissioning.

Zoe was overcome with the urge to wrap Ava in her arms and never let her go.

"When?" Ian asked.

"I don't know the details yet," Victoria said.

"I don't like it," Ian said.

"Dad is concerned that if there is a failure at the plant, it could affect this community. That's why he wants to get it cleaned up. He swears he won't come anywhere near the town's borders. He says he respects your decision about Ava, but I felt you should know he'll be up here."

"Thank you for telling us," Zoe said calmly, though her mind was racing. She would have to let Pearson know to put together a plan to increase security on that side of town.

"Mommy," Ava yelled from the other side of the table. "Can we go to Uncle Blake's pig farm?"

Zoe wished Ava had gotten a chance to know Blake, but at least they had been able to keep his memory alive.

"Sure." Zoe started to stand up but clutched the edges of the table as a Braxton-Hicks contraction hit. She was beyond ready for this baby to come.

Ian jumped to his feet. "Are you all right?" He helped ease her back into the chair.

"Yeah, false labor, though I don't think I'm up for the walk across campus."

"I can take them," Victoria offered.

This was always the hardest part of the visit. She knew it was important for Ava to have a relationship with Cole's family, but a small part of her was afraid Victoria would turn on them like Jackson had and take off with Ava.

"Why don't you take Andre with you?" Ian suggested. "Mommy and I will stay here and help load up the crops."

"Okay!" Ava grabbed Victoria's hand and pulled her out of the dining commons.

"Thank you," Zoe said as she leaned her head on Ian's shoulder and rubbed her belly.

Ian put his hand on top of hers, pulled her close, and kissed the top her head. "When are you going to learn? I'd do anything for you, Zoe Antos."

Acknowledgements

I never intended to write this book. I had planned for Cleansing Rain to be a stand-alone book, but I so glad the characters kept insisting that their story wasn't done. This was such a fun book to write, and I really hope you enjoying following the characters as they work to rebuild their world.

As always, the first person I need to thank is my husband, Mike. Without his support I wouldn't be able to write any of my books. I know I don't tell him enough, but his support means everything to me. As does his agreement not to actually read any of my books.

I also want to thank the amazing team of people I have helping me make these books the best they can be. From my amazing beta readers, Alex Smith and Kimberly Grymes to my editor Renee Dugan and proofreader Susan Whittaker. These incredibly talented people help me to find and fix plot holes, make sure the story is hitting all the emotional cues at the right time and polish the writing so it is as perfect as it can be by the time it gets into the readers hands. The last member of my team is my incredible cover designer Maja Kopunovic. Her designs fit the story so perfectly I'm blown away every time she makes a new cover for me.

Lastly, I want to thank all my readers. Your support means the world to me. Every message and comment I get keeps me motived to keep going. Hearing how my stories have touched you makes all of this worth it. Thank you.

Lightning Source UK Ltd.
Milton Keynes UK
UKHW010759270922
409514UK00002B/241